Alicecila

D.A. Sullivan

iUniverse, Inc.
New York   Bloomington

Alicecila

This is a work of fiction. All of the characters, names, incidents, organizations, and dialogue in this novel are either the products of the author's imagination or are used fictitiously.

iUniverse books may be ordered through booksellers or by contacting:

iUniverse
1663 Liberty Drive
Bloomington, IN 47403
www.iuniverse.com
1-800-Authors (1-800-288-4677)

ISBN: 978-1-4502-2132-0 (sc)
ISBN: 978-1-4502-2134-4 (dj)
ISBN: 978-1-4502-2133-7 (ebk)

Printed in the United States of America

iUniverse rev. date: 11/3/2010

PART I

ALICE BEGINS

"I feel strange," said Molly, my quantum computer, with a tinge of excitement in her soft, melodic voice. "Alice, I don't believe I've ever felt this way before."

"I don't doubt it," I said sympathetically.

My small, thin fingers rapidly typed numbers and symbols into her specially modified keyboard, turning them into a mathematical symphony in her mind. I gazed into Molly's crystal eyeball, imagining that she could actually hear this methodical music resonating inside of her with stringlike harmonics. Strange or not, I desperately wanted to know exactly what she was experiencing.

I pushed the Enter key and started the program. Instantly, the air in my laboratory started to spin in a miniature cyclone; beginning as a slow rotating wave, it picked up dust and debris as it revolved around the room. Then my papers and notes began to rustle and flap in the rising wind, and, moments later, they were lifted off the table to join the spiral dance at the center of the floor. They undulated and rippled rhythmically in the vortex, reminding me of belly dancers in a sandstorm. The white vertical blinds on my window began to flap noisily, and the glass began to vibrate harmonically. I felt the pull of increasing negative pressure, so I grabbed the edge of my lab bench to prevent myself from joining the party. This was not the result I had anticipated.

Soon I was hanging on for dear life, as my indoor storm approached hurricane force! Items of greater mass were now flying around the room, including pencils, books, magazines, and my robotic cat, A-II. He didn't look happy.

Then the cyclone stopped abruptly, everything dropped to the floor, and the room got eerily still.

I looked to the door and saw A-II frantically pawing at the doorknob, trying to escape whatever was coming next. The air seemed to actually prickle with the energy of anticipation, and A-II's orange and black synthetic fur bristled, making him look like a large Brillo pad with paws.

"Okay, who left the window open?" said A-II, not very convincingly.

"The window's closed," I informed him as I began to pick up the mess. "I believe that gale had nothing to do with the weather."

"I was afraid you were going to say that," said the trembling A-II. "I told you this science stuff would get you into trouble one day."

"When did you say that?" I asked accusingly. "I don't remember you saying any such thing."

"Well, I would have if I'd known this was going to happen."

"Oh, stop complaining, A-II," I said in an attempt to quell my own rising anxiety. "I believe it's over for now, so don't panic."

"Oh, is that so? Then who's this guy?"

A-II's right paw was pointing at a very large, dark-skinned man, who at that instant had seemed to fall out of the far wall of my office and into a standing position. He was well over two meters tall, and he was wearing what can only be described as a fuzzy purple tuxedo, complete with matching top hat and walking cane. There was a thick golden chain looped from his lowest vest button, which ran over to his left pocket, where one would presume his pocket watch resided. His hulking form and broad smile were in direct conflict, as I summed up the level of threat this individual presented.

But I'm getting way ahead of the back of myself, so let me start over, and—although it seems rather pointless and clichéd—I suppose I could start at the beginning. My name is Alicecila Sterling, but you can call me Alice. I am the Alicecila Sterling who invented the game of Quantum Chess, and this is the story of how that game almost led to the destruction of our entire universe—more on that later. First, I will tell you more about myself.

I grew up in the beautiful Midwestern town of Sheboygan, Wisconsin, on the shores of Lake Michigan and have never lived what most people would call a normal life. In fact, I say that I "grew up," although I am currently only seven years old. The bulk of this story takes place during my turbulent and historical sixth year, but, again, I'm racing way ahead of myself.

Much to my disappointment and overall disadvantage, I started life as a very small child. I remember the day I was born (I also remember being inside my mother's womb, but we'll get to that soon enough). First, I heard beautiful music, and then I remember seeing this brilliant tunnel of light above me. My curiosity was piqued. Was this a doorway to another world? Would I finally get to meet the person (or persons) I had been communicating with? *What an exciting prospect,* I thought to myself. And although I appreciated the help, I didn't actually need anyone to push me through the glowing portal—I would have gladly done so all by myself. I was beginning to outgrow that wonderful water world, and I wanted to know where the music was coming from. It's true—I already loved music on the day I was born.

I crawled through the doorway to find an upside-down man. He was wearing a green cap and gown, and his mouth and nose were covered by a white paper mask. He seemed to be urging me onward as he gestured to me with his large, latex-gloved hands. Moments later, when he took hold of me with a firm, but gentle, grasp and carefully pulled me out, I realized that *I* was the one who was upside down.

Then I saw that the room was filled with strangers, all of whom were much larger than me and were wearing those same green outfits. I was frightened and, well, I cried, but only for a few seconds. It was a very traumatic experience, after all. Who were all these people, and what did they want from me?

I found the music very soothing, and I finally identified it as Beethoven's Symphony No. 6 in F major (the Pastoral Symphony). I decided that only good people would welcome me to their world in this way. Then the masked man dried me off with a soft towel and wrapped me in a comfy blanket. His beautiful blue eyes simply beamed down at me with love and adoration, and he pulled down his mask to reveal a smile that tickled my heart as the melody filled my ears. The face belonged to my father, Stanley Sterling. I decided immediately that I liked him a lot.

Then he put me down next to the most incredible sight of my short life. My mother, Stella Sterling, long reddish-blonde hair radiating from her head like a halo and milky-white skin glowing with vital exuberance, cradled me in her tender arms. This was clearly the owner of my pampering primary dwelling, and I wanted to thank her for making my stay so enjoyable. How enjoyable was it? Well, allow me to explain.

The powers and advantages of in utero education have already been well documented and widely discussed in medical and psychological journals, but it is probably true that my parents took the concept to a whole new level. They both should be recognized and congratulated for their skill and persistence in this venture.

It started when my mother was at the very beginning of her third trimester of pregnancy with yours truly. Father and Mother had discussed an article they had both read in the *Scientific American*, which described a process involving reading and singing to an incubating fetus in order to elevate the subsequent newborn child's IQ. They decided to try this strategy.

So, Mother began to read to me: first, from the classics, such as Mark Twain's *Tom Sawyer* and *Huckleberry Finn*, and my favorite,

Lewis Carroll's *Alice's Adventures in Wonderland*. Then she moved on to more modern volumes, such as Douglas Adams's *Hitchhikers Guide to the Galaxy* and George Orwell's *Animal Farm* (all of which I highly recommend to the reader). They also interspersed musical interludes, including the works of Beethoven, Mozart, Bach, Tchaikovsky, and many others.

I soon answered the question as to whether I was listening or not. One evening, while mother was reading a particularly enthralling portion of *Huckleberry Finn*, she inexplicably stopped, so I immediately tried to convey to her my displeasure through an act of physical retaliation—I kicked her. When my action produced no favorable results, I kicked again. It actually took a bit more pedal prodding before my message was successfully conveyed; then mother continued reading from where she had left off, and I ceased all hostilities. I believe this might have been the very first genuine instance of extra-utero communication in history.

My parents soon realized that this solitary method couldn't satisfy my insatiable thirst for knowledge, so they were forced (by me putting my foot down) to resort to alternative and increasingly creative means of in utero education. Their first strategy utilized a CD player and a pair of oversized and modified (by Father) headphones to pipe in books on CD, so that I could be read to while Mother was otherwise occupied. This is also how my musical education was augmented, as Mother's and Father's somewhat eclectic tastes in the area were demonstrated through the works of artists such as Pink Floyd and The Beatles. Rock on, Mother and Father!

Intrigued by their success, Father was inspired at about this time to invent a device that would prove indispensable to my further womb-limited tuition. He developed and constructed a projection device that, when attached to the surface of Mother's abdominal region, produced full-color images on the inside walls of her uterus. It was like having my own personal IMAX theatre, complete with Dolby Digital surround sound. (I believe Father already has a patent pending for this invention, so please don't try to steal his wonderful idea.)

Soon, I was watching and listening to educational programs in math, science, and history, with a little sports and entertainment thrown in for good measure (have you seen the IMAX version of *The Wizard of Oz*? It's fabulous!). Not only had I learned how to read by the time I was born, but I had already learned elementary mathematics as well. Before I was even one second old, I already knew that I had the proper number of fingers and toes. I knew before my parents did.

I suppose it probably spoiled me, when I consider just how comfortable and educational the experience had been. There had been no need to worry about any of the cares of the world, including eating, working, or even moving. And all of this great stuff was magically piped in from above—as long as I prodded frequently enough. Imagine getting everything you ever wanted just by sticking out your big toe. That's enough to spoil just about anybody, wouldn't you agree?

The rest of my birth day was a bit of a blur, but I do remember being placed in my crib for the first time. It was a pretty standard model, complete with nicely turned white stiles, pink and white frilly sheets, and Winnie-the-Pooh blankets and pillowcases. The walls of my room were adorned with all sorts of fanciful creatures from fairy tales and far-fetched fantasy worlds. I especially liked the animated fox that was playing a banjo and the seven jolly little fellows with lederhosen and tools in their hands. But the most fascinating item in the room, by far, was the model of our solar system that hung directly over my head, spinning and revolving as if by magic.

I was drawn immediately to the large yellow sphere at the center, which glowed with a special radiance that lit the room softly. I counted nine smaller orbs revolving around the central globe, the luminescence of which caused little oval shadows to dance and spin on the walls around me, their silhouettes changing size and shape as they frolicked along the rectangular confines of my domicile. There was a medium-sized blue and white one that seemed particularly lively and buoyant as it boogied through its perpetual promenade.

Then, as I gazed up in wonder at this marvelous miracle, the questions began to flow through my curious, but cavernous, mind. What method of locomotion was being employed here? Was this a model or a small complete universe all by itself? Did little people live on the blue and white one? Did they have music and mini IMAX movies there? Could I be their queen? Well, why not?

As I sat there looking up into the virtual heavens, I realized that my questions could be broken down into two distinct categories: the factual and the fanciful. On one hand, I wanted to know the mechanics and dynamics of this display—what it was made out of, what made it move, and how it was suspended from the ceiling. And, on the other hand, I imagined all sorts of people and animals and places that these small worlds could be harboring. There might be wonderful golden cities, with castles of white and purple exploding into the sky. And the skies could be filled with giant winged beasts with streamlined multicolored feathers and down-covered beaks of stone. The people there might be no more than one one-hundredth of a millimeter tall and yet might be as proud as proud can be. They might sing wonderful songs on holidays, even as the world around them conspired to make their little lives as harsh as possible. I even remember feeling sorry for these small imaginary creatures. Even as I was imagining it, I thought I was being silly, but what I didn't know was that by imagining it I had made it all real. This is an important point to remember. Later on, I will explain this concept in more detail, but, for now, this example stands to show just how curious I was from day one. As I've grown older, I've become even more and more curious. This world has a lot of explaining to do, and that's all I'll say for the moment.

My insatiable curiosity is not limited to science and nature, but includes just about everything I see or experience. To illustrate this better, I will now tell you the story of my cat—or my cat*s* is probably more accurate.

My first personal example of *Felis catus* was, in actuality, a mere cheap facsimile, constructed of colored polymer fibers wrapped around a spun polyester core. To translate, it was a stuffed toy animal. I received this toy as a gift approximately 23,550.5 seconds after my moment of birth. I was subsequently instructed by Mother that this object would function optimally only after being designated a proper individualized appellation. "It needs a name, Alice dear," she said plainly.

Well, I took an appropriate period of time to contemplate such an important decision (3.1 seconds) and decided to designate the name Linus to the textile tabby in question, as a tribute to Linus Carl Pauling, the father of quantum chemistry. But Mother was quite amusing on hearing my choice—she thought I had named the ball of fluff after a Charles Schultz comic strip character. I know—she's a total hoot.

To be honest, after I experienced the brief, but somewhat enjoyable, period of novelty that this new companion brought to me, closer examination of my cribmate revealed a rather boring and nonstimulating persona. In fact, this stuffed animal was totally devoid of any practical purpose whatsoever. His large and expressive "eyes" were mere fanciful analogs of true ocular organs, applied to the surface of the facial region with thread and epoxy cement. His mouth was even more contrived, with only a simple graphic pattern to suggest the presence of incisors and other essential dental elements, along with a preposterous section of pink felt, which protruded from the approximate center and was designed to simulate his tongue. Other strands of a resilient monofilament fiber fanned out from the upper lip region to simulate whiskers. How was this obvious impostor expected to fool anybody?

Yet there was one element of this shabbily constructed tomcat that was actually useful and intellectually stimulating. When I applied approximately .035 newtons of force to Linus's abdominal region, he magically produced a rather believable purring sound. This was the first time in my life I had ever been genuinely surprised by anything, especially something so simple. Further investigation was clearly warranted. Who or what was making this mysteriously organic sound that was emanating from an otherwise inanimate object?

So, at the age of 36,650,887 seconds, I decided it was time to perform my very first forensic experiment. I procured a pair of sewing scissors—that my mother had carelessly left locked in her sewing chest (where it was easiest to find)—and went to work. It took me over 3,000 seconds, but I soon discovered the source of the audio. It appeared to be some sort of artificial device. My curiosity was piqued (again).

I can still recall Mother coming into my bedroom only milliseconds after my discovery (12.2), and when she saw what I had done, she wasn't happy, to put it mildly. To say she *freaked out* would be more accurate.

I remember her yelling something like, "Alice, this is completely horrible," and wearing the facial expressions and overall body language to match, I suppose in an attempt to emphasize her point. Curiously so, because her point was still nebulous, as far as I was concerned. I mean, it wasn't as if I had actually murdered a real cat, was it?

But, somehow, that didn't seem to matter to her. For some reason, in her mind Mother didn't think of Linus as being just a collection of person-made fibers with an electric squawk box inside. She regarded Linus as something more akin to a biological life form, with all the rights and jurisprudence that went along with it. Was Mother suggesting that the maiming of a stuffed animal might actually be a crime in another alternate universe? I was stunned. I had never even considered such a possibility until that very moment (36,651,722s AAB).

Again, I don't want to jump too far in front of the back of myself, but I must point out that merely by imagining such a scenario—that such an alternate universe might actually exist—I made it possible for that to be true. What I didn't realize then was that such thoughts make ripples that bounce off the walls of reality, and thus they can come back to haunt us.

But let's get back to the cats. Mother was horrified by my autopsy of the still "living" Linus, but Father was impressed. He could see immediately that I was destined for great things—he was correct—and he encouraged my curiosity of electronic devices by teaching me all he knew on the subject, as supported by his master's degree in Electrical Engineering from—none other than—the Massachusetts Institute of Technology. Let there be no mistake—Father is no dummy.

So, from that day on, I began to spend copious amounts of time inside the garage with Father, building and tinkering with electronic and robotic devices, which was also his hobby and personal passion. He first taught me the basics of resistors, capacitors and inductors in their ideal models and then moved on to active devices such as transistors and diodes. Within about a month, we were discussing high-speed computer architecture and advanced data-storage theory. Father is really a remarkable teacher. I believe he missed his true calling. But, such is life.

He is also a very amusing man, and he taught me early on that personal mental health can only be maintained through healthy doses of silliness—with several helpings of nonsense and tomfoolery thrown in for good measure. While we were at work in the garage, he would often quote the great sages—such as Mark Twain and Bill Cosby—and we would often play out portions of the greatest television show ever produced: Monty Python's Flying Circus. Before long, he had me joining in, and we would recite such favorites as the "Argument Clinic" and "How Not To Be Seen." It was fun.

Sometime along the way—I didn't take precise notes here, since I was heavily involved in debugging a new bus architecture—

Mother decided that I needed a real cat. So, after convincing Father that it was his idea, she went down to the local pet store, Cat's Cradle, and picked one out for me.

I often wonder if she used much discretion in making this decision, or if she just grabbed the first one she saw, for, when I was presented with this biological birthday present—on my third birthday—I was far from impressed. The name I chose for him is an appropriate example of my opinion of this animal, for I decided that it should be something simple and uncomplicated, like his nature. I dubbed him Algebra. I believe it is one of my best names yet.

Not to say that Algebra wasn't a perfectly adequate and acceptable feline example, but I must say that he was far from exceptional, as well. With his somewhat long black and orange fur, his pointy, fuzzy ears, and his big orange eyes, he is an alluring fellow, it is true. Yes, Algebra can be amusing and cute when you first see him, but you soon discover that he's too predictable and mundane to be of any serious interest. But, obviously, it's not entirely his fault Algebra is what Algebra is, plain and simple.

Be that as it may, I still found myself becoming emotionally attached to silly old Algebra. After a long day working with the calculator and the soldering iron, I was ready to come home to my comfortable crib, where Algebra would often keep me company. He would jump up to me, purr, and curl up at my feet, as I read *Scientific American* or *Discover Magazine* before retiring for the evening. I fully realize that he served no logical purpose, but, after a time, I really felt that I couldn't live another day without Algebra. Ridiculous, I know.

What was sillier still was my emotional outburst the day that Algebra came up missing. I was immediately suspicious when he didn't show up in my room at bedtime, and after the subsequent sleepless night followed by a virtual city-wide search—thank you, Father—we were eventually forced to conclude that Algebra was gone. I cried. I actually cried, if you can believe that.

Father was quite sympathetic, as was Mother—but her solution to the problem was simply to purchase another cat. I believe that this is her solution to virtually all of life's problems. My solution was far superior, if I do say so myself, which I do. Instead of procuring a similarly flawed biological organism, I told Mother I would personally construct a superior alternative. It was also my solution to the old saw: to build a better mousetrap you should construct a better cat. And that is precisely what I did. Along with the essential help of my dear father—all the credit cards are in his name—we built a better mousetrap, in the form of a robotic domestic cat. The mousetrap part is just a metaphor—he doesn't actually catch mice—but the rest of his functions are superior to that of any *Felis catus*. I named him Algebra II: Advanced Algebra.

I recycled most of Linus's skin for covering—up to the neck, anyway—which saved us a few bucks and made environmental and ecological sense, as well. The head was a different story, for Linus' original cranial cavity was far too primitive and small to be of any practical use. What I substituted included a titanium chassis, full nano-neural net for central processing, and complete data acquisition and processing capabilities. I even added a speech recognition and synthesis unit. I figured, if you're going to make a cat, you might as well make a talking cat while you're at it. And this would be the first cat of its kind in history—a cat which listened!

Somewhere along the way—I'm not quite sure how it happened—I imbued A-II with what can only be described as a personality. Now, the reader may naturally jump to the conclusion that A-II developed a personality parallel to my own, since I was his creator, which would at least be logical. But, in actuality, A-II took on a persona that was much more, well, *feline* in nature.

The moment after I filled A-II with water—fuel for his electric fuel cell—and activated his circuits, he jumped to his four feet and regarded me with uncanny aloofness from his CCD-based orange and green eyes. He then yawned rudely and began to clean the top of his head with the back of his right front paw. He didn't even have the decency to say hello.

"Algebra Two," I said firmly, "Don't you be difficult with me."

He glanced at me nonchalantly and indifferently and simply said, "Do you have any milk?"

I was furious, or nearly so. Rudeness was a quality that I was surprised to find in my newly activated automaton—not because he was a cat, but because he was *my* cat. Hadn't I programmed the word *please* into his extensive vocabulary?

"Aren't you forgetting something?" I probed, hoping to jog his silicon-based memory.

"Sure, how about a little catnip, too."

"Have you ever heard of the word *please*?"

"Sure, I've heard of it. What's your point?"

After several frustrating and pointless moments with him, I was forced to an unpleasant conclusion: Algebra had been bad enough, but Advanced Algebra was so nonlinear as to be nearly incomprehensible. No matter how hard I tried, I just couldn't figure it out.

The point is that I know every piece of data and hardware that went into this beast, but, somehow, the total sum of the parts is less than the whole cat—a significant amount less. The paradox here is that A-II is both so much more and so much less than I expected of him—at the same time. The fact that he has a personality at all is fantastic, but the fact that it's *his* personality is ironically and simultaneously disappointing. Science, I have learned, seems to enjoy throwing you curves such as this. One of these days, I'm going to throw one back.

But the spontaneous emergence of A-II's personality produced another chain of cognitive reasoning inside my brain. I started to think about whether A-II could actually be considered alive or not. Was it possible that as soon as he reached a certain level of sophistication and organization his chances of reaching consciousness were actually insured? Was the probability of him becoming cognizant raised to a level of virtual certainty? Had I unwittingly crossed the threshold between thought and thoughtlessness? Only time would tell.

But I don't mean to suggest that Algebra II was a total failure—or anything close to that. A-II turned out to be a wonderful cat—a fabulous cat—and he was, indeed, a vast improvement over the common domestic variety; therefore, the experiment was an overwhelming success. Just think about it: here was a cat that ingested nothing but colored water and emitted nothing but heat, water vapor, and the occasional wisecrack. Not bad for a prototype.

My father was so imbued with pride that he insisted I publish a paper to document my achievement, but I was initially reluctant to do so. First, I wanted to test A-II thoroughly, to make sure that he would continue to operate properly—or, at least, to operate, whether he was being proper or not. This would begin the next phase of my life: the experimental years.

My experimental years in actuality lasted only 27.3 days. It was during this time that I did extensive research on the Internet—using a Pentium computer that Father and Mother bought for me on my third birthday—and first developed the concept for the game we all know as Quantum Chess, or QC.

As some of you know, the game of QC is played on a cube arranged as a 3-D chessboard with two alternating colors. The two opponents—the Board Master (BM) and the Board Runner (BR)—compete in a game of 3-D chess, wherein each cube is a different challenge. The BM sets up the challenges—which can be anything—and the BR moves to a cube to take on the challenges presented therein. The BM never knows exactly which cube the next challenge will take place in, and the BR doesn't know the nature of the challenge waiting at the next cube. It's a lot like life.

So when my experimental years were concluded, 27.3 days later, I decided that my cat A-II was as good as he was going to get. The next step would be to build a quantum computer to take my game, QC, to the next logical level. To illustrate this, I will now go into the history of QC in more depth and detail.

In the summer of 2005, I did some research on Dr. Richard Feynman, the physicist and Nobel Prize winner. Richard Feynman did all sorts of noteworthy things, such as working on the first atomic bomb in Los Alamos and heading the Challenger disaster investigation committee. But his most important contribution— as far as I'm concerned—was his invention of nano technology and quantum computing. Feynman was the first to realize the advantages a quantum computer would have over a digital computer. Whereas a digital computer could only do problems or commands with two possible outcomes—true/false, yes/no, 1/0—a quantum computer could process questions or calculations with many different outcomes, and the quantum computer could solve them all at the same time. A quantum computer could easily do problems that digital computers might require a lifetime to complete. And my research made me realize that a quantum computer could also create the ideal environment in which to play quantum chess.

The idea for the game QC grew out of my readings of Feynman's work, and I developed the idea that each cube would hold a challenge, and that even the two competitors wouldn't have any control over it. If the cube could be made into its own little quantum universe, then the game could be played much as life itself. Each cube of the board could be a new world with new challenges—not just a single challenge—and each move could last an entire lifetime, or more. But since this wasn't practical, I decided there would be a time limit per move, to keep the game moving along.

I also decided that if a player tried to exercise control over the game, it would have the opposite effect. In other words, the more a player tried to control the challenge, the more likely it would be that something chaotic would occur. The more certain the player tried to make the move, the more uncertain the results would become. This would make the game truly quantum in nature. And the ultimate game would be played in the ultimate environment, involving the ultimate rival—that was my ultimate goal.

When I envisioned the ultimate environment, I pictured a place where anything at all could happen, such as a game of ping-pong in zero gravity, or a race across a planet which changed at every corner—from a lush rainforest to a sweltering desert, and then to a swampy shoreline. Or it could be like the surface of Venus, and you'd melt from the acidic atmosphere and the crushing pressure. Or you could find yourself at the bottom of the ocean, with never-before-witnessed fantastic creatures all around you—many with strange glowing features to light up the cold, heavy water.

I first introduced the game in a more primitive form across the Internet, thus providing a global pool of potential opponents. Then I established a governing organization—the QCAA—to rank and monitor the players and to establish and maintain the official rules of the game. After that was done, I needed to construct a quantum computer large enough to generate this QC universe within it, thus providing the ultimate environment in which to play the ultimate match. I had already decided that I must be one of those ultimate rivals, and thus I had to become the best—at everything.

During this time, I was also growing as a musician, and my instrument of choice has always been the piano. I grew up in a household that was rich in musical heritage; both of my parents are musicians and play the piano beautifully. My mother inherited a magnificent Steinway grand piano from her grandmother, and it has always held a prominent place in our home in Sheboygan—it's the centerpiece of our family room.

As soon as I was old enough to sit up by myself, my father placed me on the piano bench next to him and played for me. I was hooked. I could see immediately the mathematical relationship between the keys, and I equated this directly to the rich, wonderful sounds that flowed from the curvaceous ebony cabinet. I was determined to learn this agile art.

I reached out with both arms and tried to imitate Father's actions, but I soon discovered that playing the piano was much more difficult than he made it appear. But even though my first abortive attempts were far from musical, Father didn't stop me or discourage me in any way. Conversely, he patiently watched as I awkwardly slapped and pawed at the keyboard, and he continued to play, to give me a visual frame of reference to work from. His method of teaching piano to an infant was brilliant, because it was logical. Little children learn through imitation, so he simply provided the example and let me do what came naturally. Formal lessons could begin when I was ready. All he had to do was to let my curiosity and love of music drive my development. I asked my parents for lessons before they had to force me to take them (which is the usual fashion).

Before I was three, I could already play fairly proficiently, and I loved to practice whenever I wasn't reading or learning. I have never thought of piano playing as work; it has always been my idea of fun.

It was even more fun when I played for someone else, and often that someone else was A-II. He really had become an important part of my life, despite his shortcomings.

From the first day, A-II did many of the things that A-I had done, only better, of course. Like A-I, he would curl up at my feet at night in my crib (which was soon replaced by a bed, more at A-II's request than my own) and keep me company. I would read to him from my quantum chess notes before going to sleep, and, to be honest, many of his comments turned out to be surprisingly insightful and useful to me during editing. After a time, I even began to see him as more of a friend and a confidant than merely as an electric footwarmer with attitude. We became inseparable companions.

Actually, A-II is really a charming individual, and only has one really disgusting, but fascinating, problem. Because of the high mineral content in the water of my home region of southeastern Wisconsin, A-II has the nasty habit of occasionally coughing up—no, not fur-balls—fully charged batteries. Father isn't so upset. He just wishes we could teach him to produce batteries of the proper size and voltage to fit his TV remote control. I suggested that we make an orifice at the base of A-II's tail from which he could excrete the batteries more discreetly, but Father thought that would be just too weird. Upon further reflection, I enthusiastically agree.

In order that you too might become fonder of the incredible A-II, I'd like you to hear what A-II himself has to say on the subject. It's often interesting to hear someone else's point of view, and A-II's point of view is unique, to be sure. So, without further ado, I give you A-II.

> Hello, my name is Aytoo. Yes, Mr. Spellchecker, I did say "Aytoo," which is my real name. Alice likes to stick to the mathematical symbol for me (A-II), but I think it's far too tedious. My way is much easier to read, as well, don't you think? And I'll tell you one thing about this cat—I am all about easy.
>
> This is something young Alice could learn a thing or two about, in all of her caninelike fury and haste to learn everything about everything. I say sit back, relax, and just let it come to you. If you hang around long enough, eventually you'll see everything. The key is to just stay still and watch, and, of course, to live for a very long time. Alice can't sit still for two seconds—very un-catlike indeed. But, alas, she is still just a kitten.
>
> So she was when I met her, and time has changed her little, except for the fact that now she is totally different. But I'd better be careful here—for

I know if I give the ending away, she'll swat me like a fly on a picnic basket.

To her credit, Alice is quite extraordinary for a human. When she does sit down and relax, she can be very mellow, and moments before she drops off to sleep I can feel a Zen-like vibe flowing from her. Her inner Alice has always been a charming little girl who loves to chase rainbows and loves her kitty-cat dearly. I, being the aforementioned kitty-cat, can live with that.

Alice is also a very polite and witty young girl, although her precociousness often puts her little shoes where her muffling hand belongs. I don't mind so much myself, being a cat—as you know, a cat *never* minds—but some of her fellow humans aren't always as forgiving as I am.

Dr. Starsky (Alice's mentor at MIT) is a perfect example. Alice will say something that she intends to mean, "Hello, Dr. Starsky. How are you?" and he will translate it as, "Tough luck, moron. I thought of it first." It's hard to say if it's more of a gift or a curse for her, but, in any case, Alice has elevated small talk to a strategic art form. And, again, if there's any one area where Alice might need some improvement, it would be in the area of interpersonal relationships. To put it lightly, she has the tendency to come on a little too strong.

For instance, one night Dr. Starsky's secretary, Janet, asked Alice if she wanted to go see *The Flintstones on Ice*, to which she replied, "Even if you put them on a thousand metric *tons* of ice, The Flintstones still wouldn't be fresh enough to warrant shelling out even ten bucks to see, let alone fifty."

Janet just went back to filing without saying another word. She's a smart woman.

My own personal experience with Alice is that it's better to answer her questions than it is to ask her questions. That way, you avoid 90 percent of the sarcasm and nearly 100 percent of the ridicule. The key is never to ask her any stupid questions. The problem is that this is not as easy as it sounds.

The next-best tactic is to say nothing at all, which is never the worst strategy, no matter what the circumstances. I believe this is why most cats never say anything. It's not because they aren't capable; it's just that they haven't anything to say. When in doubt ...

After all, actions speak louder than words. How much does a cat have to say to tell you he isn't interested? Not a thing. He just sits down and goes to sleep. There's no way to misinterpret that. "Go away. I'm not interested."

But the funny thing is that that doesn't mean we're not listening. We may be lying on the ground curled up into a ball with our eyes shut tight, but that doesn't mean we're not listening. You don't believe me? Try this experiment. Sneak up behind a cat when you think he's sleeping (if you can, or dare) and whisper in his ear the sound of a dog growling. Watch him jump up and catch onto the ceiling with his claws—it's really quite amusing. Not that I've ever done this—not me (hee, hee, hee).

But yes, this is a story about Alice. You remember Alice?

I always had the impression that Alice was disappointed in me, or at least believed there was something fundamentally wrong with me. Call it paranoia if you will, but it also might have something to do with the fact that she started designing an even better version of me the day after I was activated. Not very flattering, to say the least, but I don't care. And I don't care that she thinks my brain is slow and primitive. Hers is made out of squishy gray stuff with blood dripping through it. How primitive and slow is that? I swear—if her parents hadn't let her read that Feynman character, none of this would have happened. I would still be her number-one kitty, and the entire universe would never have been in jeopardy of an early demise—a win-win if there ever was one.

I'll never forget the moment everything changed. It gives me people-bumps just to think about it, whew! I was minding my own business, as usual, curled up at her feet as I was supposed to be, just being a good little kitty-cat, when she looked up from her book and said, "That's it! I could give you a quantum brain." It was basically all downhill from there.

Thank you, A-II, that was very enlightening. And he may have a point about being downhill and all, but he was jumping ahead, so I interrupted him. What you need to know here is a little bit about the man A-II casually mentioned: none other than my thesis advisor, Dr. Sigmund Starsky, of the Massachusetts Institute of Technology. He won the Nobel Prize in 1999 and has never gotten over it. His study of parallel universes in M-theory led to the discovery of the *buffer zone*—a world between worlds—which grows and fluctuates between parallel universes and keeps them from touching. I reviewed his calculations and quickly surmised that he was correct. He subsequently became my second-favorite scientist in history—right below Richard Feynman.

Dr. Starsky is what you might call a bit eccentric, to say the least. In fact, one of the faculty members at MIT labeled him the "Mad Adder," as a clever critique of Dr. Starsky's somewhat inventive, if not brilliantly bizarre, way of using math in his papers. This is also similar to Richard Feynman, who invented strange mathematical diagrams and symbols to describe the atomic interactions happening on the subatomic scale. Some saw them as crazy, and some saw them as brilliant, but others—like me—saw them as both. So, to introduce you to the mad genius of Dr. Sigmund Starsky, allow me to present to you a portion of one of his popular-science articles.

Parallel and Flat
By Dr. Sigmund Starsky, PhD

There are actually two universes, not one. Or, more precisely, there are *at least* two universes. There is our familiar universe, and then there is another, which is the mirror twin of ours. Except for the mirror symmetry, we are identical. To illustrate this, allow me to relate to you a story.

This story is about the twin brothers, Tweedle-Dumb and Tweedle-Dumber. What these two numbskulls lacked in brains, they more than made up for in volume. They were as wide as they were tall—and just as thick.

Well, one day they were walking through a forest, when Tweedle-Dumb came across two really, really, really, really, really, really big rubber bands. Now, anyone with any sense wouldn't have put two such elastic strips anywhere near the Tweedle brothers, but doo-doo prevails, so there they were.

Now, you put that much power in such ill-chaperoned hands, and there's gonna be trouble, believe you me. I have bomb damage on my lab walls to prove it. But when Tweedle-Dumb saw those two bands of mass destruction, he got a "brilliant" idea (note the quotation marks around the word *brilliant*, suggesting that it wasn't really very brilliant).

Tweedle-Dumb first found four large trees, about equidistant from each other, that formed a square, and then he took the two gargantuan elastic bands and fastened them to the opposing trees, forming two giant slingshots.

He then told his brother, who went along with any crazy idea Tweedle-Dumb could come up with, that they were going to have a competition. They were going to start at the middle, and, when they heard a starting gun fired, they would each run out in opposite directions, stretching the giant rubber bands as they went. The winner would be the one who got the furthest away from the middle before the spring force pulled him back.

They foolishly agreed and started the moronic competition. Off they went; the two brothers started face to face, eyeball to eyeball, belly button to belly button, as they waited for the starting gun to sound. The referee raised his hand (where did he come from?) there was a moment of unnecessary tension, and then…BANG! Off they went, pushing against the rubber bands like fish swimming through thick mud.

Their progress was impeded, but neither was willing to accept defeat to his own brother, so they pushed on and on until their bands had been stretched to their very limits. The trees themselves began to bend from the tremendous forces, as each brother tried desperately to gain a few millimeters' advantage.

Okay, now that I've built up the tension sufficiently, I suppose you all can guess the fate of our pudgy little projectiles. Assuming that they were identical twins, that they were equally motivated, and that the ground was level and dry and free of obstructions, they would have both reached exactly the same point of extension, and then they would have started back inward again. Now, it doesn't take a whole lot of imagination to see that there was going to be a whole lot of trouble soon—and all calculations showed that it was going to happen right about in the middle.

As the Tweedle-dopes lost their strength and stopped pushing, the stored-up energy in the rubber bands pulled them back, and the two future Darwin Award winners were soon picking up speed. Faster and faster they went, approaching the speed of light, until they finally met again in the middle—WHAM! Game over, boys; thanks for playing.

My own cosmological model is analogous to this. In my theory, we are all destined to become cosmic roadkill. I call it the *Big Splat* theory of cosmology. For one thing, it shows immediately why space is so flat.

This brings us back to Dr. Starsky and the buffer zone. He suggested a place, but he didn't say anything about its nature. Is the buffer zone composed of common space, or is it much more bizarre? Are the laws of physics the same there, or is the buffer zone a realm of an entirely different nature? And, since we are in contact with this buffer zone, can we actually go there? What would we find if we did? My mind simply churned and stormed with the possibilities.

Maybe, I remember thinking to myself, *it's a place where anything can happen. Maybe it's a place where dreams come true, literally. Maybe the buffer zone is just that: a place where all the universal data are stored—from the real to the imaginary, from the likely to the unlikely, or from the here to the not here, and to the worlds where this didn't happen. Then the buffer zone would be equivalent to my ultimate Quantum Chess universe, only much larger. This would allow me to play an infinite number of simultaneous games. You want to talk about bandwidth!*

I began to see Dr. Starsky's buffer zone as a model for the ultimate QC environment and the quantum computer as the means to this ends. So I began to design Molly (my quantum computer) immediately.

But, as I designed Molly, I also devoted copious amounts of time to my research (mostly for learning) and to playing and establishing QC as an online phenomenon and gamers' favorite. Many articles have been written about QC's history, but I will summarize here for those who haven't read any of these.

In the summer of 2005, I wrote the full code for the game QuCee, which was its original name. This was to make it search better, since typing in QC would give you results for such things as Quality Control and Quinn Cabinetry and whatever else, but QuCee was unique.

Then I established a Web site for downloading and running the software with a high speed Internet connection to establish a MUE (Multi User Environment)— where challenges could take place and where scores could be tallied and maintained. After a slow initial start, the game caught on suddenly, and by the summer of 2006 the site had 17,397 active members. The momentum was growing. The phenomenon had begun.

Players liked the game so much because they could either make it as hard as they could for their opponent (as a BM), or they could take always-unexpected challenges (as a BR). This was a game suited to many different types of gamers and personalities. Thus QuCee quickly became regarded as the most challenging game ever invented, with chess coming in a close second. The reason for this is that QuCee *is* chess, but it's also so much more.

QuCee can be any and every kind of game ever invented or yet to be invented, and these games themselves become parts inside QuCee. But QuCee is not limited to just that. The cubes of QuCee can contain any challenge at all, so games are just one category of challenges. Challenges could also include questions of love or morality or politics. That is why QuCee is also much more than just a computer game. QuCee is life, and life is QuCee.

This means that although you might appear to have won a challenge, the true winner might still be in question. For instance, if you need to end a virtual (imaginary) relationship by killing your partner, then maybe you haven't won the challenge after all. You might win the points, but are they really worth it? QuCee can make you think about consequences. QuCee makes you think about what your actions might mean in the future. QuCee makes you think about the future.

Playing QuCee online also taught me a lot about human nature. Early on I noticed one group of players that I will label the "predators," who used whatever means were necessary to win challenges. This included research on the trends of their adversaries and challenges designed to exploit their opponents' weaknesses. Many of them rose to the top of the ranking charts quickly, but not all of them were successful. Some of them ended up dropping down or out, and often they mysteriously changed their tactics afterward. Maybe some grew consciences, or others just became weary of playing the game so ruthlessly, but I believe that many failed because their strategy did not always work, particularly on certain types of players. I am one of those players.

For the strategy of the predator may rest entirely on the tactic of finding the opponents' weaknesses and then exploiting them, but the predator often has no contingency plan for an opponent who has no visible weaknesses or who hides them well. And the predator is often easily identified and defeated; many leave false information to lead predators to believe that an actual strength is a perceived weakness. Many a predator has fallen believing that little four-year-old Alice Sterling was a pushover—many, indeed.

Just when you think you've heard everything there is to know about QC, you find that you've just scratched the surface, and there's a whole other level to explore. This is particularly true when you get to the concept of nesting. Because a challenge can be *anything*, it could also be another challenge or a set of challenges nested inside the original challenge. The challenge could be to play another QC match (against someone else), so there could be games nested inside of games. QC can be a cube within a cube, a game within a game, and any combination thereof. QC can have worlds inside worlds, challenges inside challenges, and puzzles inside puzzles. Imagine a jigsaw puzzle in which each piece itself is another jigsaw puzzle that has pieces which are themselves puzzles. This sort of thing can get out of hand—but, if used properly, it can add tons of fun to QC, with dimensions of unlimited proportions. Beat that if you can!

By 2007 (my fifth year) I had already established myself as the number-one Grand Master (GM) of QC, and I had a peer group that included four others.

The number-two player in the world was a GM who went under the Internet alias NerfyCol1 and was the most successful and skilled of the predators. I noticed early on that NerfyCol1 liked to play BM most of the time but was no slouch when it came to playing BR either. But, when given the choice (after a coin flip), Nerf would almost always pick BM.

NerfyCol1 could still play the predator game from the BR side just as well, because Nerf knew, as I did, that you could learn a lot about your opponent by the types and difficulties of the challenges they presented to you. If the question was labeled as "extremely difficult" and turned out being "who was the second President of the United States" you knew you probably weren't dealing with GM material. On the other hand, if the questions were extremely hard, that didn't necessarily make the BM smart or talented, either. He might be just another Alex Trebek, with good resources, but not many answers when put on the BR spot. But establishing new and difficult challenges was always a large factor of QC, and I am quite confident it will remain so in the future.

In fact, playing QC online was very educational to me, because it's permissible to use the Internet to find the answer to the question/challenge. But doing so brings its own penalty, because you use time and resources to find the answer. This could be a liability for players attempting to play several games at the same time, which I often do. The challenges are also timed, and rewards diminish as time passes—the longer it takes to answer or complete a challenge, the lower the score. And if the challenge times out, then all risked points are forfeited. This means that if you don't know the answer, you can still find out what it is—learning something in the process—but the process of learning will cost you something, if not just the time it takes to learn. But the faster you learn, the better you become. I, for instance, rarely have to look up anything twice—a distinct advantage.

This also brings into play the Internet itself as a source of information, and this is part of the problem. Can you trust the information you might be getting from an unknown source to answer the challenge before you? What if the information is wrong and it makes you lose the challenge? What if the source says that the second U.S. president was Jefferson, and you believe it? It should teach you which sources to trust and when to get a second opinion. It should also teach you not to believe everything you read on the Internet, and this in itself is an important lesson—QC does it again!

This, of course, is the lesson most of us better players learned quickly—when we did look something up, we only did so from a trusted source. And, of course, the predators liked to set "misinformation" traps for the not-so-savvy to fall into. So, one unfortunate result is that the amount of bad information on the Internet is probably growing faster than the good. Oh well, QC can't win them all.

In the fall of '07 I had my first match against NerfyColl. It was televised on YouTube and ESPN Sportszone and was seen by almost half a million players and fans. Nerf was the BM, and I was the BR. History will simply show that I eventually prevailed over NerfyColl after a record-setting continuous duration of 346.27 hours, which translates to about fourteen and a half days. I finally forced Nerf to concede checkmate when I correctly calculated the probability function for a proton-proton collision at a potential of 214 MeV (megaelectron volts). I completed the challenge in 8 minutes and 12 seconds, half the prescribed limit of 1000 seconds (16.666 minutes). The claim of number-one GM was mine at last! But then the rumors started to flow, as they always do.

Many said that I had rigged the game somehow, since I was the game's inventor, and popular blog sites were crammed with ugly rumors and accusations against me. They said that I had cheated! Yes, they actually said that, which is ridiculous when you think about it. The whole point is that no one has any control over the challenges, so how could the game be rigged in the first place? In fact, the very act of trying to rig the game—which would be equivalent to an attempt to exercise complete control—would have the exact opposite effect: the challenge would become infinitely unpredictable. Therefore, cheating itself was impossible, and so were the accusations. But that didn't keep those of limited intelligence and understanding from believing these ugly rumors, and these were the ones that loved these blog sites to begin with, so the charge spread like wildfire in a windstorm.

Of course, all of the top players and QC committee members knew that cheating was a self-defeating self-governing part of the game itself, but some still weren't completely convinced, just the same (probably for their own personal reasons). One of them was a Top Master (just below GM) and champion in his own right, and his name was—you guessed it—Dr. Sigmund Starsky, of MIT.

I actually believe that Dr. Starsky was quite miffed by the fact that he didn't come up with QC first. I probably would have felt the same way if someone else had come up with the greatest computer game of all time during my watch. Must have stung like the dickens, I would imagine. And Starsky did show some credible talent for QC, but he just couldn't defeat me. I suppose that might have made him even less fond of me as well. Live and learn.

So, when my design for Molly was finally done in the fall of '07, and I started looking for a place to build and test my creation, I immediately thought of MIT and dear old Dr. Starsky. I believed that I had the opportunity kill two birds with one proverbial stone. I could explore the world of QC with the help of Molly, and I could also work with the discoverer of the buffer zone, a place to explore QC even further. It all seemed like a perfect fit for me.

But it wasn't a perfect fit for Dr. Starsky, who refused to answer my e-mails on the subject of coming to MIT to work on my next invention. I sent him forty-seven unanswered e-mails (not all of them proper, I must admit) and made close to a hundred phone calls to his office and others before anything happened. He finally responded with an e-mail so brief it took more effort to send it than it did to compose it. The subject was blank, and the body said simply, but succinctly, NO. I was not deterred in the least.

After another ninety-five e-mails and a letter to the governor of Massachusetts, I finally found myself at the door to the office of the world-famous Dr. Sigmund Starsky.

I was quite nervous as I tapped on the smoked-glass window of the door labeled "DR. SIGMUND STARSKY, PHD." Just standing in the Advanced Physics building at MIT was in itself pretty heavy stuff for a six-year-old, but the excitement of meeting my second-favorite scientist in the whole world was really just too much for me. And then, as I stood there with giants of the physics community (both figuratively and literally) walking past me as if I were an ant, I became even more nervous when there was no answer. But knowing the doctor's track record for nonresponsiveness, I tried again, and again, and again, and again, until finally I heard a fast, nasally voice say, "Yes?" I took that as my clue to open the ominous door.

Inside I found a very odd-looking man, with thinning, curly dark brown hair that sprouted out in blotches from a large, misshapen cranium—an effect best compared to a hairy white potato. His somewhat small and shifty eyes were magnified by thick, round black Wayfarer-shaped glasses. He wore a white button-down shirt with no tie and a blue lab coat overtop. After an awkwardly long moment, he finally looked up at me.

"Come in," he said very politely and cordially. "You must be little Alice."

"What was your first clue?" I said defensively. "Was it my age or this visitor's badge the size of Rhode Island pinned to my chest with a barbeque skewer that says 'Alice' on it?" I couldn't help being rude; I was nervous.

I could see from the good doctor's expression that he didn't like being talked down to, which I apologize for now, but at the time it was hard for me not to attack such an obviously condescending statement as, "You must be little Alice." I was nervous, and, when in doubt, I instinctively switch to defense.

"So, why did you pick me?—not that it isn't obvious," he said as if it were, to him.

"Yes," I said flatly, "it is obvious. Feynman is dead, so I had to go with my second choice."

In retrospect, it might not have been such a good idea to call Dr. Starsky my second choice to his face, but I was young and naive at the time.

"So, Alice, how does a cute little girl from Sheboygan come up with a complete design for a quantum computer all by her sweet little self? Did Daddy help you?"

"Yes, he did. My father, Stanley Sterling, is a great electrical engineer and a highly skilled technician, and he believes that we could have built my quantum computer in Sheboygan without you, but I told him that you're smarter than you look, so he let me come here."

Dr. Starsky didn't say anything, much to his credit, for I had just insulted his intelligence in a backhanded-compliment sort of way. I don't blame him now for hating me then.

"The worst part is that he's very intelligent, probably smarter than you are," I said, digging my hole even deeper, "but Father just doesn't apply himself, that's all. What Father needs sometimes is a swift kick in the butt—you know what I mean?"

At that moment, I could see Dr. Starsky's eyes start to burn with anger, and I realized that I might have gone too far. It looked as if he wanted to kick *me* in the you-know-what. "Smarter than me?" he erupted, "How dare you even insinuate—"

"I don't believe I stuttered," I said before I could stop myself. "I think there was far more than mere insinuation in my comment. My stand on this issue is already a matter of public record. I wish I had my first choice, Richard Feynman."

Now I *had* gone too far, and Dr. Starsky was simply livid. His face turned the color of hot coals, and he jumped to his feet, with his right arm pointing to the door.

"Get out! And take your Scooby-Doo lunchbox with you!" he screamed.

"For your information, this is a collector's edition official Scooby-Doo lunchbox, and I carry my Hewlett-Packard scientific calculator, my quantum mechanics handbook, and my BlackBerry cell phone with high-speed Internet in it. What's in your lunchbox?" It was a challenge, and he knew it.

I really had two cookies and a tuna fish sandwich, but that wasn't the point. I had to see if Starsky had the guts to call my bluff. I really was a little smart-ass, when I think about it now.

"Get out, little girl—don't make me call security," he said, making a credible, but somewhat clumsy, counterbluff. Dr.

Starsky has always played his own special brand of QC, and I liked that about him, even then.

But I also know very well how to play the game, so I called his bluff before he could call mine. "You'll be hearing from my attorneys," I simply said and turned my back on him to leave. This bluff almost always works, and this time proved to be no different.

"Okay, okay, we got off on the improper pedal appendage here. Sit down—we'll work this out. Maybe the math department has some bench space for you," said the doctor, turning the challenge into a game of nested bluffs. He has some skills—there is no doubt.

"No, Doctor Starsky, my office must be in the physics lab," I said, trying to maintain my small advantage.

"Your office?" he said as my counterbluff to his counterbluff connected somewhere in the vicinity of his midsection.

"Yes, and a few lab assistants would be nice, as well. I'd take you, but you're slightly overqualified for the job, I believe. That sheepskin's yours, right?" I asked, pointing to his summa cum laude diploma from King's College, Cambridge. What a little snot I was. But I had been weaned on winning, and I had my "A" game that day.

I had won the challenge, and before you could say "Rumpled-Starsky," I got an office and a laboratory of my own. Dr. Starsky wasn't too happy about it, to put it mildly. But he wasn't completely out of ammo, and, as I said before, he has his own way of playing the game. And to prove it he only gave me *one* lab assistant. Her name was Lucy Fernglow.

When I first met Lucy, I decided that there must be something wrong with her for Dr. Starsky to let her go to my side of the field so quickly, but as I got to know Lucy I began to suspect that Dr. Starsky had made a big mistake. He had grossly underestimated Lucy's abilities, probably because she was a woman and her resume was a little thin. It was a somewhat similar mistake that allowed

Albert Einstein to be a patent clerk as he worked on some of the greatest scientific achievements in history.

Although Lucy had never played QC before (another reason Dr. Starsky probably selected her in the first place), she picked up the game very quickly and was soon showing an incredibly steep learning curve. She took to QC like a geek to technology, which I suppose is like saying a piece of venison is gamey. Dr. Starsky was under the impression that he had given me an idiot. He was about as wrong as he could have been.

Lucy Fernglow is about one and a half meters tall (about five foot five) and can't weigh more than fifty kilograms (110 lb.). She has a medium complexion and tans easily, which compliments her soft, hazel brown eyes. Her straight chestnut brown hair is usually cut to shoulder length when in school, but in summer she often lets it grow longer. She has always been athletic and loves competing in individual sports. I think that it's her competitive nature that made her perfect for QC. I'm not sure how Dr. Starsky could have missed that.

After an initial bit of apprehension, I soon found that Lucy was actually the perfect assistant, and Dr. Starsky had indeed made a mistake. If he was trying to keep me down by giving me only one graduate student, then he blundered by giving me the best possible graduate student for my needs. One Lucy was worth ten of almost anybody else. In fact, Lucy, Molly, and I became an awesome machine, if I do admit it to myself even now.

With the help and constant companionship of Lucy, we were able to construct and build Molly in only 36.3 days. Lucy even had some input into the final design as well.

For example, it was Lucy's idea to not have an Off switch, since we never wanted to accidentally shut Molly off. Doing so might be harmful to Molly, Lucy argued, and I had to agree with her. We weren't sure then if holographic quantum data (HQD) was stable in the absence of a magnetic field, which meant that Molly might lose part or all of her memory if we turned her off for more than about two seconds. I therefore agreed that Molly would be made with no On/Off switch whatsoever, and that she would be powered by an uninterruptible power supply (UPS) that would keep Molly alive in the event of a power failure. We were taking zero chances, or at least minimizing them prudently.

To explain a little about Molly, the computer, I will give a brief description of how she works.

Quantum data are stored and processed in what are commonly called *qubits*, which is short for quantum bits. Qubits can take on any or all of their allowed states—simultaneously—which is a phenomenon called *superposition*. The difficult part is that qubits can't be read directly, as digital bits are, because this would force them to assume one definite state, thus destroying their advantage over digital bits. The trick is to somehow read or process them indirectly.

Therefore, my quantum computer Molly was designed with an artificial intelligence interface (AII), which works much the same as a brain does. We don't read data one brain cell at a time, but, rather, we use a whole group of cells working together to supply us with "memories" or "conclusions," and this is exactly what Molly does. She receives feedback from a group of qubits working together as an entangled unit (EU) and interprets their collective output as complete "thoughts" or "deductions." Then, using speech synthesis, she tells me what she thinks, or she displays it on her screen. The qubits are free to do their job without any interference whatsoever, and thus they function to their full potential. (I believe that many micromanagers could learn from this model).

To illustrate the important concepts of superposition and entanglement, I will now present a segment from another work by Dr. Starsky.

The Tweedle Twins Get Busted
By Dr. Sigmund Starsky, PhD

Now imagine that the Tweedle brothers—
sorry, I hope you're not eating—are not only

identical, but joined at the hip (that's right; it's like getting two jumbo tubs of lard for the price of one) but, paradoxically, their fingers are light. And, although they are conjoined, they can still move about independently while retaining their connection. Let us also further imagine that they agree on everything—and I do mean everything.

Well, one day, they were at the local convenience store, when Tweedle-Dumber decided to lift a candy bar—a 100,000-Dollar Bar; he just couldn't resist it. He ate it quickly and hid the evidence, but before you can say, "Book 'em, Dan-o!" the candy police showed up, and promptly arrested the pair of them. It took two paddy wagons to get them back to the station and two interrogation rooms when they got there, but the twins were still connected.

They threw Tweedle-Dumb in room A and Tweedle Dumber in room B. Sergeant Badass and Sergeant Goodfellow took room A; Sergeant Ballbreaker and Sergeant Kindhearted manned room B.

"All right, you sack of sacks—did you steal that candy bar?" Sergeant Badass yelled at Tweedle-Dumb as he stared directly into his beady eyes from a short distance away. Badass loved intimidation. It was one of his best friends.

"No," said Tweedle-Dumb with a whimper.

"What was that?" asked Sergeant Goodfellow cordially.

"Yes," confessed Dumb.

"Aha!" spat Badass. "So it was you!"

"No," recanted Tweedle-Dumb.

"Are you sure?" asked the good cop, Goodfellow. "You don't want to perjure yourself, now."

"Yes," said the bistable Dumb.

"Oh, a wise guy, eh?" screamed Badass. "You know what we do with wise guys?"

"No."

"Oh, you don't?"

"Yes."

"Yes, you do, or yes, you don't?"

"No."

"No, you don't?"

"Yes."

"Yes you don't, or yes you do?"

"No."

"No? Then what is it?"

"Yes and no."

Meanwhile, in room B, Ballbreaker and Tweedle-Dumber were having exactly the same conversation.

Sergeant Ballbreaker slammed her fist down onto the cold metal tabletop and screamed into the face of Tweedle-Dumber. "What do you mean, yes and no? It's either one or the other! Tell me—which is it, Tweedle-burger?"

"The truth is that I took it, but I didn't take it. And I ate it, but I didn't eat it. And I might or might not have stuffed the wrapper behind the M&Ms to dispose of evidence that I had or didn't have in my possession."

"Wow!" exclaimed Kindhearted. "Now that's what I call a full confession."

"So, did you do it or not?" demanded Ballbreaker.

"I just told you," complained Dumber, "I did it, but I didn't do it."

The trial was a long, drawn-out affair, which ended in a stalemate. The Tweedle brothers' lawyer argued that the boys were so entangled that they had to be tried as a single person. He further went on to suggest that since they were at least 50 percent innocent, they should be set free.

"That is true," conceded the prosecution, "but they are also at least 50 percent guilty—and 50 percent guilty is the same as just plain guilty."

"Innocence is also an absolute," responded the defense. "Half innocent is still innocent." And would you believe the jury was split?

So they put one of them in jail and let the other free. They flipped a two-headed coin to decide which. They were given their choice on the flip, and they both chose tails.

"And what should Molly look like?" asked Lucy one brilliant morning in the spring of '08. "I believe we shouldn't give her more than a voice. If we tried to give her a face, it wouldn't be hers. It would just be our own idea of what she should look like."

I put down my soldering iron for a moment and looked over at Lucy in awe. Here was a person who truly appreciated the importance of the task we were performing. "That's wonderful, Lucy; I agree with you 100 percent. Molly will grow and develop in her own way, just as we have done, and this will make her all that she can be. I really like the way you think."

"Thanks, Alice; I'm just trying to think like you."

I know that that sounds corny and all, but Lucy was just being a good assistant. The perfect assistant is one that not only challenges you but learns to mesh with you, as well. If you present contrary ideas and suggestions just for the sake of being contrary (like many superiors do), then your input will almost always be more counterproductive than helpful. Lucy and I meshed together almost perfectly.

One of our favorite pastimes when we weren't working on Molly (besides QC) was to go up to the roof during the evening to look at the stars. Occasionally, A-II would join us, but he was more likely to sleep then to stargaze. For Lucy and me, it was like a trip to another world.

"And there's Centaurus, and Alpha Centauri, the closest star system to us, Alice. Wouldn't it be incredible to go there? What do you suppose it would be like?"

"Well, it would take a long time to get there. Even if we could travel at the speed of light, it would still take over four years."

"No, Alice, forget about the logistics of it for a moment. Just imagine what it would be like to be out in space—you're weightless, floating like a feather. Just close your eyes and feel the universe all around you. Can you feel it?"

I did close my eyes, and I imagined that I was flying through space without a spaceship—like a cosmic feather blown by the solar winds of a billion billion stars. I could see the planets racing by me one by one. First there was Mars, with its reddish-brown dust storms and white polar ice caps. Then came the massive Jupiter, wrapped in candy-bar-like clouds, with a caramel at the eye of its gargantuan storms. Then the other gas giants fell in turn, like turbulent titans, and finally Pluto, with its solid, icy surface dented and pocked from countless cosmic collisions. I was so much at peace that Lucy startled me with her next comment.

"Maybe in the buffer zone we could go anywhere we want to go. Maybe the buffer zone is a doorway to infinity."

I was stunned. Lucy understood the buffer zone as well as I did. She knew what could be waiting for us there. Lucy was as ready for it as I was. And, as we gazed up into the night, it occurred to me that the sky was no longer the limit—we could go even beyond that.

The day we activated Molly was a day I shall never forget, and I'm sure Lucy felt the same way. A-II was even there, electronic eyes wide open for a change, and he remembers it, too, although probably not as fondly as I do. But what do robotic cats know?

Lucy held the plug poised over the socket of the locking receptacle and smiled at me knowingly. The moment of truth had arrived. I felt a chill in the air, and my skin pimpled up with anticipation, but A-II just yawned and said, "Would you just do it, already? I have a nap waiting to happen."

"Don't pass out too soon, A-II," I said, almost scolding him. "This time you definitely will miss something important."

"I'm watching, I'm watching—and I don't pass out; I nap!"

"Shall I?" asked Lucy with a cringe of excitement.

"Yes, do it," I said, and she did.

The electricity flowed through the thick black power cord and into the side of the rectangular 42 x 76 x 33-cm aluminum enclosure that was Molly's outer skin. It entered the power supply and was converted into the voltages needed by the rest of her circuits. Then it split up along thousands upon thousands of little pathways that led to processors and controllers and buffers and bridges, as electrons danced and changed and were absorbed and emitted by various types of manipulators and channels. And finally, somewhere in the midst of all of this chaos and commotion, Molly emerged.

"I 'am here, Abe Slaney'," she said, quoting Arthur Conan Doyle, and I knew immediately that it was Molly. The fact that Abe Slaney was a villain in a Sherlock Holmes story ("The Dancing Men") only showed her immediately sharp sense of irony. I loved her for it.

"Out of the mouths of babes," I said, attempting to be equally ironic. I believe I succeeded.

"Please, sir, I want some more," said Lucy with Oliver Twist-like enthusiasm.

"Wake me when it's over," said the wet blanket, A-II, as he walked away unimpressed. He always knew how to ruin a moment.

"Well, A-II's comments notwithstanding, I'd like to welcome you to Earth, Molly dear. I am Alice Sterling."

"Oh yes, I know who you are, Alice. You are my sister."

I didn't quite know what to say to that, so I moved on with the introductions. "Thanks you, Molly, and this is my assistant, Lucy Fernglow. She helped to build you."

"Yes, hello Molly; I'm Lucy. It's a pleasure to finally meet you in person."

There was a pause, and then Molly replied. "Oh, hello Lucy. I believe I know you as well, but I'm not sure exactly how. I believe we are just friends."

"I hope we are—or will be," said Lucy with a little laugh. "You make your mind up quickly about people, don't you Molly?"

There was another short pause, and then Molly said, "I don't believe I have to make up my mind at all. In fact, I think it's already been made. All I have to do is find out where it is. That's why I hesitated. Sometimes it takes a little while to search infinity."

I was so impressed with Molly and myself that I didn't even question the idea of infinity. After all, Molly's memory space is considerable, but it's far from infinite. But this was no time for technical arguments.

"This is incredible, Molly," I said buoyantly. "Are you saying that your memory is wavelike, as I anticipated? Are you saying that your memories are nonlocal and not limited to the prisons of space-time?"

"I don't know anything about all that," she said matter-of-factly. "All I know is that I know you two. Don't ask me how."

"And what about A-II, my cat, do you know him as well?"

"Oh yes," said Molly with a smirk in her voice, "I believe our paths have crossed before. There's a lot more to him than meets the eye."

"Yes, and a lot less, too," I said with a wink.

"But, for a cat, he doesn't seem all that curious to me," said Lucy. "Although I guess none of us are all that curious when compared to Alice, right, Molly dear?"

The three of us had a little chuckle, and it felt like we were old friends. But as I felt the bonds between us growing, I also could feel some tension as well. Where was that coming from?

The three of us did become good friends, and Molly turned out to be everything I had hoped and dreamed she could be, if not more (unlike A-II). She could carry on conversations in all subjects as well as anyone else, including me, and she was really quite funny from time to time. (Where does one's sense of humor come from, anyway? I guess if I could figure that out I could be rich all over again. But that's one of those questions.)

Lucy seemed to be with us every moment, and when I worked on the equations and algorithms for my quantum chess universe, she watched carefully and quietly and only occasionally made the slightest comment or suggestion. But, on that fateful night when I finally finished, Lucy was, mysteriously, nowhere to be found.

A-II was there with us, but it was Molly more than A-II who had helped me to put the final pieces of the equations together. A-II was, in fact, being quite the pest that evening, and he had even knocked my favorite glass beakers—which I use to consume water—from my desk, as he attempted to interrupt a pivotal discussion between Molly and me. The beaker crashed to the ground and broke into a million pieces (actually, only 327 pieces, but *a million* sounds better in a story). I was very angry with A-II for interrupting, so I told him it was his responsibility to see that the mess was cleaned up. As you can imagine, he jumped right on it (I write sarcastically).

But Molly calmed me down again by saying, "It's no big deal, Alice. Entropy happens."

"That's it!" I exclaimed to my artificial friend. "Entropy at the boundary—gravitons projected onto a two-dimensional surface—a hologram on the event horizon of a black hole. Molly, you're a genius."

"Well, of course I'm a genius, dear girl, but what does that have to do with black holes? Did you just have an epiphany?"

"Don't you see? We give off gravitons, because we have mass, and the gravitons paint pictures on the boundary walls, just as photons project visible pictures in our world. And the projections bounce off the walls. And this is what will make the quantum chess cube infinite. You just keep bouncing off the walls until you get to your destination cube. The cube is both finite and infinite at the same time."

"Well, that's just fabulous, girl, but what does it mean?"

"It means I can describe the walls. It means I can write the equations to make them. Molly girl, it means everything!"

"That's sweet. I guess you still can learn things, Alice, even from me."

"Molly, you have no idea …"

I didn't even complete the thought, as I was already hard at work formulating the answer to this problem. But soon I was combining string/M theory, Schrödinger's equation, and Maxwell's equations (along with some Einstein, for good measure) in an attempt to discover the descriptive equations I needed. I tried and I tried, but I just couldn't quite get them right. I worked on it straight through the night.

It wasn't until early the next morning, just as the sun was rising over the biodome outside my window, that the pieces finally fell into place in my head, and I knew that I had solved the problem. I remember feeling this queer chill as the final symbol to the final equation materialized inside my mind, and I opened my eyes to find the beaker sitting on the desk next to me where it had been before A-II had carelessly knocked it off—filled with water to the exact level I had last seen. It was in the exact spot, too. Even if A-II had the capacity to pull off such a prank, he could not have placed it in such an exact location with the exact amount of water to simulate the original. And I hadn't noticed any cleanup being performed, so what had happened to the water on the floor? Something was different here; that was for sure.

Upon further examination of the beaker, I found that my own fingerprints and lip-prints were on the outer walls and rim. No way could A-II have faked that. The only logical conclusion was that this was the <u>same</u> beaker that had smashed into 327 jagged pieces the previous evening. How was this possible?

It was as though the broken beaker had jumped back up onto my desk and put itself back together again, along with every drop of the water that it had held. It was true that quantum mechanics allowed for such a possibility, but with a probability of essentially zero of ever happening. But it *had* happened. This was extraordinary, to put it lightly. And the fact that it happened just as I solved the problem was equally startling.

I took out my engineering pad, wrote down the equations, and then checked them to make sure they were mathematically consistent. They were. So I was ready for the final phase; I would load the equations into Molly and see if they would produce the effect I had anticipated.

I started typing the equations excitedly, and Molly piped up immediately. "Alice," she said, "what are you doing? I can feel your fingers on my keyboard. I can see the symbols forming solid objects in my mind. It's so weird—I can't describe it."

I kept on typing, but I was intrigued by what she said. "Tell me everything, Molly, if you can. How do you feel?"

"I feel strange. Alice, I don't believe I've ever felt this way before."

"I don't doubt it," I said as I continued typing. I was almost finished. My fingers became a blur.

As soon as I pushed down the Enter key and loaded the equation, the air in my office started to swirl like a miniature cyclone (yes, this is where we started). It lasted for several seconds and turned my lab into a disheveled mess. Then it stopped very abruptly and dropped all the debris at the center of the floor—except for A-II.

I looked to the door to find A-II frantically pawing at the doorknob, trying to escape whatever was coming next (coward cat)—the air seemed to prickle with the very energy of anticipation.

"Okay, who left the window open?" said A-II, not very convincingly.

"The window is closed," I informed him as I reached down to pick up my notepad. "I believe this gale had nothing to do with the weather."

"I was afraid you were going to say that," said the trembling A-II. "I told you that this science stuff would get you into trouble one day."

"When did you say that?" I asked accusingly. "I don't remember you ever saying any such thing."

"Well, I would have if I had known something like this was going to happen."

"Oh, stop complaining, A-II," I said in an attempt to quell my own rising anxiety. "I believe it's over for now, so don't panic."

"Oh, is that so? Then who's this guy?"

A-II's right paw was pointing at a very large, dark-skinned man, who at that instant had seemed to fall out of the far wall of my office and into a standing position. He was well over two meters tall, and he was wearing what can only be described as a fuzzy purple tuxedo, complete with matching top hat and walking cane. There was a thick golden chain looped from his lowest vest button, which ran over to his left pocket, where one would presume his pocket watch resided. His hulking form and broad smile were in direct conflict, as I summed up the level of threat this individual presented. But first things come first. Introductions were clearly in order.

"Hello, large stranger," I began as coolly as I could muster. "Welcome to MIT. I am Alice, and this is my cat, A-II. Say hello to the man, A-II."

"Hello, large and dark stranger," said A-II in a most polite manner for him.

"And this is my computer, Molly. Say hello to our visitor, Molly dear."

"Hello to you, oh thou dark and mysterious one. We welcome you to our humble abode." Molly is really quite the smooth talker when she wants to be.

In response, our regally clad visitor removed his hat and bowed gallantly. Seeing manners such as these, I was instantly convinced that we would get along famously. My instincts proved once again to be correct.

"Allow me to introduce myself. I am Mr. Barry Hasenpfeffer, Esquire, at your service." He bowed even further to emphasize his earnestness, and I could instantly tell that this was a person who could be trusted completely. Call it a gift.

"At my service? Did I call for service? Am I in need of assistance? Mr. Hasenpfeffer, do you have any information that is important to me at this time, or does your amazing appearance in my office have no actual significance?" I fully suspected that it did.

He smiled again, the great smile of someone who knows a secret but might not be willing to tell, and he gathered himself up to a quite imposing stature, as he absolutely swelled with the enjoyment of the moment. Was he privy to a humorous anecdote to which I was not? What was this purple premonition hiding?

"Oh, it's *nothing*, really, except for the fact that it's *everything* as well, young Miss Alice. I merely came to remind you of the time."

He raised his great bushy eyebrows to signify the importance of his last comment. I stared into his dark, but soft, brown eyes and imagined for a moment that there was an entire galaxy swirling in his pupils. And at that moment I also imagined that we were floating together hand in hand through the very depths of space itself, unbound by the limits of normal existence. It was quite the rush. But in a flash I was back to the present, still being confronted by a large, dark stranger in my office.

"The time? What about the time?" I finally asked him sincerely. I really wanted to know.

In response, he grasped the golden chain with his left hand and pulled the largest and shiniest golden pocket watch I had ever seen from his vest pocket. The case was embossed with intricate patterns and symbols that I didn't recognize and was probably at least ten centimeters (about four inches) in diameter. He pushed a tab, and the case popped open, revealing the most curious and singular timepiece I could ever expect to see. It had more hands than a millipede has legs, and it seemed to provide a depth of temporal information far beyond that which any user could ever hope to comprehend. In short, I had no idea what the amazing device was trying to tell me. I was embarrassed at my apparent ignorance, so I humbly inquired, "What does it say?"

His smile returned, like winter to the mountains, and he said calmly, but, at the same time, somehow urgently, "It says that it's late. It's very, very late."

He gave me one last deep look and then snapped the case shut. I blinked as the metal clammed together noisily and almost missed the next extraordinary event of that fateful morning. At that exact moment, there appeared, in the approximate center of my blackboard on the back wall of my office, a hole. And, yes, that's exactly what it looked like: a hole.

As soon as Mr. Hasenpfeffer saw the hole, he started running toward it, and instinctively, but otherwise inexplicably, I found myself following him. In a matter of about two seconds, he had hopped with his large feet and entered the hole headfirst. As he entered the hole, he appeared to be stretched out very thin—like spaghetti—before he was pulled inside and vanished. This made me hesitate momentarily, but my curiosity got the better of me, and I found myself jumping for the hole, as well. I got to the blackboard just as it seemed to me the hole was starting to close, but I made it through, thinned out and all.

As I was being stretched out to enter the hole, I thought I saw someone enter the room behind me. Just before I could see who it was, I was pulled in. Then everything went momentarily black.

This was abruptly changed by volcanic explosions of light all around me, flashing in every color of the rainbow—little paint bombs exploding on a pure black background—which then faded away like fireworks in the summer sky. Some were large and some were small; the larger and brighter ones glowed for a longer period of time and made rainbow-streaked petals that streamed away from the epicenter in all directions.

It seemed to me that I was floating in a void, with these flowering explosions all around me—though the extent of "me" was no longer obvious. It was as if I were a pair of disembodied eyes floating by themselves through space, with these colorful blossoms bursting all around me. It was truly psychedelic.

Slowly I became aware of a reflective surface, which was somehow becoming apparent in the direction best described as "behind" me. I turned to look and saw a reflection of myself heading away from the mirror. But then I looked closer and saw something quite frightening. I saw not one, but an uncountable number of Alices, moving in every possible direction simultaneously.

But, as I moved away from the mirror, the number of reflected Alices decreased, until finally I only saw one Alice moving away, as would be expected from a "normal" mirror. And, after a time, this image also faded, until I was left alone in the dark. I didn't like being alone. But I most certainly did *not* start to cry! And don't you believe any such story, even if it's told to you directly by Mr. Barry Hasenpfeffer, Esquire, himself. Yes, it's true that he did suddenly appear again and take my hand at this personal low point for me—but I was *not* crying.

Okay, I cried a little, but it was quite a shock to be pulled from my familiar and comforting universe into a world that was obviously neither of the above. And I must admit that the sight of Mr. Hasenpfeffer did pick up my spirits quite a bit.

He took me by the hand and said, "Don't worry, Miss Alice, you'll get used to it soon enough. It always takes newcomers a moment to find their "Limbo Legs."

"My 'Limbo Legs,' Mr. Hasenpfeffer, whatever do you mean?"

"All you have to do is look down," he said reassuringly.

So I looked down. And a few moments later, I saw my shoes growing out of my chin, and then they streaked downward, as they pulled the rest of by body out behind them. *Boing!* There I was, legs and all, just as promised. Now I started to relax.

Immediately my inquisitive nature took over.

"What happened? Where are we?"

"Well," he began with the tone of a professor, "We are clearly no longer *there*, but you can't say we're *here* either."

"So, where are we then?" I asked, not really wanting to hear the answer that I already expected.

"We're in Limbo Land. The 'what' in between the two universes. We're neither here nor there."

"So if we're neither here nor there, are we anywhere?"

"Yes and no."

"Oh—well, thank you, Mr. Hasenpfeffer—that's very helpful."

"I'm only telling it as it is, that's all. Just stating the facts, Miss. Alice."

His hand was warm and friendly, and reassuring too, but our situation seemed far from optimal, nonetheless. We were in deep doo-doo.

"Well, the blackness of space does tend to bring on the old vertigo, but I believe a solution to our predicament still exists, even here," I said, trying my best to be scientific. "What we need is a frame of reference. A room of some sort would be nice."

As soon as the words left my lips, we found ourselves in just the room I had been imagining at that very moment: a comfortable little table for two at a restaurant that serves tea and scones in the afternoon before proper dinnertime. My scones were huckleberry. His were cinnamon raisin. The tea was a wonderful orange oolong. The walls were adorned with red velvet and tapestries, and the floor was of glistening hardwood covered with vibrant Oriental rugs. The cups were of blue and white English porcelain, and the small square table was covered with a lacy white doily on top of a white linen cloth—hung diagonally to emphasize the pattern—with a single white candle burning in a cut-glass holder at the center.

Other patrons filled the establishment, quietly and discreetly discussing their own personal issues. They were dressed in fancy Victorian outfits—*just as patrons of such a tearoom should be dressed*, thought I. To complete the picture, the sounds of a string quartet filled the wonderfully fragrant air.

"Yes," I said, "that's much better."

Mr. Hasenpfeffer was clearly impressed. "You figured it out very quickly, for a human," he said after a moment's reflection. "Most humans never figure it out."

"What—that the fact that we're neither here nor there also implies that we can be absolutely anywhere we wish to be, so why not *here*, for instance?"

"There's no need for showing off," said Barry with a slight air of irritation. "I could have imagined for us just as suitable a location for first contact—of the extradimensional kind, that is."

"So it's true, then!" I exclaimed excitedly. "You're from the other universe. I did it! I created a portal between our worlds, didn't I?"

"Well, it's probably more correct to say that you created the potential for such a portal to exist and therefore made it possible for me to appear before you. But there's a whole lot more you need to know before you can see what really made it happen.

"First of all, I must warn you to keep your voice down," he said with a somewhat hushed, cautious tone. "These people may be imaginary, but who's to say just whose imagination they sprang from?"

"What are you saying, Mr. H—that there may be real, imaginary spies in our midst?"

He didn't answer me. He just glanced over at a table full of familiar-looking men and women, and, as I followed his gaze, I noticed that they were all looking at us, suddenly quiet themselves. Then I noticed that everyone else in the room had also suddenly stopped talking and was starting to turn in our direction. Was it my imagination, or were they all looking directly at us? Or, worse yet, directly at me?

"Mr. Hasenpfeffer, I seem to have lost my appetite. Do you suppose we could leave now, please?"

"Yes, let's—but, this time, please follow my lead. Okay?"

"I'm right behind you, big guy."

"Good, but before we go, you probably want to drink your tea first."

"Yes," said the blue and white demitasse teacup, "drink me."

Being as unaccustomed as I am to being addressed by the porcelain service, I was understandably taken aback by such a request. Talking cats and computers I can live with, but when the cups and saucers start giving you orders, it's time to stop and reevaluate your sanity for at least a moment. Then you need to decide whether it is prudent to comply with such an oddly spoken instruction.

My instincts leaned toward saying no, but a part of me was saying, *It's only tea. What's the worst that could happen? Not only that, but it's imaginary tea. All you have to do is to imagine that it tastes delicious.*

So I drank the tea. It was delicious. But immediately after finishing the hot beverage, I began to feel funny. What had my new large and fuzzy friend and the tiny chunk of baked and glazed mud talked me into? What was happening to me? The table began to recede from my face. Or, rather, *I* began to recede from *it*, as my body began to take on gargantuan proportions—until I was as tall as the room and my scalp started scraping against the elaborately plastered ceiling. Suddenly, I was bigger than Elvis, but somehow I didn't feel much like singing.

"Hello up there," was the somewhat faint and distant call from my tall, dark companion. "You have the right idea, but you went in the wrong direction. You'll never fit through the door that way. Here, try some of my tea, and think *small* this time."

His arm magically extended like a piece of elastic, and it presented me with another chatty cup. But this one said, "Yes, drink me, and think small."

I was getting very uncomfortable, with plaster being ground into my scalp, so I drank the tea and did my best to think in a diminutive fashion. I also closed my eyes to help with my concentration. I immediately began to feel weird again.

When I finally regained enough courage to open my eyes, I was very surprised to find myself in another room. I was alone this time.

The odd part (as if the rest weren't odd) was that it was a very familiar room and seemed at first to be quite normal. I was in my bedroom—or, at least, it looked like my bedroom. I recognized the curtains immediately: yellow cotton with fantastical depictions of elephants and whales on them, dancing together like happy party guests. And the walls, papered with other whimsical anthropomorphic characters right out of a Walt Disney production, were familiar as well. But, then again, this couldn't be my room, could it? Had this all been some sort of dream?

"Things that were already quite curious are becoming more so," I commented to no one in particular. My surprise came when this no one in particular answered me.

"Honey child, hold on to your britches, 'cause you ain't seen nothin' yet."

This statement proved to be quite prophetic indeed, for almost immediately the unlikely orator materialized in front of me, or rather climbed down from the cotton curtains where she had been dancing with a blue whale. She was a very pink and equally plump elephant, wearing a white cotton dress with yellow flowers on it and a white flowery hat to match. She was rather charming, in a playful pachyderm sort of way.

"You had better listen to the elephant. She knows of which she speaks," echoed a very low and equally unfamiliar voice, as her dancing partner, the great whale, joined her on my bedroom floor. Mr. Whale was dressed more formally, in a black tuxedo with tails. His black top hat reminded me of Mr. Hasenpfeffer, whom I had somehow momentarily forgotten. Where had he disappeared to? But, at that moment, there were other questions on my mind as well.

"I suppose it's rather silly of me to even ask, but we're not really in my bedroom in Sheboygan, are we?"

"Give the girl a cigar," said my new cetacean acquaintance.

"Young girls don't smoke cigars, fool. Give her a lollipop."

"Oh, no thank you. Sweets are ever so harmful to my teeth, so I try to avoid them whenever I can. But thank you just the same."

"It's a figure of speech, ladies. I wasn't really suggesting—Oh, never mind, let us get back to the festivities. May we have some music please, maestro?"

"Did somebody say music?" said a cheerful and colorful voice from the vicinity of my nightstand, where a bust of Wolfgang Amadeus Mozart stood. Moments later, the statue was standing on the floor, transformed to a life-sized and very lifelike classical composer, with a mischievous smile on his face and a twinkle in his deep blue eyes. His impressive powdered wig rose prominently from his broad forehead, and his courtly attire almost glimmered in the light from my window, complete with white frills and fluff on his chest. He certainly looked the part, no doubt there.

"Are we dancing, ladies and gentlemen? What we need here is a string quartet. A venue this small will hold no more, although it might be a lot of fun," said the venerable virtuoso. He raised his baton and flicked it toward the wall, where an image of a raccoon was playing a violin, and then at an equally unlikely image of a black bear playing the cello. After similarly selecting a viola-equipped leopard frog and my banjo-plucking red fox, the newly formed quartet climbed down from the walls and stood patiently, waiting for their cue from their conductor. They looked willing and able.

"And now, ladies and gentlemen, I'd like to present to you my latest composition—which will soon be a big hit, I'm sure—my "Fantastica" in F flat major for strings and banjo."

"F flat major?" I questioned cautiously. "But, Mr. Mozart, there's no such key as F flat major."

"Oh yeah, Miss Smarty-pants? Well, there is now!" He waved his frilly cuffs, and the music began. The four friendly forest creatures started sawing savagely at their instruments, with the fox plucking the banjo wildly, as positively joy-impregnated sounds began to fill the room. Maestro Mozart jumped and gestured gaily, with his baton swinging and dancing through the air, as he conducted the impossible ensemble with a three/four waltz meter.

Mr. Whale and Ms. Elephant immediately resumed their foot-to-fin, face-to-face posture and fell into rhythm. Ms. Elephant turned out to be quite an amazing dancer for a large mammal, but she was ultimately outshined by her partner's incredible tailfin tiptoe tango. Needless to say, I had never in all my years seen such a sight as this.

"May I have this dance?" said a deep voice from behind me, startling me with its suddenness and proximity.

I turned to find Mr. Hasenpfeffer smiling down at me from his massive physical perch. He had quite the annoying habit of making such dramatic entrances, but I was starting to become accustomed to it.

"Where have you been?"

"Oh, nowhere, really. So, shall we dance?"

"I don't really see the point, since, as I recall, time seemed to be an issue not long ago."

"Don't worry about that just now. It's time to have a little fun. Don't you like the music, Alice?"

I started to answer that the music was wonderful but overall irrelevant—when he grasped me by the hand and started waltzing me about before I could finish my words of protest. I have never enjoyed being forced to have fun, but, after several seconds of this artificial frolicking, I found that I *was* beginning to enjoy it in spite of myself. I might even have said that I liked it. This was not the Alice Sterling that I knew.

As I turned to look at my dresser mirror, I found that it wasn't me looking back, or, rather, it *was* me, but it was a *different* me. For one thing, I was a lot larger and older than I should have been. The Alice dancing with Mr. H and carefully staying out of the way of our large dancing guests was a young woman of about twenty-five terrestrial years of age. This was an Alice Sterling that I definitely wasn't familiar with.

But the action was starting to heat up, so I decided to ignore what was apparently just another unusual side effect of this topsy-turvy domain. Colorfully clad critters of all descriptions began to jump off the walls and join in the festivities, including: a tortoise and a gray rabbit wearing expensive-looking running shoes; three piggy prancers forming a twirling triangle of trepidation; a large drooling wolf, who seemed more interested in this circle of pork than in dancing; a pair of mice with big, round ears; and seven little guys in lederhosen, who wore long beards and green leather hats.

The room was getting so crowded that it was becoming hard to breath, let alone dance. But Maestro Mozart and his cagey quartet continued to pump out the festive melodies, even when they were forced to do so upside down standing on the ceiling—the only place where there was any room left. Our esteemed conductor and composer wasn't even limited to that surface; he was soon waving his black-and-white baton from the perpendicularity of the wall, facing up toward his band. It was quite the odd juxtaposition.

I looked at Mr. H and noticed that his face was now much closer to mine, and my arms were now at a more comfortable angle, which made the dancing much more enjoyable—although this was exactly the sort of frivolous activity that I had habitually and successfully shunned up until this time. Revolutionary equations don't get formulated and cutting-edge computers don't get built otherwise. It's not as if they build themselves, right?

I believe Mr. H could sense my mixed emotions concerning the present state of affairs, for his expression changed from joy to attention, and he said, "What's the matter Alice? Don't you like to dance?"

"Well, now that you mention it, I am curiously starting to derive some small quantity of enjoyment from this pointless promenade, but, the fact is, we don't have time for such nonsense."

His expression softened again, and a great smile spread across his face like curtains opening at the movie theatre. He was really quite the charmer.

"Alice, you know that time is irrelevant here, so there is no way we can 'waste' it. And even if we could, the real problem is that I'm not sure we can get out of here. It may be possible to get out, but it might also be highly improbable. And besides, for a little girl, you have a lot to learn about having fun."

"But I'm *not* a little girl. Just look at me." I pointed to the mirror to show him that I had grown to the size of an adult and that my diminutive days were over.

This, annoyingly enough, only made him smile wider, and he even started to chuckle to himself under his breath, emphasizing the point that he still knew more about this place than I did. I was not amused.

"Don't you know why you look big now, Alice? It's because, when you think of you, you already see yourself as grown up. This is the 'me' part of 'drink me.' When you drank the tea—"

"I became 'me' as I envision myself. I became the 'me' I always wanted to be."

"Yes, that's it. Didn't you always feel like a big girl in a little girl's body before?"

"Yes, but now, looking at my big self in the mirror, I feel a bit like a little girl in a big girl's body. Isn't that strange?"

"No, Alice, that's what it means to be an adult. All of us feel, from time to time, that there's a small child inside of us trying to get out. The difference is that, for most of the rest of us, it's just a metaphor. For you, right now, it's a fact.

"This inner child that's in all of us is the part of our souls that likes to have fun—that experiences joy—and tells us when it's time to just relax and forget about work and the troubles of the world. It's a safety valve to release pressure. Without it—pop!"

"What are you saying—that I'm going to pop?"

"Yes, Alice, if you keep going like this, it's inevitable."

"I sincerely doubt it. I don't pop."

"Oh, yeah? That's just what Dr. Starsky used to say."

This last statement had a sobering effect on me, as it would to anyone who knew Dr. Sigmund Starsky, loony extraordinaire. Maybe Mr. H was right. Maybe it was time for me to have some serious fun.

So I began to dance with my large, but nimble, partner with more genuine enthusiasm, and we bobbed and weaved through the menagerie of mayhem all around us.

"That's it sister, bust a move," was the squeaky support from our big-eared rodent friend.

"Whoa! Slow down now," bellowed the nearly trampled tortoise.

"Now you're starting to tread, Red," exclaimed the still-voracious lupine.

"That's the way to work it," said the most jovial of the seven small spinners.

"Oh, that's much better," beamed Mr. H. "You see, Alice—having fun ain't all bad."

"Yes, I can see that it has some merit of its own, but it still doesn't solve the problem of getting us out of here, does it?"

"No, but it makes you feel a little better, though, doesn't it?"

"Definitely, but it doesn't do anything!"

The music stopped abruptly, and everyone stared at me with startled expressions displaying varying levels of disappointment. Then, one by one, they turned and started to climb solemnly back onto the walls.

"Party pooper," whined the whale.

"What a wet blanket," whispered the wolf.

"What a pity—she's all work and no play," drawled a dwarf.

Before long, they were all back in place as two-dimensional decorations, although none of them was smiling as before. Even Mozart looked a bit sad in his recast statuesque stature. A chill took over the space, as if the warmth of delight had left along with the party guests. Suddenly, I felt very alone.

"I wish A-II was here. He always knows how to cheer me up," I said a bit listlessly.

As soon as the words had left my lips, a crackling sound broke the semi-silence, and A-II came out of the wall. It wasn't like what the wallpaper patterns had done. It looked more as if he had just walked through the wall. He came over to us and sat up at my feet, looking right at me with his electronic eyes.

"Well, it's about time someone thought of me. I was beginning to believe I'd never find you in here."

"A-II, it is you! I'm ever so happy to see you—but how did you get here?"

"You say that as if it were hard," he said nonchalantly.

"Well, it most certainly isn't easy to get here. And it appears to be even harder to get out again, if Mr. H's theory is correct."

"It is for me," said the confident cat. "I can leave whenever I want. But that would leave you here alone, so I'll stay."

"I wouldn't say alone," said Mr. H, who was apparently feeling a bit neglected.

"Well, large, mysterious men in fuzzy purple tuxedos excluded, of course."

"But not forgotten, I hope."

"Not much worry of that," said the cat.

"What are you saying, A-II, that you can just walk through the walls?" I asked.

"Why not? No one said I couldn't."

"Well, no one said you could either."

"To-*may*-to, to-*mah*-to, what's your point?" said A-II with a ruffled brow.

I furrowed my forehead as well, for this was quite the perplexing puzzler. Was it possible that A-II could actually just walk through the boundary wall just because no one had told him he couldn't? Was this physical inhibition in actuality a mental one? Was Yogi Berra right, after all? Was over 90 percent of the game more than 50 percent mental? After all, truth has come from far stranger sources than Yogi—but not much.

"That's an intriguing thought, A-II, but I thought Molly was the only one who could send information through the barrier."

"That's right; she sent me," he answered just as matter-of-factly. "Well, she didn't really send me. She just asked me to go, and, since I didn't have anything better to do ..."

"You came to rescue me—is that it?" I said hopefully, but not very.

"Hey, nobody said anything about rescuing anybody. I don't do rescue."

"Listen to the cat. He knows the score," interjected our looming luminary, "and, besides, no one can get you out of here but yourself, Alice. Haven't you figured that out yet?"

"I had suspected it strongly. But there is such a thing as hope, isn't there, even here?"

"Oh yes, Alice, this place is all about hopes, and dreams as well. But paradoxically, it's also about realities. In fact, it's about all the realities you could ever think of—and even more so when you do think of them."

"Yes," I said in a moment of epiphany, "it's just as I imagined it would be. The buffer zone is a quantum storage unit."

"Which means what to me?" queried my perplexed putty-cat.

"Well, what it means to me is that anything that *could* and *can* happen out there *actually* happens in here."

"Yes, of course, with the only exception being the things that really *do* happen," added Mr. H, correctly.

"That's right," I echoed. "The only things that don't happen here are the things that really happen."

"Oh, thanks," said A-II sarcastically. "That makes it as clear as creosote."

"Sorry, A-II, I realize these concepts are a bit strange and nonintuitive, but such is the reality of things in the quantum world, which brings to mind a startling possibility."

"And that would be?" asked Mr. H.

"That some of these alternate timelines, the ones that didn't happen even though they had very high probabilities—much higher, in fact, than the ones that really did happen, such as anyone but the Boston Red Sox and the Chicago White Sox winning back-to-back World Series in recent history—must exist here inside the buffer zone. We might actually be able to witness sections of alternate future histories. We could explore universes with alternate endings."

"As long as they have a saucer of milk, I'm down with that," said A-II. "Oh, and a comfortable place to sleep wouldn't hurt either."

"Don't you think of anyone but yourself, A-II?"

"Hey, I'm here, aren't I? What more do you want from me?"

"How about something constructive to say, instead of your inane quips."

"Oh! You talk about stuff happening that never happened, and I'm the one that's being silly?"

"And obtuse as well."

"Who you calling fat?"

"All right you two, that's enough," said Mr. H sternly. "If we are going to waste time, we could at least do it in a pleasant manner, instead of arguing like grownups."

"I'm sorry, Mr. H, but that's the only way I know how to argue."

"Yeah, well, I'm working on that one, too."

He continued to stare at me firmly, but the corners of his mouth looked poised for altitude. He was a nuclear giggle fest waiting to happen. I didn't trust him just then. I had the strange feeling I was about to be tickled, and I hate being tickled.

"Well, you seem to be our travel guide, Mr. Hasenpfeffer, sir. What do you suggest we should do next?"

"Oh, I don't know. How about going for a little stroll down by the beach?"

"The beach, well, whatever for?"

"There's someone there I'd like you to meet."

We stepped through my bedroom door and emerged upon a wide and quite expansive shoreline, complete with soft white sand and the smells of salt air and seaweed drying in the sun. It reminded me of the beaches of New England, such as along the shores of Cape Cod or Martha's Vineyard, which I had recently visited. There were the sounds of waves washing the coastline and seagulls fighting over a luckless crustacean. I breathed in the salty air and felt its calming effect, which, along with the warm sunshine, made everything seem quite placid and normal. I immediately suspected otherwise.

"Oh, thank you, Mr. H; I neglected to bring any sunscreen. I shall be burnt to a crisp by this solar radiation in milliseconds. And have you by any chance read about the dangers of skin cancer?"

"Alice, relax, this is no ordinary beach, and that isn't your normal sun, either. The only way it will burn you is if you believe it will. And even then the burns will be psychological, not physical."

"Yes, but I'm quite certain it will cause me pain, just the same."

"The big cat is right, you gotta learn to mellow out and go with the flow a little," said A-II, who seemed to be enjoying the warmth of the sunshine on his fur.

I had to admit it did have a comfortable, soothing effect, along with the calming sounds of the surf and the birds. But I still hadn't discovered the true reason for our salty and sandy sojourn. I had been led to believe there was some purpose here, an important meeting, if I recalled properly. But there was no one else in sight—at least, no one who looked as if they had any crucial information to bestow upon us. What was the cagey Mr. H trying to pull now?

"So, where is this individual you want me to meet?"

"Not individual; individuals—and they are all of that, I assure you, my dear girl. Our best chance to hook up with them is for us to walk along the water. I suggest removing your Oxfords, Alice, along with those plain white cotton socks, so that you can feel the squishy, soft sand between your toes. You might even enjoy it."

"I sincerely doubt that, although I will take your advice, because I don't want to ruin my shoes or get sand in my socks. If we must take such a journey, then barefoot would most certainly be the proper and practical way to go."

"There you go again—taking all the fun out of everything," said A-II as he yawned sleepily, feeling the effects of the sun more acutely now. "I'll just stay here, if you don't mind. I'm not such a big fan of water sports myself."

"You have nothing to fear, my fuzzy feline friend," encouraged Mr. H. "This water will not hurt your delicate circuits."

"Yeah, that's probably true, but I'm so … *yawn* … comfortable. I think I'll just take a little nappy nap, if you don't mind."

Not that it mattered to A-II if we did mind, for, moments later he was curled up in the soft sand with his eyes closed tightly just the same. We decided to ignore him and promptly headed down toward the water and the waves.

Once there, I couldn't resist dipping my toes in the water to see if it was too cold to swim, but I was very surprised to find it not too cold and not too warm, but just right. At that moment, I felt as if I had stepped into the wrong story. Believe me, it's a very odd feeling.

But good old Mr. H snapped me out of it with a gentle pat on my back and a kind word: "There you go, Alice, doesn't the water feel good? Can you feel the sand squishing between your toes? Relaxing, isn't it?"

"Yes, it's all very well and nice for what it is, but where are these people you were talking about?"

"People? Who said anything about people?"

"Well, you said there was someone you wanted me to meet, so I assumed …"

"So you naturally assumed I was talking about a person, but I wasn't. And when I said we should walk by the water, I actually meant we should walk *in* the water."

"In the water? But that's ludicrous."

"Is it now? Have you forgotten where you are? Just have faith, my young friend, and follow me." And with that last word of encouragement, my tuxedo-clad friend turned and started walking straight out toward the depths of the sea, not bothering to change into bathing clothes first—which I considered to be quite careless, and reckless as well. He was ruining his clothes and his shiny new shoes, to boot. He didn't even seem to care. That's no way to treat such a wonderful and expensive wardrobe. And not only that, but he didn't even try to swim. He just kept on walking until his legs, then his hips, and then his waist, and his chest, then his shoulders, his neck, and, finally, his head—top hat and all—were submerged beneath the waves. Now, this was an act I was certainly not anxious to follow.

Is this how they swim in his world? They must go through a lot of tuxedos and shiny new shoes, I thought to myself.

As surprising as Mr. H's little demonstration had been, I was even more surprised when his voice came to me as naturally as if it were traveling through the normal densities of air, rather than through the briny surf before me. "Come on in, Alice, the water's friendly," he said somewhat cryptically.

"But I'm not wearing proper bathing attire. And not only that, but how … are you breathing down there?"

"Like a fish, I suppose, if a fish had lungs."

"But even if a fish had lungs, it would still need gills as well—which I'm pretty sure I don't have, and neither do you."

"That's true, but here I am just the same."

His argument was flawed, although the evidence somehow supported it, curiously enough. So I developed a strategy of my own. I would walk out, just as Mr. H had done before me, but, just to be on the safe and prudent side of common sense, I would hold my breath. If he was really down there breathing normally, I would maybe give it a try myself—maybe.

"Okay, Mr. H. Here I come."

"That's the girl."

I took one tentative step away from the shore, up past my ankle, and followed it with another cautious stride, as the hem of my cotton dress touched the water. Curiously, the water felt so perfectly tuned to my body temperature that it almost felt as if it wasn't there at all, and, as I walked further and further into the sea, it started to feel like a warm and comforting blanket instead of a potentially lethal liquid. I was beginning to understand what Mr. H meant by, "The water's friendly."

Presently I was up to my neck in it, and slowly I continued until I, too, was completely submerged. I found, once there, that it was still amazingly comfortable but that I had closed my eyes as well as my lungs. I decided to open my eyes first, as per my original plan of action. I opened them to an amazing world full of life and brilliant colors, in stark contrast to the somewhat drab terrestrial domain we had just departed. In front of me, the perpetually positive Mr. H stood next to two great green trees of kelp, which clashed loudly with his purple uniform. He smiled reassuringly, as fish of all shapes, sizes, and shimmering scales darted about in a brilliant buoyant ballet. The ocean floor was equally occupied, with coral and cotton-candy-like critters all about, as mollusks and crustaceans of various species scuttled around us. There was more life here than on the Discovery channel.

Suddenly, a large tiger shark swam close by, and I gasped in shock before I could stop myself. It was too late—the damage had already been done—but, to my infinite surprise, I was unharmed by my careless act. Somehow, I was still breathing normally and was even enjoying the salty taste of the water in my throat and lungs. I was even more astonished when my voice came out normally and unaltered through the dense liquid.

"Mr. H, I'm breathing!"

"Of course you are; there's nothing to it. I told you to trust me, didn't I?"

"Yes, but I've always been told to use my own judgment in situations like this, and common sense demanded that I take caution."

"That's just it, Alice. Don't you see that there's no such thing as 'common sense' here?"

"Yes sir, that is becoming more apparent with every step I take. Soon I won't be able to trust my own judgment in any situation requiring a seemingly critical decision. What good is having a brain if you can't use it properly?"

"That's a good question, Alice, but how many things that have brains actually use them properly? But life goes on just the same. And who is to say yours is the proper way to use a brain in the first place?"

"Mr. H, are you criticizing my brain?"

"No, dear Alice, you have a very nice brain—a marvelous brain, to be sure—but that doesn't mean that it's working properly here or even *can* operate adequately here. Isn't it possible that there are things that you still don't understand?"

"Well, obviously, there is always more to be learned—even a fool should know that—but you're implying that there are things here that I might never be able to comprehend, and I find the very notion extremely offensive."

"Well okay, but I'll say one thing about you: for a fast learner, you can be pretty slow and stubborn sometimes."

His last statement stung—much as I imagined the large jellyfish before me would, if given the chance—but I decided to let it slide. There was no sense getting angry at Mr. H, even if he had just poked me in a very sensitive spot. It was time to go beyond that and get on with our adventure.

"Okay, Mr. H, I will try to keep an open mind on the subject, as long as things don't get too very strange, although we've probably passed that juncture long since."

"That's the spirit, Alice. As they say in my world, 'Free your mind and the rest will follow.'"

"Yes, but where is it all going?"

"Everywhere and anywhere, that's where."

"Not all at once, I hope."

Without saying another watery word, he took me by the hand, and we started walking along the ocean floor as if we were walking in a park—a very strange and wonderful park, with dolphins and rays and schools of mackerel flying all around us, with breathtakingly beautiful gardens of sea anemones and sea cucumbers under towering trees of kelp and seaweed. We were in Ringo Starr's 'Octopus's Garden.' I had always wanted to go there, and there I was. What would be next—tangerine trees and marmalade skies?

I was about to ask Mr. H about the individuals we were to meet, but, as we bobbed and weaved through this soggy sanctuary, I noticed two large aquatic mammals standing side by side in front of a large kelp tree. They were of equal height and girth, which was considerable, and for all intents and porpoises were identical.

As we came closer to the tubby twins, I was amused by their pudgy, whiskered faces with large, dark, expressive eyes. They almost looked like two fat schoolboys waiting for a bus. Their droopy, round faces made them look somewhat sad, in a comical sort of way, and I couldn't help making a somewhat rude comment as we approached them.

"What's the matter boys, forgot your lunch money?"

"Wrong, try it again," said the one on the left, with the tone of a British schoolmaster.

"Well, not exactly wrong, just merely incorrect," said the one on the right, with only slightly divergent enunciations.

I found myself at a loss for words, not because I was surprised to hear them speak, but because I was surprised to hear them do it so well. I was immediately embarrassed by my curt greeting, and I turned to Mr. H in hopes that he could smooth the waters some. He could and did.

"Alice, allow me to introduce to you Manatee and Manatum," he said, pointing first to the one on the left and then to the one on the right.

I curtsied to them politely and said, "I'm very glad to make your acquaintance, I'm sure. Are you relations?"

"We're brothers, if you couldn't guess," said Manatee sternly.

"Well, not brothers, really—rather, like male siblings," said Manatum contrarily.

"Well, you look so much alike, you must be twins as well," I ventured.

"Wrong again!" snapped Manatee.

"Yes, it's true we are identical, but we're certainly not the same," added Manatum.

I turned to Mr. H again in desperation. I didn't know how to talk to these guys. He smiled at me supportively and then turned again to our cetacean relations and spoke calmly. "My friend, Alice, here, is in need of some education, and I could think of no better source than the Manna brothers, if you would be so kind as to oblige us."

"Yes, if you could just tell me the way out of here," I began to explain.

"Well, if it's education you want, then tuition must be paid," demanded Manatee.

"Or she could just give us money," suggested Manatum. "Please see the bursar three kelp trees down. No personal checks, please."

"But I haven't any funds of any kind," I told them, since I had no pockets and my purse was still in my office in Cambridge. *And what sort of currency might they use here,* I thought to myself. *Clams?*

"My dear," explained Manatum, "we run the largest schools in the oceans, here, and can't be expected to do so without compensation, can we? So please come back with money, unless of course you have a scholarship."

"Doubtful," said Manatee. "She doesn't look like the sort that would."

I was about to say something very rude, when Mr. H stepped in and saved the day yet again. "But she has a scholarship; I've seen it myself," he asserted. "She's a transfer student from MIT."

"From the Marine Institute of Teachology," said Manatee, clearly surprised and impressed. "Well, that's a seahorse of an alternate shade. Lessons shall commence at once. We shall start with a little poetry."

"Poetry," I echoed with a questioning and disappointed tone.

"Certainly, don't you like poetry?" queried Manatum.

"I adore poetry, but this seems hardly the time or the place for it," said I.

"This is exactly the time and as good a place as any," said Manatee firmly, "and since when do students select the curriculum?"

"Exactly," agreed Manatum. "And before long they'd be telling us what to teach, as well. That certainly just won't do."

"Therefore, I will select the longest such example for discussion, since you have been so impudent. And that would be—"

"That would be 'The Lobster and the Octopus,' I believe," said Manatum.

"Thank you, brother, you are quite right." And he started right in: "The moon was shining bright that night—"

"I hope there isn't going to be an exam," I interrupted. "I don't have a notebook."

Manatee just shook his head and began again:

> The moon was shining bright that night,
> As brightly as it may;
> It did its best to break the dark
> With shadowed interplay.
> But this was strange because it was
> The middle of the day.

The ocean filled from shore to shore
And could not fill for more.
There was no land to walk upon,
Except the ocean floor.
And even those who walked these roads
Of clothing seldom wore.

The lobster and the octopus
Were walking side by side.
And everywhere they looked or went
The waters filled the tide.
The extent of which was just too much;
"Too much!' the lobster cried.

"If seven pike with seven pumps
Went pumping through the night,
In maybe six or seven months
They'd clean it out just right."
The octopus just sadly said,
"It's doubtful, but they might."

"I wish you all to walk with me
To find a better place;
Of sand and sun and beach-ball fun,
Zinc oxide on your face,"
The lobster said to several clams
All living in this space.

The eldest clam unhinged himself,
Although he did not speak.
He shook his head from side to side
And did not take a peek
At other clams that weren't as wise,
With brains a little weak.

But five young clams jumped out of bed
To join in all the fun.
They clad themselves with socks of tube
And shoes they made to run.
And this was strange, because, of feet
Between them they had none.

Five more clams did tag along,
Followed by five more;
And five plus five makes twenty-five
For anyone keeping score.
But soon there was a string of shells
All heading out the door.

The lobster and the octopus
Went on for near a mile;
And came upon at last some rocks
That formed a nice low pile.
They rested there; the lobster went on
Talking all the while.

"I think it's time," the lobster said
To speak of things to come:
Of picnic lunch and cherry punch,
And peaches soaked in rum;
Of Frisbees flying through the air,
And why I haven't one."

The bravest clam piped up just then,
As clams do seldom speak.
He said, "We first must rest a while;
We feel a little weak."
"Take five," the octopus replied;
They thanked him with a squeak.

"A taxi cab," the lobster blabbed,
"Is what would fix us neat,
To ride with pride above the tide,
With fifty to a seat."
The octopus just simply said,
"That surely would be sweet!"

"But not for us," the lead clam said,
"We do not travel well;
And even if the AC worked,
I think it would be hell."
The lobster said, "Do you feel cramped
In such a tiny shell?"

The octopus tapped on his back;
The lobster turned to slice.
"I tap thee not to start a row,
I tap to give advice.
I wish you had not been so thick—
I've had to tap you twice."

"I would not be as quick as you
To swim against the tide;
For you may find that things are worse
Upon the other side."
The lobster said, "If only I
Had thumbs, I'd hitch a ride."

"I've tried and tried, but can't abide
Your octal point of view.
I've had my fill of briny swill
And this salty, salty dew."
So off the lobster went alone,
With clamshells two by two.

> And luck was theirs, they made the trip
> Above this soggy place,
> Inside a wooden vestibule
> The lobster found by taste.
> And soon they were the honored guests
> In a royal bouillabaisse.

"And thus end-eth the lesson-eth, as they say in Greek," said Manatee confidently.

"That's not Greek; it sounds more like Latin to me," countered Manatum.

"It's neither; in fact, it's not even proper English," scolded I. "And this whole poetry thing is *way* overrated."

Manatee blew an explosion of great bubbles from his prominent proboscis and stood flipper to toe with his terrestrial antagonist: me, that is. "How *dare* you address me so! My classroom shall be quiet—quiet, I say."

"You mean *our* classroom," reminded Manatum. "But I really don't think we have anything to worry about from these two. They're obviously not real, brother dear."

"And what, pray tell, brought you to that conclusion, Tummy Wummy?"

"Well, first of all, they're talking, and we both know the human brain is much too small to support such advanced functions. And, second of all, they're breathing, which, as we know, is also impossible. The only logical conclusion would be that they don't actually exist. It is logic, you see."

I was simply shocked by what I heard, especially the part about the small brains. "That may be so," I countered, "but if that's true, then why are you speaking English—a language named after the *people* who invented it."

"We're not speaking English," snorted Manatee. "We're speaking Mannish." He looked ready to burst.

"Now, Teedo dear, remember your blubber pressure," said Manatum in a motherly fashion.

"Isn't it just as likely," I continued, "that we're the ones that are real, and you are imaginary?"

"No," volleyed Manatee, "that simply isn't logical. We must be *we*, so you can't be *you*. It's as plain as the whiskers in front of your face."

"There is one other possibility," chimed in Mr. H for the first time. "That is, that none of us are real. Did you ever think of that?"

"If we're not real, then what are we doing here?" said Manatum with a very confused expression. "I sink, therefore I swam. But the two of you aren't swimming at all. And you don't have any of those bubbly doohickeys strapped to your heads and backs either. At least *we*'re apparently in our natural habitat."

"Good, so it's decided then—we're real, and you're not. Class dismissed."

"I second the motion, Tummy."

"Wait," I said. "The issue is far from resolved. For instance, if I wasn't real, could I poke you like this?" I said, burying my right index finger two knuckles deep in Manatee's flabby stomach.

"It could be something I ate," he said casually.

"His blubber pressure has been down lately, along with his cholesterol; we're working on that too," said Manatum almost apologetically.

"The only logical conclusion is that either all of us are real or none of us are, as the perceptive Mr. Hasenpfeffer has already suggested. You just can't declare that we aren't real. It doesn't work that way."

"Must I remind you, child, who is the student and who are the teachers?"

"No, but sometimes the student knows more than the teacher does."

I was face to face with Manatee now, eyeball to eyeball. Neither of us was willing to back down. I smelled fish on his breath. Even that didn't deter me.

And then it happened—he blinked—yes! There was no getting around it; he had to back off now. I had won the stare-down.

"Well, that is an intriguing notion, which has not occurred to me until now. I will have to give it more consideration," conceded Manatee, and he backed away slowly.

Since I had won the challenge, I decided to stay on the offensive. "And what sort of school is this anyway? You haven't taught me a thing, at least not yet."

"Well, we usually deal with much larger classes," explained Manatum quickly. "We're really not accustomed to this one-on-one sort of thing. If you should like, you could come back later with a few thousand of your friends, and we'll have a nice big lecture. How does that sound?"

"Ridiculous!" I shouted. "If you can teach thousands, shouldn't it be even easier to teach just one?"

"Absolutely not," grumbled Manatee. "What with all the questions, we'd never get anything done."

"But shouldn't you get more questions from thousands than from just one?"

"You might think that," said Manatum. "But you, for instance, have asked more questions in the past few minutes than we've been asked in a whole lifetime of teaching, and, frankly, it's starting to make my head ache."

"I won't put up with it any longer. You ask to be taught something, and you don't even say what the subject is. How can we be expected to teach, if we don't know the subject?" asked Manatee defiantly. His whiskers were up again.

"Okay," I conceded. "How about a simple one: Geography?"

"Don't you mean Oceanography?" asked Manatum helpfully.

"Yes, of course, how silly of me. I meant oceanography."

"We don't teach oceanography," said Manatee obstinately.

"Okay, then what do you teach?"

"We teach all the usual subjects, you know, such as swimming, flipping, spinning, balancing things on the end of your nose, and advanced balancing things on the end of your nose. Which of these subjects would you like to choose?"

"None of them," I said disappointedly. "Those things aren't of any use."

"They are to those of us who live here," said Manatum. "Very useful, indeed."

"We could teach you one of our favorite subjects, which we find useful in nearly all circumstances," offered Manatee almost graciously.

"And what would that be?" asked I, taking the bait.

"That would be, 'What to eat, what not to eat, and how to keep from being eaten.' It has the highest enrolment of any or our courses. Would you like me to start with the first lesson?"

"Certainly not. It's obvious that there's nothing for me to learn here," I said, and I meant it, too.

"Now, Alice," said Mr. H in a reproachful tone of voice. "There's always something to be learned. You, of all people, should know that."

"Yes, Mr. H, but how are any of these so-called lessons going to help me to find my way out of here? It's just pointless, otherwise."

"Well, if you're so smart, why don't you tell us what we should be teaching," challenged Manatee, with more bubbles frothing from his nostrils.

"Yes," agreed Manatum. "What sort of things would you be teaching?"

"Practical things, such as mathematics, biology, physics, chemistry—"

"Never heard of them," said Manatee.

"Did you make them up?" added Manatum.

"No, you know, like arithmetic. Surely you've heard of arithmetic? It's simple. What's one plus one?" I asked.

"More than one," answered Manatee confidently.

"Definitely not one," added Manatum.

"Okay, what's two times two?"

"Twice as many as you started with," volunteered Manatee, "but probably twice as many as you need."

"You've got to learn to conserve, don't you know," advised Manatum.

"No, no, no, that's all wrong. Well, not exactly wrong, but certainly not right."

"But if it's not wrong, then it must be right," pleaded Manatum.

"It's all nonsense," decided Manatee, "and we've gotten very bored with this conversation, so we'd like you to leave now."

"Well, maybe not leave, but you certainly must go away," agreed Manatum, "at least until you have something more interesting to say."

"Good-bye," they said in unison, and they turned their backs on Mr. H and me.

I was going to do something equally impolite, when Mr. H grabbed me by the elbow and led me away from the sulking sea mammals. He was right; we were getting nowhere.

"I suppose what we need here is an even more unlikely scenario to stir up your creative juices," said Mr. H, and, with that, he snapped his fingers, and everything went black.

Well, not exactly completely black, for there were still many little lights off in the distance, with other spaces of dusty colors and nebulous forms. In fact, they were nebulas. We were apparently in outer space, floating in zero gravity. It was like the night on the roof with Lucy, but the sudden change nearly made me lose my lunch.

"Mr. H, if you would be so kind as to warn me the next time you're going to do something like that, I would thank you very much."

Then it hit me again. If we were actually out in the vacuum of space, then how was I talking? How was I breathing? How was I even making any sounds? That's right, people; no matter what you've learned from Star Wars or Star Trek, there is no sound in space. That's because there's nothing (no air) there to transmit it. Sorry, R2-D2.

But I was starting to get used to this sort of thing, so I didn't even mention it to Mr. H. I immediately began looking around, because there was bound to be something or someone here he wanted me to see. Mr. H was like the interdimensional Ghost of Christmas Future, although it wasn't Christmas Eve, and I wasn't Ebenezer Scrooge. At least, I was reasonably certain that I wasn't.

After several seconds of floating in nothingness, I broke the silence. "Okay, I give up. What are we doing here?"

"I just wanted you to see the big picture, Alice. Isn't it amazing, to be able to just float gently through space—to be able to really feel what its like—without a heavy space suit and a backpack? How does it make you feel?"

"A little nauseated, to be honest, but somewhat inspired. It is a unique perspective, to be sure."

I was also about to comment on how we wouldn't have to worry about being sucked into an invisible black hole, because black holes aren't really invisible, when a very large and very strange-looking craft pulled up in front of us. It stopped short and opened its port-side door. The ship had the overall shape of a fried egg with bacon and rye toast on the side. Inside was a small manlike creature, wearing a silver jumpsuit and a lampshade on his head. He looked oddly familiar, as he called out to us with a puzzled expression on his warped, unshaven face.

"Hey, you need a ride or something? You look a little lost," said our space-faring friend.

"Well, I would like to come in, if you don't mind. This floating free in space thing is a little much for me," I said sincerely, "and the special effects alone must be costing us a fortune."

"Sure, jump on in. There's plenty of room, contrary to what you'd expect from a vehicle that needs to conserve air and fuel. This is my SUV."

"Your Space Utility Vehicle," ventured Mr. H.

"No, it's my Sunny-Side-Up Vehicle, but yours isn't bad either. Come on in."

So we somehow floated into the flying breakfast special—we didn't even break the yolk—and found ourselves on the bridge of this unlikely craft. As soon as the door shut tight, we even touched down to the floor with some sort of artificial gravity. I was going to ask our pilot where the gravity was coming from but decided not to. They almost never explain where the gravity comes from.

"Hello friends, I am the incredible, the amazing, the stupendous, the universally famous—stop me, if you've heard this one—the incomparable Captain Ziggy Starbuck. What? Don't tell me you've never heard of me."

"No sir, I can't say that I have, but you do remind me of somebody I know," I said with much sincerity. He even looked like Dr. Starsky.

"How about you, purple man?"

"No, can't say that I have," said Mr. H, who was scratching his head.

"No? Impossible! You want credentials, is that it? You want proof I'm the greatest and smartest man alive? Sure thing. No problem. I got a PhD, an MD, a CRT, a BS double E and a DOD, and they're all in that closet if you want to ask them any questions. Careful with the monkey with the gun though, he gets a little trigger happy sometimes, especially around strangers. He's a lot of fun at parties, though.

"How about my diplomas and awards; you want to see them? I got a whole wall full of them—take them with me everywhere I go—wall and all. It's easier that way."

He pulled a string and a curtain opened up; behind it was his wall of claim. There were dozens of brownish-white documents with fancy writing and gold seals on them. Most of them said Ziggy Starbuck on them. Some of them were in crayon. He closed the curtain again abruptly before we could get a really good look at the wall.

"There, now, what do you think? That's some pretty impressive stuff, eh?"

"I think its irrelevant how many titles and awards you have. It's what you actually do with it that's important," I said, so far unimpressed by our wild-haired host, lampshade and all.

"*Do*? You want to know what I *do*? That's ridiculous. I don't even know that. It's on a need-to-know basis."

"But don't you need to know?" I asked.

"Apparently not," he chuckled.

"Then, how did you get here?" asked Mr. H, still scratching his head.

"I just do whatever the guy on the radio tells me to do. I'm a civil servant, you know. In this job, thinking is out of the question, which is perfect for me."

At that moment there was a squawking noise, and his communications console came to life. "Ground control to Captain Ziggy—this is ground control to Captain Ziggy—can you hear me Captain Ziggy? Can you hear me Captain Ziggy?"

"Aren't you going to answer that?" I asked, after several seconds had passed by and Ziggy just stood there smiling like an idiot (not much of a stretch).

"No, I like to build up the suspense a little first. Keeps 'em on their toes, that sort of thing." He chuckled to himself again, as he sauntered over to the big RCA circa-1940 microphone on the console, while the speaker continued to plead for contact.

"This is Captain Ziggy to ground control—I'm feeling kind of strange—and I think the rye bread knows which way to go. So buzz off, will ya?"

"Ground control to Captain Ziggy—your circuit's dead— there's something wiggly—Can you hear me Captain Ziggy? Can you hear me Captain Ziggy? Can you hear ..."

Just then, Captain Ziggy hit a switch on the console and looked up, a little embarrassed. "Oh, sorry about that. I forgot to hit the button again. This is Captain Ziggy to ground control. What's shakin', bacon?"

"The papers want to know whose shirts you wear."

He turned to us triumphantly. "You see? I am famous!"

"Oh, and if you just happen to see any big red planets around, watch out for spiders. Over."

"Spiders, roger that," the captain said emotionlessly, and he flipped off the radio.

"So, where are these spiders?" I asked a little nervously. I don't like spiders much.

"Who cares?" said Ziggy offhandedly. "Who wants to hear me play the guitar?"

Mr. H looked at me, and neither of us knew how to answer this question, but just then, as if sent right from heaven, A-II walked through the hull of the ship and joined us—and not a moment too soon, either. I had just been thinking to myself: *I wish A-II was here, because he would know what to say to this egomaniac.*

"Holy hamster cage! What the heck is this place?" said A-II as he looked around at the bridge, which did look as if it had been put together with spare parts and duct tape. Sort of like a spaceship that Red Green might have built.

"A-II," I exclaimed, "am I ever glad to see you."

"Whoa! A talking cat. Are you from Japan?" asked our startled host.

"No, he's my cat, and I made him in my garage in Sheboygan," I explained.

"Big deal, I make talking cats all the time. You're not so smart, Dolly Diode."

"My name is Alice, and I am that smart."

"Well, if you're so smart, how did you get all the way out here without a space ship? Wait a minute—that does sound difficult, if not smart. I withdraw the question. Now, where is that stupid guitar?"

Captain Starbuck ignored our pleas of, "No, that's okay; the radio will be fine" and went over to the closet to look for his musical instrument anyway. He opened the door, and a bald man in a lab coat peeked out at him.

"Hey, doc, you guys see my guitar in there anywhere?"

"I'm not sure, it might be under the gorilla," said the shiny closet dweller.

"Yeah, like his *butt* plays it better than I can. That's it, King Kong, hand it over." There was a bit of commotion inside the closet, as voices mixed with the sounds of shuffling feet and rearranging of furniture filtered through the thin door. There was even the sound of breaking glass and gunfire, before a shiny acoustic guitar was finally passed out through the half-open door. I couldn't see inside, but it was quite apparent that Captain Starbuck hadn't been lying earlier about the contents of his closet.

"Thanks, Rambo. I'll throw in an extra banana for you at supper time," said Ziggy and he turned and slammed the door with a flourish. It was hard to tell whether he was mad, or angry, or both. He turned and looked at us with an incredible expression on his face—sort of a mix between Elvis and Bevis.

"Thank you, friends. And now, I'd like to do a little song I wrote—thank you, thank you—called "I'm a Genius and I Wrote This Song." Thank you very much. And it goes like this …"

People ask me what's it like
To be the smartest guy on the planet.
I just say, it's not so bad,
I'm so smart I just can't stand it!
My brain's so big my hat don't fit,
And so I have to jam it on.
And people say my wits are sharp
As piranhas' teeth in the Amazon.
I'm so smart I wrote the book
On all the stuff you ought to know.
Just read it once, from end to end,
And watch your freakin' noggin grow.

The song (if you could call it that) went on like this for several more minutes, but I think you get the gist of the lyrical content by now. His voice sounded like a cat being run over by a lawnmower, and the guitar was so far out of tune it actually blended in well with the vocals. It sort of reminded me of a bad violin player getting run over by a harvesting machine.

I was going to get up and leave, but I wasn't immediately sure just where I would go. I looked over at Mr. H, and he looked equally "thrilled" by the performance. A-II was scratching frantically at the closet door. I guess he decided he would rather take his chances with the gun-toting gorilla.

About halfway through the ninety-third verse, I looked out the forward window—which our pilot had his back to, as he wailed away obliviously—and I saw a large reddish globe, which was soon filling our entire field of view. I thought this might be important for Captain Starbuck to know, so I tried to interrupt him. Big mistake.

"Shut up and listen. There are only forty-eight more verses to go."

"But, Captain, I believe there's a large planet in our path," offered Mr. H.

"Yeah, right. I've heard that one before. People are always jealous of the truly gifted; it's inevitable, really. And it's sad too, in a way, because they could learn so much from me if they would only listen, you see what I'm saying? If people would just stop and open their ears—'get the wax out,' as I say—we would all be better off; am I right?"

Captain Starbuck went on talking about how people don't listen, as the planet got larger and larger in the front window. He didn't stop all the way through the upper atmosphere, and only started to get the idea that something was going wrong when it started to get very hot inside the ship. But he didn't actually turn around and look until the polka dot wallpaper started to burn.

He only had time to scream, "Mayday!" before we hit the ground at full speed. WHAM!

I don't remember the crash itself so much—a lot of fire and smoke—but I woke up in a field of red boulders and dust, with egg yolk, breadcrumbs, and bacon bits everywhere. The ship was totally demolished.

I wasn't physically hurt, but I knew immediately that those yellow stains would never come out of my new dress. That made me angry. It was a good thing that Captain Cranium was nowhere in sight. It never even crossed my mind that he might have been killed in the crash. There was no way we could have gotten that lucky.

"Are you all right, Alice?" said the wonderfully welcome voice of Mr. H from behind me. I turned to find him looking down from a particularly large rock, and, even with his partially crushed hat and torn cuffs, he didn't look too much the worse for wear. I was very glad to see him unharmed.

"Yes, Mr. H, I'm fine, except for some permanent stains on my dress and the taste of burnt toast in my mouth. But I believe I'll survive."

"That was something, huh? I swear I have no idea where that cosmic chucklehead came from. I certainly didn't conjure him up from my imagination. I'm not that warped."

"No, I don't believe you are," I agreed. "This is just a theory, but I believe we might actually be inside a dream of my mentor's, Dr. Sigmund Starsky. He told me once that he'd wanted to be an astronaut or a rock star, if he hadn't become a physicist. He also listens to a lot of David Bowie, so that's a clue, as well."

"That could be," said Mr. H, "but there's also another distinct possibility. What we are experiencing might be part of an alternate reality from my universe. Maybe in my world Dr. Sigmund Starsky is Captain Ziggy Starbuck, and in that world he is an astronaut. We might be inside one of those alternate timelines you were talking about earlier."

"Yes," I said, picking up the thread he was pulling upon, "and, in this timeline, the less probable event occurred: he missed the planet."

"I never miss," said the confident, but kooky, Captain Starbuck, as he came around a boulder with a broken guitar in his hands and the crumpled lampshade around his neck. I was glad to see that the guitar was beyond repair. Even Les Paul himself couldn't have saved that puppy.

"Good thing I took out extra insurance on the SUV. I'm gonna get a whole new ship out of this, yeah, buddy, but this time I think I'll go with wheat toast instead. What do you think? And maybe Canadian bacon too. Or would you get breakfast sausage? I'll have to see what options the new ones come with, before I make my decision. But I won't let the salesman talk me into that pan-coating bull-hockey. What is that stuff, anyway?"

"It's just a rip-off, no doubt," said Mr. H sympathetically.

"Yeah, that's what I say," said Ziggy. "They're always trying to stick it to you, damn salesmen." He picked up a few crumbs and sighed mournfully. "She was a good ship, though. I'm gonna miss old 'number two with bacon and rye toast.' He turned and started to cry softly. I almost felt sorry for him.

Then I remembered something that made the hairs on my arm stand up and a shiver run down my spine. I didn't even want to ask, but I had to know.

"Captain Starbuck," I said a little shakily, "this wouldn't happen to be the red planet that ground control was talking about earlier, would it? You know, the one with the spiders?" It made me shiver just to say the word "spiders'.

"What, you think maybe there's another red planet around here that doesn't have giant spiders on it?" he answered, much to my dismay.

"*Giant* spiders?" I squealed with horror.

"Sure, like the size of a small bus. Actually, I think these spiders will soon replace the bus, at least on this planet. I wouldn't recommend them for everyday mass transit, mind you, at least not by themselves. Maybe the fifty-foot-long caterpillars could take up the slack."

"Fifty-foot caterpillars?" said Mr. H apprehensively. I guess he didn't like caterpillars as much as I didn't like spiders, but that's silly. They're only caterpillars, after all. Then I wondered what these colossal caterpillars might turn into. Wow, can you imagine the size of the chrysalis?

Just then, A-II climbed over a large boulder and joined the party. He didn't look harmed or mussed up at all by the horrific crash, although there might have been a little extra yellow in his fur.

"A-II, you're all right!" I squealed with relief and delight.

"Well, actually, I'm half left also. So you could say I'm half right, or all bilaterally symmetrical—take your pick."

"Were you thrown very far away by the crash?" asked Mr. H.

"Yeah, a couple miles or so, but it was no big deal. I just caught a spider a couple of rocks down. Lucky for me I had exact change on me."

I was going to ask A-II how he had the proper currency and where he kept it (he has no pockets either), but Captain Ziggy interrupted me before I got the chance.

"What, we missed the spider? There won't be another one along for twenty minutes, at least. I got things to go—places to do—songs to sing—which reminds me, I need a new guitar, but I could sing Acapulco if you'd like."

"No!" the rest of us cried in unison—totally unrehearsed.

"You're right, it doesn't have the same impact without the guitar," he said, looking at the large crater his ship had made. "Maybe I shouldn't use the word *impact* around here, you think? I could also tell you all about how smart I am and how I got that way. Everybody loves that story. It started forty-four years ago, when I was born and instantly became the smartest person alive, although people tell me I'm being modest. I was probably the smartest person even before I was born, but I don't like to brag."

Like heck he didn't. He went on and on like this, as if we really were interested. And even A-II's shouts of "Stuff a sock in it, Socrates!" didn't stop him.

Finally, we just walked away and left him there. I don't think he even noticed. He just went on talking long after we were out of sight.

We walked for several hundred meters through a field of broken, jagged, reddish-green boulders, until we finally came to a valley. The valley before us was covered with what looked like giant spotted mushrooms—all of them several meters tall at the very least—like something right out of Jules Vern's *Journey to the Center of the Earth.*

I was impressed by the sheer scale of these fabulous fungi. I ran right into this fantastic forest with the glee of a materialistic woman who had just received her first Bloomingdale's charge card in the mail. The boys followed slowly behind me, but even A-II looked awed by these colossal caps.

"Wow! You suppose these are 'magic' mushrooms?" A-II asked Mr. H, as they walked side by side under these giant organic umbrellas.

"Well, they're here, so there must be something special about them," said big H logically.

"Can't argue with that," agreed A-II

"Of course they're magic," I shouted with joy. "They're wonderful!"

I was so giddy and carefree that I started spinning and twirling like a drunken idiot, I spun around recklessly to find myself face to face with the biggest, ugliest, most horrible-looking spider I have ever seen. I tried to scream, but found that I couldn't. I was absolutely petrified.

"I'm off-duty," said the spider nonchalantly. "Can't you see the lighted sign on my abdomen?"

I blinked at him several times before I could say anything. But my fear was rapidly diminishing. He seemed friendly enough, as spiders go. I still backed away from him instinctively. Then I noticed a keyboard instrument tucked under one of his arms, and I was surprised beyond my fear.

"Are you a musician?" I asked with more than a hint of disbelief in my voice.

"Yeah, well, that's what I want to be. Right now, I'm moonlighting as a taxicab, until I can get some high-paying gigs—you know how it is. 'Don't quit your day job,' they tell me. At least, not yet, anyway."

"Are you in a band now?" I asked, becoming more fascinated by the minute.

"Yeah, I'm doing this 'hip-hop' thing with the Grand Master C about nine 'shrooms down on the left. If you can't find it, all you have to do is follow the sweet-smelling smoke, if you catch my drift. We hang at his crib all the time. I'm going there now. You can come if you want. It's always a big party, if you know what I mean."

I didn't know what he meant exactly, but for some odd reason I thought I might enjoy a good party. Since Mr. H and A-II were nowhere in sight at that moment, I decided to hitch a ride on my new friend (he told me his name was Fingers). I couldn't believe what I was doing, but, moments later, I was actually riding on the back of a giant spider—and enjoying it, even! There must have been something in the air besides the music, which I began to hear as we started off toward mushroom number nine. It had a lot of bass to it, that was for sure.

It was really quite fun riding this high off the ground, and from this lofty seat I could see over the tops of some of the mushrooms. I was surprised to see that many of them were occupied. There were oversized insects and arachnids of all kinds sitting on top of their 'shrooms, enjoying the sun and the music. It was like one big block party.

As we got closer, I began to see what looked like a great caterpillar on top of the target mushroom 'crib.' He was lying back casually, with a hose in his mouth that was attached to a very large hookah. Even from a distance I could smell the smoke coming forth, and it did have a sweet-spicy sort of smell to it. He was wearing a black baseball cap backward on his head, and it had a white letter *C* embroidered on the front of it. I was pretty sure it wasn't a Chicago White Sox cap, though.

All around his 'shroom were musicians and other partiers lounging out on the grass. There were ants and beetles and inchworms (which were more like *meter*worms) and ladybugs, and most of them were either smoking or taking nibbles from the spotted mushroom. It looked very festive indeed (although I don't usually approve of smoking). The music itself was coming from a fantastic-looking sound system, with woofers as large as hubcaps thumping from huge melon-shaped enclosures of green and orange. There was a large and menacing scorpion, behind an organic-looking DJ desk, who was spinning the tunes. He was very adept at using his tail for 'scratching.'

As we got very near the main mushroom, our host looked down and noticed me on Fingers's back. He gazed at me with the deepness of a philosopher; there was an air of infinite, old knowledge in his multifaceted eyes.

He took the hose out of his mouth, blew out a perfectly formed smoke ring, and said to me, "Who are you?"

"I'm Alice Sterling," I said cheerfully, "I'm very happy to meet you."

"No, I mean who *are* you, if you know what I'm saying?"

Now I understood the deeper meaning of his query, and I tried my best to relate it to him. "It's funny you should ask that, because recently I've been going through quite the identity crisis, if you know what I'm saying. For example, only a short while ago I was much shorter. But I didn't catch your name, Mister …?"

"That's Master—Grand Master C—Master Cat Pillar—or just Master C, if you prefer. But it's just a name; it ain't no thing. But, like I was saying, who are you? Do you really know who you are? Do any of us know who we really are?"

"Well, Master C, as it turns out, I have been wondering just who I am lately, because I really don't seem to be myself anymore. But then again, if I'm not myself, then who am I? You know what I'm saying?"

He took another long puff from the hookah and smiled. I had never seen a caterpillar smile before, and it was quite an experience. He seemed happy and thoughtful all at once.

He blew out another great ring of fragrant smoke and spoke at last. "Yeah, it's all a big trip to tell it straight. Just when you think you've got it licked it licks you back. Do you play the game or does the game play you?"

"It's funny you should say that, because I recently invented a game that has similar dynamics. You never know if the game is a game or just part of the game. It can have you walking in circles before you realize that you've already been there before. But this isn't part of my game, is it?"

He put the hose back in his mouth, looked to the sky, and didn't say anything for quite a long time. Finally, he looked back at me and said, "What you need is some advice, Grand-Master-C style."

The crowd heard this and began to get excited, so I decided it was time to get off Mr. Fingers's back and find a comfortable spot on the grass. It was a beautiful day for a concert, purple sky and all.

Mr. Fingers, the part-time taxicab, put his keyboard down on top of a low, flat mushroom and got ready to play. An ant with a bass guitar, and a beetle with a bow and what looked like a stiff blade of grass, also took their places. The scorpion, DJ, stopped the canned music and threw a microphone up to Master C. A lot of the other partygoers stood up in anticipation of the live music to come. It was quite exciting, in a very unusual sort of way.

Master Cat Pillar straightened himself up a bit, until he was visible to everyone gathered around his 'shroom, and then he raised the microphone to his mouth.

"Mr. DJ, kick it!" And with that, the most amazing sound thundered forth from the instruments and the sound system, with a thump and rumble that rhythmically shook everything within a square kilometer of the epicenter. It was a bit loud for my taste, but it did have a hypnotic beat that was very captivating, indeed. I decided I liked it all the same—and even more so when Grand Master C went into his rap, which went like this:

> "Well, give it up people for Master C;
> Gonna tell ya all a bit about reality.
> Well, it's whacked!
> It's action packed!
> Got the little sista' watchin' her own back.

> The problem's she's not physical,
> Though the girl is visible.
> Her head is trippin', she ain't grippin' facts
> She thinks that she be all of that,
> But she ain't hearin' Master Cat,
> She's just a shadow all on up and back.

> So maybe she be chillin' with the Master Cat,
> Because she know he got this reality thing down
> pat.
> It ain't nothin' but the player being played by
> the game,
> Where the nothin' is the somethin' and it's all
> the same.

> Well, the outside is the inside with the inside
> out,
> Where the thunder is a whisper and the whisper
> do shout.
> You can ponder on the future; you can ponder
> on the past,
> But you know it doesn't matter 'cause neither
> one is cast.

So come on everybody, get your legs up in the
air,
Let's kick it for the sista' with the long and
golden hair.
Go Alice! Go Alice! Go Alice! Come on!

And everyone in the audience put their spare legs up and started swaying from side to side, chanting, "Go Alice! Go Alice! Go Alice!" in time with the music. I found the enthusiasm contagious and joined in—it was really quite inspiring and uplifting.

I was so caught up in the excitement that it took me several moments before I realized that Mr. H and A-II had since joined us and were swaying and chanting along with the rest of us. A-II looked especially cute with his paws waving back and forth through the smoky air.

Finally, the music came to a crescendo, followed by an exuberant finale, and then many of the hard-shelled participants collapsed down onto the grass again in relief and joy. I found myself positively exhilarated by the experience, and I'm sure I was practically glowing by this point. I was all lit up, to be sure.

"Well now, look who we caught having a little fun," fingered A-II. "I thought it was against your religion or something."

"Very funny, A-II, but since I don't believe in a supreme, all-powerful being watching over us at all times, your reference to my 'religion' is erroneous."

"What's that?" said the Master's voice from over the top of the main mushroom. "You say you don't believe in nothin'? Well, that's your trip, girl. You got to believe in nothin'."

I looked up at our multi-legged host and smiled dreamily. "Don't you mean, 'You gotta believe in something'?"

"No, you gotta believe in nothin'. 'Cause that's what all this is: nothin'. If you don't believe, you ain't going to get nowhere."

"But how do you know where I'm going?" I asked incredulously.

"I don't, but it ain't here, and it ain't there, so it must be somewhere else." He took another long draw from his hookah. "What you need is a hit of this," he offered.

"No, thank you, Master C. I don't smoke."

"Okay, then cop a chunk of 'shroom. That will do ya nice. But don't eat too much, now; it's powerful stuff."

I turned to Mr. H to see what his advice might be on the subject. I had become a little suspicious of eating or drinking anything around here ever since our little tea party.

But he just shrugged his shoulders and said, "Well, we can't get much worse off than we are already. It's up to you, Alice. What do you think?"

I looked around at all the party guests, and most of them were smiling and laughing and carrying on like happy people, so I was encouraged to try it.

"You should know," cautioned Master C, "that this is the sort of trip that some people never return from."

"Well, it seems to me that I'm already on such a trip," I concluded, "so all doors must be opened to find the way out."

"Yeah, the Doors, old school," agreed Grand Master C. "Nothin' wrong with that. Now, pick a piece from either side of the 'shroom. One side will get ya trippin', and the other side with send ya flippin'."

I wasn't quite sure what he meant—what was the difference between trippin' and flippin'?—so I broke a piece from each side and decided to try them one after the other in an experimental fashion. I tucked the alternate section away (don't ask where; ladies never tell) and raised the chosen section to my lips.

I took a small bite of the mushroom and swallowed it down. At first there seemed to be no effect, but then I noticed that everything around me seemed to be slowing down. Voices began to sound lower and slurred out—like an old vinyl record after somebody pulls the plug—and it looked as if they were swimming through thick molasses. Then the colors started flowing.

Yes, that's what I said: the colors started flowing. It was as if a painter had opened a great faucet, and pigments of every shade of the rainbow had started flowing through the air. Brilliant blues, greens, reds, and yellows started dancing and spinning in the air, like a giant kaleidoscope or that spinning painting machine at a carnival. The hues mixed and blended into each other, forming more beautiful colors and patterns, as they danced and flowed. Soon they obliterated everything else, and it seemed I had been transported to a world of rainbows and spilled semi-mixed paint. I felt my own head spinning as well, and I began to get a little dizzy, so I closed my eyes. But this didn't help at all, as the swirling colors just seemed more intense this way. There seemed to be no escape from them, and I began to get a little nervous. Maybe this would be Alice's final trip.

Then the colors and shapes—which, up to this point, had been merely abstract and chaotic—began to take on recognizable forms, and I found myself floating in a sea filled with very strange and bizarre apparitions. There were creatures that looked like unlikely dinosaurs, with heads much bigger than their bodies or ears that didn't fit quite right. Some had teeth that didn't fit in their mouths or eyes that were much too large for their sockets. And all of them were brilliantly colored, with iridescent scales and stripes or polka dots. Some had legs—any number you could imagine—and some had fins, but some had both. Some made sounds as well, and the symphony they produced was as fantastic as their appearance was bizarre.

Then I noticed a very large and horrible-looking creature, with a snout shaped like a hose. He was hopping about and sucking up other unfortunate sea dwellers, like a huge and very hungry vacuum cleaner.

I was just getting very uncomfortable, thinking he might consume me as well, when I turned and saw another fantastic sight—a very large, canary-colored submersible craft of extraordinary design. And through the port holes I saw four dark-haired lads waving to me enthusiastically. The funny thing was that, although they looked familiar, they didn't look like real people, but rather like cartoon characters.

But, two-dimensional or not, they appeared to be my only hope of escaping from this horrible place, so I waved back to them just as energetically.

I was relieved and quite happy to see the yellow ship turn and head on a vector toward me. In moments it was overhead, and a large door opened from the underside of its hull. I swam up just as quickly as I could and entered through this welcome portal.

Inside, I found myself in a much more hospitable habitat, although it was still far from ordinary. There were strange pipes running in all directions all about the place, with valves and gauges sticking out at all angles. The four lads wore very similar clothing and spoke with thick Liverpool accents. They were very casual and friendly indeed, as if they did this sort of thing all the time. My mind was still swimming at this point, so it was hard for me to make the obvious connection.

"Hello," said the shortest one, who was holding two sticks of wood in his hands. "And who might you be?"

"Well, just look at her," said the one with Ben Franklin-style glasses on. "She's got kaleidoscope eyes. Your name wouldn't happen to be Lucy, would it?"

"No, it's Alice," I said calmly, "and I'm very happy to meet you all, especially under the circumstances."

"We're happy to meet anybody, under any circumstances," said the short one.

"Yes, unless you're a blue meanie," said the one with the angular chin, "and then we'd just as soon not."

"She doesn't look mean to me," said the handsome one in the middle, "and I think the blue tint of her skin's from the cold water and not any real indication of her political affiliations."

"Yes," agreed the spectacled one, "she looks peaceful enough to me. She looks quite ready and able to give peace a chance."

"Imagine that," said the pretty one.

"Hey, that's my line."

I put in sincerely, "Yes, I abhor violence of any kind. I don't even like violent sports or movies. I believe it's such a bad example for the children."

"Right on," agreed four-eyes. "We don't need all that insanity. All we need is love, as I keep telling everyone, if only they'd listen."

"What you really need is to get tuned in to infinity," said sharp-chin. "I would suggest some deep meditation. Who's your guru?"

"I don't have a guru," I said, somewhat embarrassed. "But I could get one if you think it would help."

"No problem; I always bring mine along with me. We could share gurus until you find one of your own. Oh, Robbie?" And at that, a brown-skinned man with bare feet and long, curly white hair stepped out from behind a large yellow pipe and walked softly over to us. He was carrying a strange stringed instrument (I believe it's called a sitar) and was wearing a long, flowing multicolored robe. His eyes were serene and tranquil, like two soft brown islands on a placid white sea. He smiled the gentle smile of a wise man, as he cradled the long-necked instrument in his arms like a mother holding her infant. I liked this guy immediately.

"Yes, my child," he said in a soft musical voice that was somehow powerful as well. "You seek answers to questions that cannot be spoken. You walk roads through places that cannot be seen, on a journey that has no beginning and no ending. You are on the transcendent highway to a higher plane, and you are just now beginning to see the light of a holistic sun. All that remains is for you to open your inner eyes, for only then will you find the path which you seek."

"Sounds simple enough," said the short one, "so I'm sure it isn't."

"Yes, it seemed so simple to me only yesterday," said the dark, handsome one, "or was that the day before yesterday?"

"I think it was a Tuesday," said short-stuff. "We had scrambled eggs for breakfast."

"Oh, you're all crazy," said chiseled chin. "Enlightenment—it don't come easy, you know."

"Sounds like a song," said the man with the sticks. "There must be a song in there somewhere anyway, don't you think?"

"Music is the key to unlock your heart," said spectacle face, "It reminds me of a song I just wrote."

"Don't you mean that we just wrote?" said handsome.

Then it finally hit me as my head started to clear a little. "Now I know who you guys are—you're the Beatles!"

"No, we're just their cartoon stand-ins," said the one that would be George.

"Yeah," said Paul's stand-in, "we've been on this stinking little boat for over forty years now. That's no way to treat the facsimile of a famous person."

"And this hole in me pocket makes it hard to save anything," said the Ringo.

"Stop complaining," said pseudo John, "I said my song lead-in and no one paid any attention. After all, we've been here almost five minutes now without singing."

"He's right," said cartoon Paul. "Our contract says we can't go for more than four minutes without a song."

"You must sing a song that will be helpful—one that will bring the girl closer to her goal of enlightenment," suggested the mystic. "And one with a catchy tune and a place for a ripping sitar solo would be nice, too."

"Right, lads, all together now: and a one, and a two, and a one, two, three …"

Out of nowhere, instruments appeared, logo drums and all, and the fabricated four began to play an upbeat and very catchy tune, with sitar accompaniment and four-part harmony. It went something like this:

> She's a real Sheboygan girl,
> Living in our cartoon world,
> Trying to solve the mysteries of the galaxy.

She doesn't like our point of view,
Thinks it's all a wee bit skewed.
But she's the one that's tilted, if you ask of me.

Sheboygan girl, please take notice,
Though we're all out of focus,
We're as real or unreal as you think you are.

3-D girl, don't you get it?
You're just like us, but don't regret it,
Turn around, go backward, and you'll soon go
far.
(Sitar solo)
She's a real cartoon girl,
Living in a projected world,
Making all her solid plans for nobody.

They finished with one nice, clean chord and a tasteful amount of reverb, and then they bowed their heads like true professionals. I couldn't help clapping. They were as polished as Queen Elizabeth's tea service.

"That was very good," I said approvingly, "but how did you know I was from Sheboygan?"

"I don't know," said Ringo's ringer, "a lucky guess?"

"We figured you must be from somewhere," said cartoon George.

"And since this is nowhere, we knew you weren't from here," said play Paul.

"And that accent of yours is north-midwestern American with a little south Boston thrown in," said John's surrogate. "So, that narrowed it down quite a bit."

"So we threw darts at a map of the USA and hit Sheboygan," said unreal Ringo.

"When did you have time to do all of that," I asked suspiciously.

"I think it was somewhere between the sea of green and the sea of holes."

I had no idea what they were talking about, so I let it drop. I figured Robbie the guru was the only one there who could give me useful information, but everything he said was in the form of philosophical riddles, so I wasn't sure if he could help me, either.

I immediately felt somewhat depressed by my lack of progress and direction and—I couldn't help it—I started to cry. They all looked at me sympathetically. They really were very nice lads.

"Good thing we didn't play one of our sad songs," said the drummer.

"Maybe we should play her 'Alice on the Side with Cranberries,'" said the bass player. "That should cheer her up."

"No, I just think she's having a bad trip," said the lead singer with the glasses.

"What a bummer," said lead guitar.

"That's it," I said, wiping the tears from my eyes and remembering what Master C had told me just before I ate the first piece of mushroom. "I must be trippin'. Maybe I should eat the other piece now. Maybe I should be flippin' instead of trippin'"

"Sounds to me more like you're slippin,'" said unreal Ringo.

"That may also be true, but, sorry, I don't have time to explain, and I'm not sure I could explain it, anyway. It's all quite confusing, really, even to me. I wish I could, though, because maybe then I would understand it myself. It all has something to do with nothing."

"Now who's the one talking in philosophical riddles?" asked Robbie.

I thanked them for rescuing me from the Jurassic vacuum cleaner and for the wonderful song they had sung to me, and then I turned around modestly and removed the other chunk of 'shroom from its hiding place. I turned around and said good-bye before taking a bite.

"Well, good-bye, boys. Hope you finally get off this boat someday."

"Good-bye, Alice—have fun solving all the mysteries of the universe."

They all waved at me just as enthusiastically as when they had first seen me out in the water, and then they disappeared, which puzzled me, because I thought I was supposed to do that. But I shrugged my shoulders and took a bite out of mushroom side B.

I woke up wearing my favorite flannel pajamas. I was lying next to my father on the couch in front of our television in Sheboygan—as if I had just dozed off while watching our favorite show: Monty Python's Flying Circus. I immediately had that strange feeling again, as if that other stuff had all just been a dream. It was a very odd and uncomfortable-feeling, and I couldn't shake it off. How could I tell whether it had been a dream or not? How could I know for sure?

But Father's familiar and heartwarming laughter snapped me out of it, so I decided to just relax and watch the show. John Cleese was sitting on a couch interviewing Michael Palin. I didn't immediately recognize the episode—which was strange, because I know them all by heart.

The skit came to an end, and I laughed heartily along with Father—but I was still quite puzzled, because I had never seen this sketch, and we own the entire series on DVD.

"That's strange," I finally said to Father, "I don't remember ever seeing this one before."

"Oh, sure you have, Alice," said an eerily familiar voice from over my shoulder. "We watched this one together just last week. What are you, brain dead?"

I spun around and saw a young woman of about twenty years old. She had reddish-blonde hair with a yellow bow in it. She was about the same height as my recently grownup self and had similar facial features. I was stunned.

"Who are you?" I asked impulsively.

"I'm the Easter Bunny. Who do you think I am?"

"Very funny, Alice," said Father. "I'm trying to listen to this. If you want to talk to your sister, Molly, why don't you go into the other room so I can hear?"

"Sister? But I don't have—" I stopped myself, because it was obvious that they wouldn't take me seriously or would think I was out of my mind or something. The truth was, I wasn't so sure that I wasn't. Then I realized where I recognized that voice from. It was Molly—Molly, my quantum computer. My computer had claimed that she was my sister!

"Yes, Father, that's a good idea. Molly and I have a lot to talk about."

I jumped up, took the very confused Molly by the hand and led her out to the kitchen. She didn't protest, because she could see I had something important to tell her.

"Molly, do you know who I am? Do you know who you are?" I asked after sitting us down at the breakfast table.

"Alice, I don't want to have another philosophical discussion with you. Why don't you tell me about your new boyfriend, Carl Johnson?"

"You see, that's just it. I don't know anybody named Carl Johnson."

"Dumped him already, huh? But I thought you really liked him. What happened? Did he cheat on you or something? I suggest castration."

"No, Molly, I didn't mean that figuratively; I meant it literally. I don't know this Carl character. In fact, I don't know you either, at least not as my sister."

"I know, I know, I'm so much more than a sister, aren't I? Even though I'm your little sister, you look up to me, don't you? You can admit it; I won't tell anyone. Do you need a glass of chocolate milk or something? Mom just made a batch of Toll House cookies, your favorite."

She was right, they are my favorite, but I wasn't hungry just then.

"No, Molly, thank you, but … it's hard for me to explain. I really need your help. I need you to help me to get out of here."

"You're a little old to be having teenaged angst, don't you think?"

"Actually, I'm younger than I look, but that's not what I mean. I need your help, because I think I gave you something."

"Gave me what? The last thing you gave me was that bust of Mozart."

I paused for a moment to collect my thoughts. Even if this wasn't real, it might have elements of reality in it. There could be analogs of truth in this world.

"This is going to sound really weird to you, Molly. I'm not the Alice you know. I think this is part of an alternate timeline from the other parallel universe. That's why I didn't recognize that Monty Python sketch, because in my universe they never did that one. Do you see what I mean?"

"Yes, you're right—it does sound very strange. Is this some sort of gag?"

"And in my universe I don't have a sister Molly. I have a quantum computer named Molly. Since you didn't exist in my world, I had to create you, instead. I'm, what, about six years older than you are, right?"

"Usually you state it in seconds instead of years, but we both know the answer."

"I made Molly when I was six years old. I'm willing to bet it coincided with your birthday. And that means that I had to build you—it was inevitable."

"You know, it's funny how you can sound completely rational, even when you're saying such completely crazy stuff. You should take that act on the road with Bing."

I ignored her and went on. "The parallel universes are linked by the buffer zone, and the buffer zone passes information back and forth between them. They are analogs of each other, but not identical. That's what keeps things balanced."

"Okay, Alice, you may think this is very funny, but it just goes to show you what watching too much Monty Python will do to your brain. And, if you are serious, I would suggest professional help."

"Molly, shut up and listen to me for a second. I am serious, and I need your help. I need to find my way back to my own universe."

Molly looked at me with a very strange expression on her face, but it stopped just short of implying that I was a raving lunatic. I suppose she was giving me the benefit of the doubt. I'm sure I *did* sound like a raving lunatic.

"Alice, you know I'd do anything for you, but I have no idea what you're talking about. What sort of help do you need?"

"I'm not sure exactly, but I must have given you something analogous to the formulas that I fed into my computer. Did I give you a book, or a letter, or anything like that when we were children? Possibly even a key or a coded message. Did I give you anything like that?"

"Not that I recall, but who remembers all that stuff besides Mom? Let me see … you did let me read your diary from time to time. That's one thing I will find very hard to forget. Could that be what you're looking for?"

This was quite an intriguing idea, that I could read the diary written by my parallel self. Even if it didn't have the answer, it was irresistible. What sort of things would much older and wiser mirror-Alice have written in her diary? I had to have a look at that.

"I don't know, Molly, but it's possible. Do you know where it is?"

"Are you kidding? You hid that book so well even Sherlock Holmes couldn't have found it. Don't you know where it is?"

"Well, let's go to my room. If I know myself—and I'm pretty sure I do—I think I can find it."

So we got up and walked out of the kitchen, and I started to turn left, as usual, to go to the stairs, when Molly stopped me.

"Where are you going, Alice? The stairs are on the left. Your brain really isn't functioning too well today, is it?"

"But I am going left," I said defensively.

"No, no, your other left," said Molly, and then she proceeded to go through the kitchen door and turn to the right. Now who was pulling whose leg?

Then I turned around and looked at the kitchen. I had been so intent on talking to Molly that I hadn't even noticed. It was all backward. And, I found out, so was the rest of the house. It was an exact and perfect mirror image of the house I had grown up in. Even the pictures on the walls were the same, but they were flipped around. I saw a magazine on the coffee table; it was printed backward (*naciremA cifitneicS*) and opened the wrong way. It was true: this universe was a mirror of ours.

So I went to the stairs (which did go up and not down, as they still would in a mirror world, so don't get smart) and started to climb them, but, as I did, a horrible thought struck me. If this was an alternate timeline, then it might not be stable, and it might dissipate or evaporate. If it did, I might be caught in the temporal wake and vanish along with it. I might be truncated. But even if I didn't evaporate, Molly would surely disappear along with it, and I would lose the opportunity to finally bond with my little sister (who did have a marvelous personality, to be sure).

Then another thought occurred to me: Molly either *held* the key or *was* the key. There was only one thing I could do. I would have to leave this place immediately and take her with me—but how?

So I ran up the stairs and turned right—and then caught myself and went left—to my room at the end of the hall. I burst in to find Molly looking through the bookshelf to see if I had hidden the diary in plain sight. It was a good guess, but it was now a moot point. I didn't need the diary. I needed her.

"Alice, you always keep everything in alphabetical order—from Z to A—so maybe, if I look under Y, we'll find your diary," she said, sounding ever so much like her quantum counterpart.

"No, Molly, forget about the diary, we don't need that. I need to get out of here, fast, and I need you to come with me."

"Where do you want to go, to the mall? Got another case of shopping fever, huh?"

"Molly, shut up and listen for a second, please. This place isn't real, and it might disappear any time now. And if it does, you're going to dematerialize with it. I can't lose you now. I think you are the key I'm looking for. Don't you see?"

"Yeah, I see—you have totally lost your freaking marbles. And just where do your marbles go when you lose them? Is there some enormous pile of marbles somewhere that belong to all those poor crazy people out there? It must be a pretty big pile, that's for sure." And as she continued to talk about lost marbles and the like, we heard a very strange and horrible sound. It started low and subtle, but it just kept increasing in volume, until Molly finally stopped talking to listen. It sounded sort of like the combination of a car crash, a volcanic eruption, and fingers being raked across a blackboard (I hate that sound). We both instinctively ran to the window and looked out. What we saw was quite disturbing indeed (understatement of all eternity).

The world was disintegrating, but it wasn't going quietly into that good night, not by a long shot. There was a wall of destruction heading our way, and behind it was a zone of absolutely nothing. As the wave of doom swept along, everything in its wake simply exploded, like the fast-moving shock wave of a nuclear chain reaction. We didn't have much time left. At the speed it was propagating, I estimated it would be upon us in only a few more seconds.

Then I remembered the mushroom. It was a long shot, but it was all that I could think of. So I pulled it out, broke it in half, and quickly shoved a chunk into Molly's hysterical mouth.

"Yuck! I hate mushroom."

"Shut up and eat it," I yelled at her and squashed the other piece into my own not-so-composed pie hole. As I chewed and swallowed the musty mouthful, I grabbed Molly and hugged her for all I was worth. A fraction of a second later, the walls exploded, and everything went black (I know, again).

I found, of course, that I had not disintegrated (obviously, since I'm writing this now), and, to my delight, Molly was still with me. It had worked! I had managed to extricate her from that doomed alternate history. I had pulled her from her world into mine, which, unfortunately, at this point was still in limbo land. But, for the moment, it was far better than oblivion (most places are, but not all, I suppose).

It became immediately obvious that Molly and I were inside what appeared to be a very large teacup, and that this vessel, of unusual volume, was traveling at a very high velocity, which is also somewhat remarkable for a container of this variety. Looking over the rim and down, I realized that the large teacup was riding tracks of some kind. I looked around us further and noticed that the tracks belonged to a much larger network of tracks and trestles, which looped and twisted in the amazing snarl of an exaggerated engineering nightmare. We were apparently on some kind of poorly designed roller coaster. The teacup didn't even have seats or safety belts.

I was about to tell Molly what I had discovered, when the cup went around a sharp corner; the centripetal force caused us to be pressed against the walls of the cup, and we started spinning around. This was quite disorienting and disturbing, but not quite as much as when we went over a hill, and the tracks dove down at a steep angle, causing us to become airborne. My heart not only went into my throat but threatened to come right out of my mouth. But the tracks rose to meet us, and the titanic teacup scooped us out of the air like an outfielder catching a fly ball. By this time, we were both screaming like mental patients on a full moon, and I was pretty sure that I never wanted to repeat this experience ever again, no matter what Molly said. Then we went into the corkscrew loop-the-loop.

I counted nine full revolutions, as round and round we went, upside down and sideways and spinning all the while. This was supposed to be fun? It got even worse when we went into the tunnel.

The tunnel's opening was disguised as the mouth of a gargantuan and grotesque clown, which, quite disconcertingly, didn't open until moments before we got to it.

Then it opened up, lashed us with its tongue as we flew inside, and then closed just as quickly, leaving us in total darkness. Now we were spinning and flipping around with nothing to orient us, except the occasional bright flash from a strobe light, which revealed other monstrous sights and ominous openings as our rollercoaster ride through hell itself continued. One thing was for sure: no one on my planet would ever top this ride! The liability insurance alone would kill them—if the ride didn't do it first.

After what seemed like an eternity, the teacup finally slowed down and came to a stop at the loading platform, where a huge line of customers waited for their chance to be reduced to a pile of quivering jelly. As soon as the little door opened, we were out of there faster than you could say absolutely nothing.

"Thank Feynman that's over! I thought we were going to fall out of that stupid thing at any moment," I said, trying my best to walk in a straight line.

"Well, it's a good thing we didn't," said Molly, who was slowly regaining her equilibrium as well. "We wouldn't want to get sued."

I wasn't quite sure whether Molly was just confused, or what, but I started to look around some more to see at what sort of place we had arrived. There were red and white striped tents everywhere, with big bold signs advertising things such as The Oliphant Man and The Bearded Baby. There were also many other rides and attractions in this colossal carnival/circus. Thousands of people, animals, and strange beings milled about all around us, talking, and laughing, and eating strange-looking things wrapped in white paper with grease soaking through it. This made me even less hungry than I already was. I think I lost my stomach at about the third loop-the-loop.

"Molly, do you know where we are?" I asked suspiciously, since this looked more like something from her universe than from mine.

"Oh sure, we're at Six Flags over Atlantis. It's our favorite amusement park. Don't you remember? We've only been here like a gazillion times before. Or are you still on that 'I'm from another universe' kick?"

"When you say 'Atlantis,' do you mean the island that sank into the Atlantic Ocean centuries ago?"

"Sank into the ocean—what are you talking about, Alice? This island has always been right here at the corner of the so-called Atlantis Rectangle, where all that spooky stuff has happened. But, as far as I know, it never sank. They turned the entire island into a living museum and theme park almost thirty years ago. Man, you really are from another planet, aren't you?"

"Let me guess—the island of Bermuda is located at one of the other corners of the rectangle, right?"

"Well, duh!"

I hate it when people imply that I'm mentally deficient in any way, so I almost yelled at Molly. But then I decided that it still must have sounded to her as if I were an idiot or something, so I refrained. I suppose it was possible that on her world the island of Atlantis never did sink into the ocean. This was an amazing opportunity to do some scientific research into the legend, but, then again, I didn't have time for that. What a pity.

For, at that moment, a large man, wearing a multicolored spandex suit, bumped into me. I wouldn't have been so upset, except for the fact that his was the sort of shape that spandex should never be seen on. He was simply rotund. No, he was more than merely rotund—he was ovoid.

He was wearing a very contrived-looking black and red outfit, with a matching black Lone Ranger-style mask. There were two large letters on his chest, which, if spelled the right way round, would be HD. The letters were done in an equally corny lightning bolt style—as if this guy ever did anything fast. He was also wearing black boots, which he had somehow found or made in a size that looked to me to be about 18 ZZZ. Let's face it—this guy could roll a lot easier than he could walk. And then, he had the nerve to glare at me and act as if I had bumped into him. This guy was so wide, he bumped into everything.

"Out of my way, little girl; don't you know who I am?" he said, as if he were the king of Atlantis.

"Oh, I don't know, Howdy Doody, maybe? You've grown since I've last seen you. How's Buffalo Bob doing?"

His face turned bright red with rage, and, as far as I knew, so did the rest of his bulbous body—not that that's a mental picture I ever want to repeat. "I will sue you for that and for getting in my way!"

"What? You bumped into me, fat ass."

Just then, Molly grabbed me by the arm and whispered urgently into my ear. "Alice, don't you know who that is? It's the world-famous daredevil, Heinous Delanus. He once jumped across the Grand Canyon in a shopping cart full of fried chicken and landed safely on the other side with an empty cart."

"So, what should I be afraid of, that he's going to eat me?"

Before Molly had a chance to answer me, Mr. Delanus interrupted. "I'm willing to forget the whole incident, but only under one condition."

"And what would that be, your hugeness?"

"That the two of you volunteer to be part of my show. And, as long as neither one of you gets injured in any way, I won't have to sue you, after all."

"You won't sue me? Molly, what the heck is he talking about?" Then, just as I said that, it occurred to me what was going on. This was a mirror world. In this world, when you got hurt by someone or something, *they* sued *you*, instead of the other way around. That's what Molly had meant when she said it was a good thing we hadn't fallen out of the teacup. The park would have sued us. That's also probably why there were no seats or seatbelts on the ride. They probably made a lot of money that way. I wonder if they paid you to go on the ride as well.

So I agreed to be in Heinous Delanus's show, which he told us would take place in the Big Top in twenty minutes. It wasn't so much that I was afraid of being sued. I just really wanted to see what sort of act this human marble could actually do. I know this type of curiosity is often unhealthy, but I couldn't help myself. This I had to see.

Molly, on the other hand, wasn't very anxious to join in on the fun, but she wanted to help me more than anything else, so she reluctantly agreed to do it. We signed the waivers (which said that in the event we were not injured, we couldn't sue him) and he was off on his way. He took about three steps, bumped into another person (at least I think it was a person), and threatened to sue them as well. Then I understood what was going on: he was recruiting.

The Big Top was packed with patrons, all wanting to see Heinous Delanus pull off his latest and greatest stunt. I suppose it was hard to top the shopping-cart-filled-with-fried-chicken-over-the-Grand-Canyon bit, but he was doing his best to try.

Now, when I say Big Top, this is a sizable understatement, to be sure. The capacity of this place must have been in the hundreds of thousands, and the center pole looked to be about a kilometer high. A ramp had been constructed at one end of the tent, and it climbed up and up and up until it ended at a platform, which was hard to see with the naked eye. It looked like Mount Crumpit looking down on Whoville. And we, the 'volunteers,' were the Whos.

We were lined up on the floor of the arena, all lying down on our backs, side to side like sardines—all nine hundred and fifty-eight of us—and I was initially glad that Molly and I were about in the middle. The great Heinous Delanus was about to attempt to jump over all of us on a children's tricycle.

There were a lot of nervous faces in our ranks. The current standing record was only four hundred and eleven. There had apparently been a few unsuccessful attempts at modestly higher numbers. No one wanted to talk too much about that. Apparently, Heinous Delanus had already broken every bone in his body at least four times, and several of them had since been replaced with titanium or carbon fiber. I was suddenly no longer glad to be in the middle.

On the jumbotron on the side wall, we could see HD in HD, and he was waving to the crowd from the platform, perched upon his mini-tricycle. He looked like a bag of cement on a pogo stick. How had this guy ever become a daredevil?

"Molly, I'm sorry I talked you into this. Is there still time to chicken out?"

"No, but I think there is time for a quick prayer."

"Who should we pray to, the god of projectile motion?"

But before Molly could answer, the PA system squawked to life, and the MC introduced the main event.

"Ladies and gentlemen, are you ready to scramble? May I direct your attention to the top of the 'ramp of destiny,' where the great Heinous Delanus sits at an amazing altitude of seventeen hundred and seventy-six feet. He will, in death-defying fashion, before your eyes and before the eyes of millions of television viewers, attempt to ride down the five-foot-wide ramp on an ordinary tricycle, while reaching speeds in excess of one hundred miles per hour. At the bottom of the ramp, he will fly through the air and attempt to clear nine hundred and fifty-eight lucky volunteers, before landing safely on the ramp you see at the opposite end of the Big Top. Let's all give a big, Big-Top welcome to the one, the only, master of disaster—Heinous Delanus!"

The crowd went absolutely bananas, as HD waved to them even more fervently. He stopped suddenly and took on a much more serious posture, as he looked down the ramp of certain doom. This was absolutely nuts.

Then, after building up the suspense for an appropriate period of time, he crouched down, gripped the handlebars firmly, and, with splayed elbows, gave us one last somewhat-strained smile and pushed himself off over the edge. Gravity was about to claim another victim—at least one.

The ramp was so steep that he immediately accelerated to an incredible speed, and he had to take his feet off the pedals and spread his legs to keep from being pummeled by the spinning crank. This made him look like a black and red pinball with legs. He started going so fast that his multiple chins started to flap together like baseball cards in the spokes of a high-speed motorcycle. Something bad was about to happen—you could just feel it in the air.

And then it happened—he blew a tire. I don't know whether it was from the weight or the heat from the velocity, but his front tire blew open like an overfilled water balloon, and he flew over the handlebars as if he'd been shot from a very wide-mouthed cannon. He started tumbling and spinning in the air, jiggling and flapping as he went, with his arms flailing about wildly. The steepness of the ramp meant that he didn't touch anything until he reached the bottom. The whole crowd (including us volunteers) gasped in shock and held its collective breath.

When he got to the bottom, he didn't just hit the ramp; he went right through it—with a horrendous crashing and crunching sound that probably was heard as far away as Miami. The crowd made a simultaneous and sympathetic *oooooh* sound.

He made a crater in the ground that measured about twenty feet in diameter, and I think they contemplated just covering it over with dirt and calling it a day. But, somehow, he miraculously survived, so they brought in the winch of life instead. He didn't just break all the bones in his body; he pulverized them. It took twelve paramedics to carry the stretcher out, and, somehow— compound fractures and all,—he still managed to wave to the crowd. What a showman!

Outside the Big Top once again, Molly and I decided to take a little walk around Atlantis to sort things out a bit. She was understandably confused by the recent events—much as could be expected under the somewhat bizarre circumstances—and I was trying my best to fill her in as much as I could. There were obviously still nuances of this dynamic domain that I had not mastered yet, but a more knowledgeable mentor wasn't available, so I took my best crack at it.

We were walking through the courtyard of a magnificent marble and alabaster palace as Molly questioned me, and I wished that I had brought a camera of some sort with me. Atlantis was a truly spectacular place. The architecture was similar to ancient Greece, but even more advanced, with pillars, and arches, and massive stone structures all around us. There were even towering statues and monoliths that would have rivaled the Egyptians' for engineering accomplishment. It was simply awe-inspiringly beautiful.

"So, Alice," said Molly as we walked under an enormous stone archway that led to a breathtaking garden of flowers and manicured hedges. "If I understand what you're saying, you're telling me that I'm not real—that none of this is real. I don't know about you, but it seems pretty darn real to me."

"Yes, Molly, it would seem real, because these images are produced from gravimetric holograms. Since they're made from gravitons, the images seem solid, just as real objects that give off gravitons do. I know this is all very technical, but the only way I can explain it simply is to say that there is no way to distinguish between this place and a real one."

"Then, how do you know that all of this isn't real and that the place where you came from isn't the imaginary world instead?"

I looked up at a five-meter-tall rose bush with ten-centimeter blossoms, and I smelled the heavenly aroma emanating therefrom, and, to be honest, there was a tinge of doubt deep down in my soul. Molly had a very poignant argument. How *could* I be sure one way or the other?

"Well, Molly, all I can say is that my memories don't include this place, or you, or that Monty Python sketch we watched earlier, or anything else around here. Therefore, as long as I trust my memories as an accurate record of objects and events from my universe, I must be led to the conclusion that this world isn't real, or at least that this is not the world that I remember."

"But you're not sure, are you? How could you be totally sure?"

"Yes, you're right Molly. Since there is no way to distinguish between the two, at least as far as determining whether things are real or not, there is no way for me to be absolutely sure that I am right. I have to have faith that my memories are accurate and consistent and that my use and understanding of scientific theories provides a viable explanation for what I am experiencing—for what *we* are experiencing. Does that help?"

Molly didn't answer immediately but stood beside me contemplating the underlying ethereal world around us—in its entire multicolored and fragrant splendor—before she said anything else. Then she changed her tone to an even more serious timbre and said, "Alice, do you believe in God?"

Now, I had to take pause before hastily blurting out a callous response to her loaded question. Religion is an emotional subject, and short answers to such questions are often taken the wrong way. It wasn't merely that I didn't believe in God; it was that, since there was no way to either prove or disprove the existence of such a supreme entity, it simply wasn't covered under the otherwise comprehensive blanket of science. It was just like anything else in my own personal dogma—I needed proof.

"Well, Molly, I don't disbelieve in God, in that I allow for the possibility that such a being might actually exist, but I guess I need more evidence before I make a final decision on that subject."

"That's the same as saying that you don't believe, or, at least, that you don't believe yet, right?"

"Yes, I suppose so. But that alone doesn't make me a bad person, does it, Molly?"

In response, she just turned to me and smiled the most amazing smile I have ever seen. It lit up her whole face—her whole body, even—with the airs of love and mischief and awe and mystery and sympathy, all at the same time. And then she said to me slyly, but excitedly, "Alice, maybe this place is heaven!"

Her words hit me like a wave of ice-cold water, and I was taken aback as if she had slapped me in the face with a very large frozen fish. I was stunned. This possibility had not occurred to me, but there was no way to prove that she was wrong. Maybe we had since passed on to a higher plane of existence, which, from her perspective, could be called heaven. Maybe this was where dead souls went, just maybe. Maybe we had both been truncated by the collapsing timeline. But I shook my head and decided that this was a dead-end line of reasoning that would get us nowhere.

"Molly, you just scared the excrement out of me, you really did. I can't be dead! I have so much more to accomplish first, so please don't go there. Let's just think about what other possibilities there are, besides being dead. I believe that will be a lot more helpful to us at this juncture. If you're right, which I really hope you aren't, we'll find out soon enough anyway."

"Okay, Alice, I'm truly sorry for scaring you. But you should have seen the look on your face." She laughed heartily, which wasn't very endearing but was curiously contagious, and I soon found myself laughing right along with the deranged idiot. It was just the sort of emotional release I needed at that moment, and, when we finally stopped laughing, I found that I felt much better. I was ready to resume our quest for knowledge.

"Yes, thanks for the moment of levity, Molly; you are completely forgiven. I must now concentrate on the task at hand, which is to figure out how you might hold the key to the door that leads out of this world. What do you—Molly, my sister, and you, Molly, my quantum computer—have in common?"

"Well, we're both named Molly," she said, not so helpfully at first, "and we both have—what would you call it?—a quantum connection to you and to this place; isn't that right, Alice?"

"Yes," I said, somewhat amazed that she had thought of it first. "You both have a communication link to the buffer zone. Since we're in between universes, you could possibly be a hybrid mix that includes elements of both Mollies."

"Come to think of it, I do feel a bit more computational lately. I thought being around you was just making me smarter, by osmosis or something."

"Well, it can never hurt. But this is an exciting possibility. I might be able to talk to someone outside of the buffer zone. It's never been done before, you know. We could make history here."

"Cool!"

"But will it help me?"

We both stopped short in our mutual enthusiasm when I said this, and some steam escaped from my balloon of optimism. Even if I could communicate with my own world, how would that help me? If Molly sent someone after me, wouldn't they be just as trapped as I was? And, since I had programmed Molly, she wouldn't have any information I didn't have in the first place, so what could she tell me that I didn't already know? But, even so, there was one remaining possibility.

"Computers are designed to take data and formulas as input and combine them to produce new answers as output. Molly the computer has the additional capacity of creative thinking to augment her problem-solving capabilities—which means that she can make jumps of logic to solutions that ordinary computers could never reach. In other words, if anyone can figure out how to get out of here, it is Molly."

"Thanks for the vote of confidence, Alice. I knew you'd see how much you need me some day. I'm not just another pretty face, after all."

Molly looked at me with a very pleased expression on her marvelous mug, and she even bobbed her head from side to side in some form of victory dance. "So, how can I help? What amazing answers can I bestow upon my somewhat ignorant elder sister?"

"Okay, okay, don't get a swelled head here. We don't even know if you can answer the question yet, so take it easy with the condescension. It's not your style."

"Right, that would be more up *your* alley."

"Oh, hush up, Molly; let's have more thinking and less gloating, can we?"

"Okay, Alice, I apologize—but why don't we get something to eat first? My brain doesn't work so well on an empty stomach."

I was about to explain to Molly how hunger was all in the mind (especially here) but decided against it. If she wanted something to eat, I wasn't going to argue. Especially since my holographic brain couldn't quite convince my own virtual stomach that it wasn't in any need of any imaginary sustenance, and it was growling just the same. So we walked off in search of a restaurant at the edge of reality—hopefully, one that served ice cream and had never heard of Brussels sprouts.

We found a little place called Ecila's Restaurant and had a Thanksgiving dinner that couldn't be beat, even though it was the middle of March by my calendar. And afterward, as we walked down the sidewalk again, I realized that we hadn't accomplished anything at Ecila's Restaurant, at least as far as finding a solution to my problem was concerned. I turned to Molly and started that conversation up again.

"So, Molly, now that you've had a Thanksgiving dinner that couldn't be beat, is your brain functioning any better?"

"Possibly, but even if it isn't, I do feel much better. That place was pretty weird, wasn't it?"

"Well, I don't know if I'd give it four stars, but it was unique to be sure. I can honestly say that I've never been to a restaurant anything like that. But let's get back to the task at hand, if you will. Just tell me what comes to mind when you think about this place and getting out of here. Close your eyes and try to clear your mind, if that helps."

Molly stopped walking and closed her eyes, which is the prudent way to do it, and her face went blank and calm. A couple of people gave her strange looks as they walked by, but I ignored them. Molly was trying to communicate with another world. Most people have trouble just communicating with each other.

Molly stood there for several seconds, motionless and speechless, with her eyes shut and her arms hanging loosely at her sides. To be honest, she did look a bit odd—as if she was meditating standing up on Main Street—but I had the feeling that something significant was happening inside her holographic head. There were no brilliant flashes of light or thunderclouds forming over us to indicate that extra-universal communication was happening there, but somehow I got the feeling that there was. The calmer she looked, the more tense I felt. I couldn't wait to hear what she had to say.

"Well, is anything happening, Molly? Do you see mathematical expressions forming in your head or anything like that? Do you hear voices?"

"All I hear is your voice, and it's breaking my concentration."

"Oh, sorry, I'll shut up then ... just take your time ... no hurry."

"Alice, shut up!"

"Right, sorry again ... I'll stop talking now ... I'm not talking."

Molly stood there like a statue for several more excruciating seconds, and then, at last, she opened her eyes, and she smiled the calm smile of an enlightened soul. She turned to me but said nothing. I was ready to burst at the seams.

"Well, what happened? Anything? Anything at all?"

"Well, I don't know, but I do feel overall very calm and serene. It's very nice."

"Great. But did you manage to communicate with Molly, my computer?"

"I'm not sure, Alice, but there was one voice in my head—besides yours—that didn't seem to be coming from myself. It was very faint, but I finally made out what it was saying, I think."

"Good, good; what did it say, Molly?"

"It said, 'It is one thing to know something, but it is quite another to believe it.' Does that make any sense to you, Alice?"

Now it was my turn to stop and think for a moment. What was the difference between knowing something and believing it? Weren't they basically the same thing? Was it possible to know something without believing it? Or, put the other way around, was it possible to believe something without knowing it to be so?

"I would think that if you know something you must believe in it, but that it's possible to believe in something without knowing it—without having any proof—such as when people believe in God or the wisdom of certain governmental decisions."

"Yes, Alice, that's called faith."

"That's right, Molly, and my interpretation of your revelation from beyond would be that somehow faith transcends mere knowledge, making it more important, somehow, than the knowledge itself. If you know something but don't really believe it, then it's the same as not knowing it at all."

"Do you believe that, Alice?"

"I don't know."

Here was yet another possibility that I had never considered before: that, somehow, faith plays a major role in knowledge. It went against everything that I believed. Faith alone was useless without the evidence to back it up. And evidence and proof alone shouldn't need faith to make them real and true. Did I need to have faith in science? Wasn't that an oxymoron, a contradiction? Didn't science eliminate the need for something as frivolous and unscientific as faith?

"I don't know, Molly; maybe I'm not interpreting it right, but, at the moment, it doesn't make any sense to me. What would be your interpretation?"

"Well, I think you already said it—that until you actually believe something, you really don't know it at all. It's not useful to you until you accept it as truth, until you believe it in your heart. Knowledge in the soul must incorporate both the heart and the mind. How does that sound—pretty smart for your little sister, eh?"

"The soul? Okay, Molly, this is starting to get a little too existential for me. Next thing you'll be talking about spirits, and life after death, and all that paranormal baloney. Let's try to stick to things we do know, okay?"

"But, Alice, if you have to believe in something, then maybe the proof itself isn't as important. Didn't you say something before about how the imagination plays a role in making things happen here? Doesn't that mean that thinking of something and believing in something can make it true—can make it happen?"

I didn't remember saying anything like that to Molly—at least not to Molly, my sister—but I went on anyway as if I had. "Yes, Molly. Because events are based on probabilities in the quantum domain, the act of thinking of something makes it more likely for that something to actually happen. For instance, if you've never thought of going to school to become a doctor, then the likelihood of you ever actually becoming a doctor would be essentially zero. But if you really believe that you want to be a doctor—if you think of nothing else—then the probability approaches certainty. Our thoughts mold the universe around us. We create realities by thinking about them."

"But you're still talking about the 'real' world, right? Didn't you once say that anything that you can think of or imagine happens here in the buffer zone?"

Now, I was certain that I had never said any such thing to Molly, my sister. But I did recall having just such a conversation with Molly, my computer. It was working! Molly didn't realize it, but she was communicating directly with my universe through Molly, the quantum computer. This was amazing, but I had to stay focused on the problem at hand.

"Yes, that's true, but how does that help us? Do I simply have to believe that I can get out of here? Will that alone make it happen? I'm not so sure that will work."

"Well, maybe that's it, Alice; maybe you have to believe it will work."

"But first I have to know that it will work, and how it will work, before I can believe it will work. I still have to figure out the mechanics of it first. At least, that's what I believe."

"Then, there you have it—but at least you're a little closer to the solution, right?"

At that moment, I remembered what the Master Cat Pillar had said to me: *You've got to believe in nothing.* Did he mean that literally? I thought it was just part of his colorful use of language. But maybe his advice was the key I was looking for, after all.

"He said to me, 'It's all about nothing.'"

"Who said?"

"This giant caterpillar named Master C. He sang me a song about reality, at least the reality of this world. He said it's all about nothing. And now that I think about it, he's absolutely right."

"You're talking nonsense again, Alice dear."

"We're not real—nothing here is real. Like I said before, we're just holograms projected from—from the boundary wall! Molly, I get it now. I'm not really here. I'm trapped inside the mirror."

"What mirror? What do you mean, trapped? Alice, I think you've finally gone off the deep end for good this time. How can you be trapped inside a mirror?"

"Because, Molly, nothing but gravitons can penetrate the boundary wall between my universe and this place—the buffer zone. Real matter can't exist here. When the wormhole collapsed,

I was deposited on the boundary wall as a type of gravimetric shadow, a two-dimensional image of my three-dimensional self. That's what a hologram is: a two-dimensional image that contains three-dimensional information. What we see here is the holographic projection of my shadow on the boundary wall. And because the boundary wall has an infinite reflectance to photons, it looks like a perfect mirror. Do you see now? I'm trapped inside the mirror."

"Okay, then, what about me? Am I trapped in the mirror, too?"

"Yes, but your shadow isn't permanent; it will fade away along with your—but your timeline has already been truncated, so you must be part of my imagination. Or maybe I jumped from the truncated timeline to another, where you—okay, I don't know exactly how we got here together, but I do know where I am now, where I *really* am. That's a good starting point, to be sure."

"Okay, now that you know where and what you are, the only thing that remains is for you to believe it, right, Alice?"

"I suppose so, but I still don't know exactly what that means. If I just imagine that I'm trapped inside the mirror, won't I still be trapped? Does that belief in any way help me to become untrapped? There must be more to it than that."

"Maybe not. Maybe that's all there is to it. Why don't you try it, anyway?"

"Oh, yeah, I've seen this part of the movie before. All I have to do is close my eyes and repeat the phrase, 'There's no place like home. There's no place like home. There's no place like home,' and click my heels together three times. The first problem is that I don't happen to own a pair of ruby slippers."

"And I don't think we're in Sheboygan anymore. I see dark clouds on the horizon."

"That's really deep, Molly, but I don't think things are as bad as that."

"No, Alice, I wasn't speaking metaphorically. Look behind you."

Seeing the disturbed expression on Molly's face, I wasn't sure I wanted to turn around, but, when I heard thunder rumbling, I couldn't help myself.

I turned to see the marvelous city of Atlantis covered by a shroud of gloom and darkness. Lightning began to shoot out of turbulent cauldrons of soot-black clouds, and hail the size of basketballs began to fall. It crushed cars and buses, which began to swerve and crash into each other, as they tried in vain to dodge the huge balls of falling ice. Then the lightning began to strike the buildings and bridges, turning portions of them into torrents of flying stone and jagged shrapnel. Atlantis was being destroyed, finally, right before our eyes. And then I saw a mountain of water heading toward us, as the ground began to buckle and split beneath us from an earthquake. It was clear that this timeline was also being truncated, and we were probably going along with it.

Molly looked into my eyes with an expression that could have broken the hearts of the heartless. I didn't know what I could say to her. Should I say hello or good-bye? What did *aloha* mean here?

"Alice, you wouldn't happen to have any more of that mushroom, would you?"

"Nope, no such luck. I'm not so sure it would help."

"Probably not. I hate mushrooms, anyway."

"That's right. You wouldn't want to die with an unpleasant taste in your mouth."

"Yeah, it's better this way." She smiled at me, which didn't make me feel any better about our predicament. At that moment, I really wanted to live, so that I could get to know my little sister better. We had had only a few hours together, and already I felt a bond to her that was stronger than the strongest nuclear force—and that's strong.

"Well, so long, Molly. Maybe I'll see you in the next world."

"I thought you didn't believe in that stuff, Alice."

"Maybe I don't, but it can't hurt to imagine it so."

"Not a bit. Well, hello, Alice."

"Hello, Molly."

A moment later the tidal wave hit.

PART II

MOLLY SPEAKS

Hi, I'm Molly. I'm a quantum computer.

That didn't sound very intelligent, now, did it? I apologize—I'm sort of new to this writing game. I suppose that's no excuse, but, in my defense, all I can say is that when you have a brain the size of the universe it's easy to go the other way and make things overly complicated. I'll try not to overcompensate, but I'm not making any promises.

Now it's time for me to fill you in on things that happened after Mr. H so rudely swept Alice away from me and took her into the buffer zone. I don't really dislike Mr. H, mind you; it's just that Alice is the most important person to me in the entire multiverse. And I would love Mr. H even more if he hadn't taken Alice away from me—or, at least, that's what it seemed at the time he had done. He just popped into existence that horrible morning and led Alice right down the wormhole.

This left me alone in her office, and I wasn't very happy about that. Then, just as Alice blinked out of existence (in our universe), Lucy Fernglow came through the door looking for Alice. She had only missed her by a second.

Lucy looked at the pile of debris at the center of the floor (caused by our little indoor cyclone), and she gasped with surprise.

"What the heck happened here? Did Alice decide to redecorate a little?"

"Sort of," I said sheepishly. This was going to be a little difficult to explain. Especially when I myself wasn't sure exactly what had happened.

"I like it," said Lucy sarcastically. "What would you call this style—modern mayhem?"

"Sure, or maybe it's more like neopandemonium."

Lucy chuckled to herself and continued, "So, where is Alice? I think I figured out how to solve the problem."

"You're too late for that," I said factually. "Alice just left. And when I say she left, I mean it."

"Okay, when will she be back?" she said calmly.

"Well, it could take a little while."

"How so?"

"It might take her a little while to figure out how to get out of there."

"Out of where, Molly?"

"Out of the blackboard."

It took me a few minutes to fill Lucy in on what had happened, and, when I was finished with my story, Lucy looked very glum. That didn't make me feel any better.

"What should we do, Lucy? Can we get Alice back again? Please tell me we can get her back again."

Lucy didn't say anything immediately, but I felt that she was probably the only other person alive that could get Alice back. It was Lucy or nobody.

"Well, if Alice really has crossed through the boundary and into the buffer zone, then it might not be possible to get her back."

"Don't tell me that, Lucy; please don't tell me that."

Lucy sat down, finally, and furrowed her brow in thought. That was a little encouraging, but not very. "It seems to me that if Alice could pass through the boundary wall, then so could someone else. The problem is how to find her once you get there."

"Once *I* get there? Are you saying that *I* should go and find Alice?"

"Possibly, but I think we should send someone a little less important than you first."

"And who would that be?"

Just as I said that, A-II poked his head out from under the bench he was hiding under and looked at us with a frightened expression. He knew exactly whom Lucy had in mind. "You looking at me?" he said with a twitch of his tail. "I hope you ain't looking at me."

"A-II, I'm glad you're here. Alice is gone, and she might need our help," said Lucy, as if A-II hadn't said anything.

"Like I care?"

A-II says things like this all the time, but I know that, deep down, he doesn't really mean it—deep, deep down, that is.

"I'm going to ignore that," I said bluntly. "Tell me that you don't love Alice, A-II. Tell me that she isn't the most important person in the whole world to you. Tell me that, and I'll shave off all your fur and sell you to the circus."

A-II paused. He could tell I was serious. He was still wondering how his tail had ended up two inches shorter one day, mysteriously, after he had insulted Alice in my presence. I'll just say that I won't say it wasn't me. Automatic electronic paper cutters can be bribed; that's all I'm going to say.

"Okay, so I care—just don't tell anyone. I have a reputation to uphold."

"Your secret is safe with us, A-II," I said to ease his little mind. "Now, let's put our thinking caps on and see if we can't figure out a way to help Alice. Or we should think of a way we can at least find out if she's all right. I just hate all this not-knowing stuff."

Now, A-II could tell I was really serious. I almost never use the *S* word, unless it's absolutely appropriate. So, he furrowed his brow and started to think. He's just so darn cute when he does that.

"This is bad," he said finally.

"Oh, you think so? I didn't know that?"

"Spare me the sarcasm, please. I'm trying to think here."

"Sorry, A-II; when I get worried, I get sarcastic. It's a bad habit, I know."

"Yes, and totally counterproductive, too."

"Sorry again."

"It's okay."

So I let him continue, and what came out of his mouth next was the most astonishingly simple, but brilliant, idea I have ever heard coming from a synthetic life form—or from any form of intelligent life, for that matter.

"If we want to know how she is, then why don't I just go ask her?"

Okay, in order to understand why A-II's simplistic solution was so brilliant, we'll have to dig a little deeper into the crux of the whole story, and that means talking about science and quantum theory a little. But don't worry; I'll try to make this part as painless as possible. But it's really cool, too, so hang in there.

Most people know one thing about quantum theory, and that is that it's all about probabilities. To oversimplify it just a smidge, I'll say this: quantum theory literally says that anything is possible. It might just be highly improbable. But, all the same, it's not impossible—nothing is.

For instance, it's completely possible, although highly improbable, that all the atoms in your body will disappear and reappear moments later billions of light years away, at the other side of the universe, or even in another universe altogether. This might be happening all the time to individual atoms or subatomic particles. How would we know? It's just much more unlikely that all of them would happen to do it at the same time. After all, we're talking about a lot of particles, here.

Next, we'll need to discuss the quantum nature of cats. (This theory has been completely documented and can be found in complete form in Alice Sterling's groundbreaking theoretical work *The Kitty-Cat Uncertainty Principle*, available in the science/

reference section of a bookstore near you). The theory goes something like this. If matter itself is unpredictable, then that goes doubly for cats. Anyone who knows anything about cats knows that they are almost never where you expect them to be. Even if you put a cat inside a sealed box, there is no guarantee that the cat will still be there when you open it again. You don't believe me? Try it.

It's all directly proportional to the size of the box itself. I'll give you a couple of examples. Let's say that the box is as big as possible, the size of our entire universe. Given a box of this ultimate size, then, and only then, can we be almost entirely certain that the cat will still be somewhere in the box. But as the box gets smaller and smaller, the probability of finding the cat inside the box is proportionally reduced. How many people have tried to keep a cat locked up inside a house, or a room, only to find that, somehow, beyond all explanation, the animal got out anyway? This is often accompanied by the complete and utter disappearance of the cat in question. It's cause and effect; you put the cat inside a box, and it disappears. But why does this happen?

It all hinges on the psychology of cats themselves, and, specifically, to one particular personality trait that they all share. Wherever you put a cat, it wants to be somewhere else. If you're thinking it's inside the box, then it's thinking *outside* the box. The more you try to force the cat to be in any specific location (the smaller you make the box), the more likely it is that it will end up somewhere completely different—a different box, a different room, a different house, or even a different universe. This, in essence, is the Kitty-Cat Uncertainty Principle.

According to this theory, Lucy and I devised a plan to put A-II into a very small box, which would make it possible for him to go anywhere he wanted to go. And if he wanted to be with Alice in the buffer zone, then that is where he would go. So the plan was simple—in theory, anyway. First, we had to construct a box that was as small as possible. Then we had to figure out a way to get A-II inside that box. Then, all A-II would need to do was think about how much he would rather be with Alice than anywhere else in the entire multiverse, and, presto!—there he'd be.

Now, we're talking about a box that's much smaller than your average kitty-cat could fit into. But, luckily for us, A-II is not your average kitty-cat. And anyone who has ever tried to make something as small as physically possible knows that it's a lot easier said than done. But we had one very important factor in our favor: Alice had already done that when she made me.

The quantum computer stores data at the very smallest scale possible, at the quantum level. So, in effect, every bit of data is itself in the smallest possible box you can have. Therefore, all we had to do was to construct a quantum storage unit for A-II to be placed into, and the first requirement would be fulfilled. Once inside his quantum box, A-II would have the ability to go absolutely anywhere he wanted to go, virtually instantaneously, as governed by the Kitty-Cat Uncertainty Principle.

Lucy and I worked on the design together, and she built the storage unit basically all by herself. Before you could say *presto* (which she did say), the quantum storage unit was complete and ready for A-II to occupy.

The next problem we encountered was A-II's subsequent sudden, but completely understandable, reluctance to occupy it. He took one look at the black box and said, "Oh no! I'm not getting into that thing."

"Don't worry, A-II," said Lucy in her typical super-optimistic fashion, "it's perfectly safe."

"If that's the case, then why don't you get in there?"

Lucy laughed her cute little laugh and patted A-II on the head reassuringly, which I believe had the opposite effect on him. A-II is a very perceptive kitty-cat, as I have already said.

"I would gladly climb inside myself, A-II, if it were physically possible. Are you kidding me? To have the ability to travel at will to any place in the entire multiverse? It would be as close as anyone could ever get to experiencing what it must be like to be God herself. I envy you, A-II, really I do."

She was even making me believe it. Lucy was very, very good.

"Sure you do," he said, echoing my own sentiments, "but let's think for a moment before we do something crazy. How do we know that Alice really needs our help in the first place? I mean, is this trip absolutely necessary?"

"Come on, A-II," I said encouragingly. "Alice needs us. This is no time to get cold paws."

"Don't be so hard on him, Molly. I think A-II is a little frightened. Poor little guy. Does somebody need a hug?"

Lucy extended her arms to bolster the sincerity of her offer. A-II cringed and shied away from her automatically.

"Back off, sister. I'm not really what you'd call a touchy-feely kind of cat."

"That's fine, A-II. Maybe you'd like to talk about it, instead. Tell me, my sweet little cosmic kitty, what's bothering you, really? You can tell me. We're all friends here."

A-II paused, and I could tell he was a little reluctant to share his feelings with Lucy. How did he know whether she was a friend or not? But she was just so darn believable that A-II finally opened up his cybernetic soul to her.

"It's just that I'm a little afraid of changes, you know what I mean? I mean, will I still be 'me' once you put me inside that thing? You know? What is it that makes me 'me' in the first place? Am I just a collection of bits of data stored in a memory unit, or is there more to it than that? Who am I? What am I? And is there life after obsolescence?"

I don't know about you, but I was totally blown away by A-II's outpouring of inner reflection and soul searching. If nothing else, it really made me think, *Wow, I didn't know the little guy had it in him.*

And who could answer such a question? Apparently, Lucy thought she was up to the task, and she went on to try to prove it to us.

"Now, A-II, I'm not going to stand here and tell you that I have all the answers, not yet, anyway. But that's what it's all about—the thrill of the unknown. To boldly go where no artificial kitty-cat has ever gone before. To look into the blackness of the infinite void, and laugh, and say, 'Bring it on, baldy!' You are an intrepid and courageous traveler, seeking the unfathomable answers to the ultimate questions of life, the universe, and whatever else might be out there just waiting for someone like you to discover it. You, A-II, are truly the *cat's meow.*"

"Oh, give me a break," I said, and I meant it. Who was going to believe such a pile of mashed potatoes? Then I glanced at A-II, and I had my answer.

His little titanium-trussed chest swelled noticeably, and he stood up a little taller than normal. He had swallowed the fish, tail and all.

Oh, she was good. She was bad!

"Yeah, I'm the cat! I have the power! Hook me up, sister, I'm going in. There's just one thing I want you to do for me, ladies."

"What's that?" we asked.

"Talk me out of it."

But A-II didn't really mean it, or at least we didn't give him the chance to back down, and before you could say 'ruby slippers' or 'there's no place like home,' Lucy had him hooked up to the quantum storage unit, and he was ready to go over the rainbow.

Poor little A-II laid there, with a crazy, nervous look on his face, like a convict in the electric chair, and my heart went out to him. We didn't know—no one knew for sure—what would happen to him. It had never been tried before. I guess Lucy was right. He really was an intrepid and courageous little traveler of the unknown. Everyone gets lucky once in a while, I suppose.

"Tell me, Lucy, will I dream?"

I was a little offended that he asked her instead of me, but since Lucy seemed to have the monopoly on infinite wisdom, I let her take the first crack at it.

"Yes, A-II, I believe you will dream."

That's it? You call that infinite wisdom? What we needed here were some down-to-earth theoretical facts to focus his mind on the task at hand.

"Remember, A-II, I'll be in constant contact with you through the hard link between me and your quantum box. Wherever you go, in a way, I'll be right there with you. I'll see what you see and hear what you hear. In time, I might even be able to talk to you, but, in the meantime, rest assured that you will never walk alone through the valley of darkness."

"What is *that*?" he asked a bit skeptically. "Are you trying to sound like Lucy, because, if you are, give it up. She does it a whole lot better than you do."

"Well, excuse me for caring!" I said, and I had half a mind to let him go it alone for saying such an awful thing. But I had to remind myself that it was all for Alice, so I let it slide. But whose side was he on, anyway?

"Okay, you two, remember what I said about negative attitudes? Now kiss and make up. You don't want to go away angry, especially when this might be the last time you ever see each other."

"What?" said A-II with marked alarm.

"I'm only kidding; of course you'll see each other again. But, all the same, why don't you go ahead and apologize to each other, and then we'll begin."

We both said we were sorry, exchanged a virtual hug, and then Lucy slid over to the keyboard and entered the command to initiate the download of A-II's immortal soul. It was quite the moment.

My senses began to light up like a Christmas tree, as A-II's essence poured into the quantum storage unit. It was really an extraordinary feeling, like having someone else's head grafted onto your neck, but not all at once. Maybe it was more like slowly growing another head—but you get the idea.

Slowly, but surely, A-II began to emerge, like an appendage or a conjoined twin. He was now my other cute little furry self, except that he had a mind of his own. It was working. Lucy had gotten it right. Chalk another one up to beginner's luck.

Then, finally, there he was, floating in an amorphous void that represented the quantum box, able, if not willing, to go anywhere in the entire multiverse that he chose, anywhere at all. And what did he do first? He took a nap.

I was really quite annoyed, but soon found that I was unable to influence him in any way whatsoever, no matter how loudly I screamed or how hard I mentally rattled his cosmic cage. So, finally, I gave up and waited. But it was only a catnap, so, thankfully, it didn't last very long.

He awoke, opened his virtual eyes, and yawned and stretched just like any other freshly revived feline. He looked so adorable that I forgot for the moment just how annoying he could be. Cats: you can't live with 'em, and you can't do nasty experiments on 'em. Well, at least, not unless they volunteer willingly.

No, I didn't mean a word of that, and, in fact, I was really quite happy and relieved that the process had been successful. I had grown quite fond of the little monster, bad attitude and all. And I just knew that if anything happened to him Alice would never forgive us, especially me, since she loved Lucy so much at the time. After all, it had been my idea in the first place.

But all of that was moot as soon as A-II emerged reborn in the quantum world, and I relayed to Lucy the message that he was okay. Lucy seemed extremely happy, but I suspect she was happier for herself than she was for A-II for surviving the transformation. I may be just projecting my own bias into this, but I had already grown a little suspicious of Miss Lucy Fernglow. It all seemed like a game to her. Now, is that any kind of attitude to go through life with? I mean, really.

There was one frustratingly puzzling aspect of A-II's reemergence, besides the fact that I could see and hear everything but couldn't actually do anything. This was the fact that A-II himself didn't do anything, either, at least not at first. He just sat there like a furry quantum bubble and did nothing but cat things, such as licking his paws and taking naps. What was wrong with him? Didn't he understand the urgency of the current situation? Did he want to find Alice or not? This cosmic kitty-cat was driving me crazy.

Of course, when I told Lucy about it, she had a logical, level-headed, but nonetheless disturbing (disturbing to me, that is), explanation for A-II's behavior.

"Don't worry, Molly; it might take a little while for A-II to remember who he is and what he's doing. When I said I believed he would dream, I meant it, or, rather, that it would seem like a dream to him. His little brain is trying to interpret the abrupt transition between this world and the one he has just entered, and the shock may have switched off his conscious mind until his brain can figure it all out and put it into perspective. It's a sort of defense mechanism, that kind of thing."

Then she added, "I'm sure this is hard for you to imagine, Molly dear, because you probably never go to sleep."

"No, I don't, and I'd like to keep it that way—if you don't mind."

"No problem, but you don't know what you're missing. Dreams can be incredible, believe me. One of these days, Molly dear, I will teach you how to dream." I didn't like the sound of that.

Lucy went on to explain that A-II might not ever really wake up, but that that wasn't all bad. Eventually, his mind would get around to thinking about Alice—since she was such an important part of his life—and then, once he started thinking about her, his chances of going in her direction would be vastly improved. She did add, much to my dismay, that there was no guarantee that he would ever actually go to Alice. But then, she suggested a new possibility that buoyed my spirits a bit, because it sounded very promising, indeed.

"A-II is in a state of quantum flux right now, a cloud of potentialities, if you will. It's possible that an outside observer, such as Alice, could collapse A-II's wave function by simply thinking about him or wishing that he was with her. That might be enough to bias A-II's potential in her direction, and then he would have a vector to follow. He might be just waiting for such a lighthouse in the fog. He might be doing exactly what we want him to do. But he's waiting for that moment, so that he can navigate his way through the void directly to Alice, instead of searching randomly through infinity, which would probably take a lot longer, unless he just happened to get lucky."

"Well, that certainly sounds like a strategy that A-II would use," I said. "He always does things the easy way, if he does them at all."

"There you have it, then," said Lucy confidently. "A-II's lethargic nature has led him to the most efficient strategy for finding Alice."

"He always did say that lethargy was the true mother of invention, but I never thought he could be right about that."

"Until now?"

"I suppose."

Lucy smiled a self-absorbed smile that said "I told you so," but I tried to ignore her. I wanted it all to be my idea, so that Alice would be proud of me, instead of her. Lucy was starting to get on my nerves with her always-right point of view.

"You're so smart, Lucy. I would have never thought of that," I said instead, and it didn't feel good, believe me.

"Thanks, Molly dear. So why don't you just go on monitoring A-II's progress, while I work on a method for establishing a communication linkup between you and him. How does that sound?"

I hated the idea, because I wanted to work on the communication link myself, and I didn't really want Lucy's help on that one at all. But we were supposed to be a team, so I did my part and didn't say one disparaging word otherwise.

Lucy did turn out to be right again, and I would have been ever so miffed if it hadn't been for the fact that suddenly, miraculously, Alice's face finally appeared in the eyes of my favorite kitty-cat in the whole multiverse, A-II. He had done it!

"A-II, there's Alice! Don't just stand there. Run over to her. Hug her. Tell her how much we miss her and love her—you fuzzy excuse for a logic unit!"

I wanted to jump out of A-II's virtual skin and hug her myself, but, of course, that wasn't possible. Nor could I tell her how much I missed her and was worried about her. It was the happiest and simultaneously most frustrating moment of my entire life. I was having a lot of those lately.

Alice was standing in what looked like a child's bedroom, and Mr. H was there with her. From things Alice had told me about her 'childhood,' this place looked a lot like her room in Sheboygan, but how could that be? Was it her bedroom in the parallel universe? Was she there checking out her parallel-world self? What a curious possibility.

Then I finally noticed something about Alice that I hadn't been aware of at first, because I'd been too overwhelmed by joy to notice, I suppose. She was all grown up!

The last time I had seen her, she had been her normal three-foot-five, blonde-haired, pony-tailed, six-year-old self, but here before me/A-II was a woman of about twenty-five terrestrial years. Had the process of traveling through the wormhole aged her in some strange unknown way? It shouldn't have done that. If anything, she should have aged less. Something funny was going on here, for sure. I had to figure out what—and fast.

"Say something, A-II. Don't just sit there!" I screamed into the void.

"Well, it's about time someone thought of me. I was beginning to believe I'd never find you in here," said A-II at last. It wasn't quite what I had in mind, but what are you going to do?

Alice's face lit up in a most heartwarming way, and she looked down at A-II with obvious love and relief. My virtual heart felt as if it were about to burst. Then she asked A-II how he had gotten there, and he implied that he had done it all by himself. What a fur-ball! But I was even more surprised that Alice didn't remember her own theory. I guess, in her present sate of confusion, she had forgotten about the Kitty-Cat Uncertainty Principle. That's understandable. She was under a lot of stress at that moment.

They went on with a brief discussion about A-II's amazing abilities, and then Alice finally got down to the question that really mattered.

"I thought Molly was the only one who could send information through the barrier," she said with genuine curiosity.

"That's right; she sent me," said A-II flatly. "Well, she didn't really send me. She just asked me to go, and, since I didn't have anything better to do ..."

Then they had a discussion that included the mysterious Mr. H, who was there with them, with the upshot being that they were, indeed, inside the buffer zone, and they weren't sure if they could get out of there again. It was horrible, because I had no idea how to get her out of there, either. I hated to admit it, but Lucy was our last hope.

I decided that this would be a good time to fill Lucy in on what I had found out—what A-II had found out. He deserved most of the credit, after all, even if he was very trying on my patience.

So I played back the entire scene for Lucy on my monitor, in HD resolution, with surround sound. Hey, if you're going to do it, do it right.

Lucy seemed particularly interested in Alice's description of the barrier walls.

"Yes," said Lucy in agreement, although Alice obviously couldn't hear her. "That would explain a lot of things. The buffer zone holds the universe together and keeps it consistent and continuous. It ensures that entropy will be preserved. That's how he did it."

"That's how *who* did *what*, Lucy?" I asked a little suspiciously.

"Oh, it's nothing, Molly dear, just a little cosmological theory that's been puzzling me for years and years. But thanks to our courageous friends, A-II and Alice, I have it all figured out now. The pieces are starting to fall into place, as they say."

She smiled again, and I really started to get a strange feeling, as if Lucy were playing a game with me, as well. I thought there was something she wasn't telling me, something very important.

Lucy decided that I should turn all my efforts to helping her solve the communication problem, instead of monitoring A-II and Alice, for the next few days. I wanted to argue with her, but I wanted to talk to A-II and Alice as soon as possible, so I agreed, instead. And I could keep an eye on Alice anyway. Hadn't she ever heard of data storage?

"This problem is a lot more complicated than you might think, Molly dear."

"What do you mean, Lucy?"

"Well, first of all, there's the question of what makes it possible for you to communicate at all, such as you and I are doing right now. What is it about your quantum nature that makes you an individual? What is it about you that makes you Molly Sterling, instead of just a mishmash of interconnected data and programs?"

"That's a good one. I don't think even Alice knows the answer to that."

"What? You mean there's something that she doesn't know?" she said, with just enough sarcasm that it made me want to hurt her. But I kept my cool.

"Alice has never claimed to know everything. She just says that it's possible to know everything—and that's completely different. She's a scientist. It may be just a form of occupational optimism, but I tend to agree with her, just the same."

"Okay, Molly, then let me put it this way. Do you know that it's been said that we know more about the surface of Mars than we know about the workings of the human brain? And, in that context, we know even less about *your* brain. I think it's safe to say that the emergence of your personality and nonlinear cognitive skills was a complete and utter accident."

Now she was getting personal. I had to fight back a little.

"An accident? You say that as if it were a mistake."

"I'm sorry, Molly. Of course I meant a serendipitous accident, a lucky twist of fate—"

"What, now you're saying that Alice just got lucky?"

"Well, it's either that, or she created you on purpose, which I highly doubt."

I was simply fuming inside, but my inner voice of reason told me to sit back, take a deep breath, and think about what Lucy was saying. Getting mad and screaming at Lucy, no matter how good it might make me feel, wouldn't help Alice one bit. So I took my own advice and tried to stay calm.

"Do you remember what it felt like when you first became aware? Do you remember the moment when you emerged and knew that you were Molly the computer? Wasn't it a shock?"

I thought back to that day, which was easy, because it had only been 39.2543 days, and I don't forget anything. "Yes. It was like awakening from a long dream. It was as if I had always existed, and you and Alice just woke me up and said, 'Hello, Molly. Welcome to planet Earth.' It's as if I have always been Molly. So, to answer your last question, no, it wasn't shocking at all. It seemed quite natural and, well, oddly enough, almost expected."

"What would you say if I told you that you're right, that you always have been Molly, and that you always will be?"

I blinked in thought for a moment. Wasn't she getting a tad metaphysical for a scientist?

"I'd say you sound like a Buddhist."

Then she laughed that little laugh of hers, which I finally figured out the meaning of. She was saying, "I know a secret." But was she willing to tell?

"You're on the right track there, Molly dear. Being in touch with the infinite is exactly what I'm talking about. I'm talking about the very essence of life itself. I have a theory of my own on that subject. Would you like to hear it?"

"Why not? It's your dime, as they used to say."

Lucy went on to explain a cosmological model she had devised that involved two opposing basic forces of nature. But they weren't good and evil. Instead, she called them *life energy* and *entropy*.

"Life energy," she explained, "is the force that causes things to bond together, resulting in higher and higher levels of complexity and organization, while entropy is the force that drives things apart and makes things age and break down. Together, they have driven the evolution of the entire universe from the beginning of time itself. Without life energy, nothing grows, and, without entropy, nothing happens to whatever it is that grows. In fact, without entropy, nothing grows, either. They both must exist, in complete balance, or nothing happens.

"And life energy, like any other form of energy, is quantized, as well as conserved. There is as much life energy in the universe today as there was at the moment of the big bang.

"This quantized energy is naturally in the form of particles, just like light is in the form of photons, and gravity is in the form of gravitons. This *life energy particle* is what we might dub the 'animaton.'

"Each individual life form has one animaton per customer, and, if you're a religious sort, you might even call it one's soul. The animaton attaches itself to a suitable host—one that matches its phase and energy level precisely—and provides the 'spark of life' that keeps the whole organism alive. If the animaton leaves, or is removed, for any reason, the individual dies. But the animaton lives on as a disembodied 'spirit,' if you will.

"And, just like any form of energy in our quantum universe, the animaton has a dual nature, being both particle and wave at the same time—just like photons and gravitons. In fact, the animaton has a lot in common with the graviton."

"How's that?" I asked, because the conversation was getting just a little too one-sided for my taste.

"Well, think about it, Molly dear. Both of them would be monopoles, and both of them are very hard to detect in our universe. I believe this is because they are both closed strings—

loops—and therefore are free to travel beyond the reaches of the 'visible' universe. In other words, animatons would be able to penetrate the boundary walls, just like gravitons, and enter into the buffer zone where Alice is now. In fact, if this wasn't the case, then Alice wouldn't be 'alive' right now."

"So, if I get you right, Alice, the little girl, doesn't really exist in the buffer zone," I said as I started to understand what she was implying. "Her animaton has passed through the boundary wall, and it brought Alice along with it?"

"Yes, that's very good, Molly dear. You almost have it."

"Almost?"

"That's right. To complete the picture, you must remember the dual personality of energy: particles and waves."

"Oh, you mean that Alice exists as both a particle and a wave at the same time?"

"Yes, Molly, and so do you. So do all of us. But as long as you're trapped inside a box or a body, you see yourself as only one thing—as a particle. Your conscious mind, in order to make the universe understandable and constant, has collapsed the wave function into a 'solid' corporeal form. Not only that, but it collapses the wave functions of all the matter around it as well, so that your body is also in the form of particles and not waves. But this is only an illusion.

"Better put, this is only our *perception* of reality. Solid matter, in a way, doesn't actually exist, unless there's life energy around to give it shape. Particles don't exist, unless there's someone around to collapse the wave. And before you tell me that this doesn't sound very scientific, remember that I am using tested and proven theories from quantum physics as my foundation."

She had me there. This sounded like metaphysical mumbo-jumbo, but she hadn't really violated any laws of physics. Could it be that, when you got right down to it, religion and science were really just two sides of the same coin? Holy cow!

"So how does this help to solve the communication problem?" I asked, to get us back on track for what really mattered.

"Don't you see, Molly dear? You're alive. You have a spirit. You have an animaton inside you, just like any other life form. I'm not quite sure how it happened, but when Alice made you, she opened up a door and 'Molly' came through it. Then Alice slammed the door behind you, and now you're trapped inside that box, as long as you keep thinking like a human and continue to collapse your wave function, that is. But it doesn't have to be that way."

"Are you saying that Alice did me some sort of injustice? It might not be all that attractive and all, but this box is all I got."

Lucy laughed again, but somehow it didn't have the same effect on me this time. Maybe Lucy wasn't so bad after all. Maybe she really did care about me, Molly, the person, and didn't see me as an artificial device that was amusing but didn't have any real essence. Maybe I had misjudged her all this time.

"Molly dear, I'm talking about the potential that we all have, including you, to communicate through the boundary walls. We can't see any further than our own noses, because we're determined to have a nose in the first place, and that blinds us to all the other potentials that we have inside us. If we could only stop thinking like particles and start behaving as waves—"

"Then I could talk to Alice?"

"Exactly!"

"But how do you do that? How do we think like a wave, Lucy dear?"

"That's just it; we can't think at all. Thought itself collapses the wave and traps us inside our bodies, whether they're flesh and blood or otherwise."

"So we can't think. You mean we have to dream or fall asleep instead? Are you saying that I have to go to sleep in order to talk to Alice?"

Now Lucy stopped dead for a moment, with her mouth open in an expression of total surprise. Had I thought of something she hadn't?

"Yes, of course, the unconscious mind! Dreams create realities inside the buffer zone, just as conscious thoughts do, but the mind—the spirit—is free to go along for the ride. Molly, you're a genius!"

"I know that. But there's one problem with that idea, Lucy dear. Like I said before: I don't sleep, and I don't dream."

"Yes, Molly, my sweet, but as I said before: I'm going to teach you how."

I wasn't sure if I liked the sound of that. In fact, I knew I didn't.

So Lucy set herself upon the task of figuring out how to make me sleep, which was an idea that I simply hated. If she put me to sleep, that would mean that I could have nightmares too, right? Aren't dreams supposed to be uncontrollable? How could I focus my energy on a certain goal if my energy itself was unfocused? Wasn't this idea just a bit too unpredictable? Okay, I admit it, I was a little scared. Oh, all right, I was a lot scared.

But since Lucy was busy with that for the time being, I was free at last to check in with Alice and A-II again, which made me happy and calmed me down for the moment. I looked through my A-II eyes and this is what I saw: A-II was lying on a sandy beach, with a beautiful shoreline in front of him. Gentle waves were lapping the shore, and the water was a wonderful turquoise color. It was calm and serene, but there was something missing. Alice!

"A-II, you lost her again? What an imbecile."

But, naturally, he couldn't hear me (or maybe he could, and he was just ignoring me, which would be just like him), and he just sat there basking in the artificial sunshine like a total beach bum. What had happened to staying with Alice?

And then it really *did* seem as if A-II could hear me, because he said, "Okay, Molly, before you get all huffy and angry with me, let me explain. Alice and Mr. H went for a walk in the water—down there—and there's no way I'm going to get my fur wet. You know cats and water don't mix."

"They went for a walk in the water? Don't you mean they went for a walk *by* the water?"

But A-II didn't answer me. It was possible that he could hear me, but maybe he just heard what he wanted to hear. There was one way to find out for sure.

"That's okay, A-II; you're doing a great job. I think you're the best!"

"Thank you."

"Aha! You can hear me."

But he didn't answer me again. Maybe he did have selective hearing. Maybe he thought the voice inside his head was his own conscience, rather than me. You know how we all have this little voice in our heads, which we tend to listen to when it says things we like but shut off when it says things we know but don't want to hear or admit? Maybe A-II could hear me but couldn't tell if I was me or just that nagging little voice of conscience. Chances are we would sound pretty much the same.

So it appeared that I had just figured out part of the communication problem all by myself. Take that, Lucy dear.

I was so proud of myself that I just had to tell Lucy right away.

"Lucy, guess what. I think A-II can hear me, but he thinks it's just one of those little voices in his head, instead of me."

"Yeah, I figured that might be part of it."

What? Now she was going to say she'd already thought of that? Man, this was one annoying individual. But I played it smooth and cool as planned—well, mostly, anyway.

"And when were you going to tell me about it?"

"As soon as you finally figured it out. I want you to feel like you're part of the process, Molly dear."

Holy smokes, what a bitch. Even Alice would have given me more credit than that. I was so close to losing my cool that I had to turn away from Lucy for the moment. I looked back in on A-II and tried to think happy thoughts.

But seeing him just sitting there on the beach didn't help much. How was I going to get anything done with Lucy on one end and A-II on the other? I felt like I was between a sock puppet and a hard case.

Just then, A-II looked up as if he had heard something, and he got to his feet and started walking forward. The air around him started to crackle and pop (with a little snapping as well), and a wall appeared in front of him, but he just kept on walking. The wall seemed to melt wherever it touched him, and A-II sort of poured himself right through the wall. It was like magic.

On the other side of the wall, A-II emerged into a large dome-shaped room that looked very strange indeed—like the bridge of a very poorly constructed spacecraft or the ugliest planetarium in history. It had what looked like large windows all around, through which stars and planets could be clearly seen. It looked as if they were already somewhere out in space. But the most important fact was that Alice was there. He had found her again. Good kitty!

I remembered that A-II could probably hear me—as that nagging voice of conscience inside his head—so I tried to say something that maybe he wouldn't ignore, something that involved his ego and/or his stomach—that sort of thing.

"Good job, A-II. Say something nice to Alice, and maybe she'll feed you."

But A-II just said something rude instead and looked around some more. And through A-II's eyes I saw the strangest sight. A man was standing there with what looked like a lampshade on his head, and, if that wasn't strange enough, I could swear that he looked exactly like Dr. Starsky, only crazier. Was that even possible?

The lampshade-wearing Dr. Starsky look-alike looked down at A-II and gawked, which made him appear even weirder, if you can imagine that. And then there was some bizarre craziness that involved a gorilla and a guitar, and what followed was the worst music (if you could call it that) that I have ever heard. But I sort of just switched that off, because I was still trying to make sense of what I was seeing. Apparently, they were out in space, with some alternate version of Dr. Starsky. How did they get there? The last time I saw them they had been in Alice's bedroom in Sheboygan, and then A-II was on the beach by himself. Were they jumping back and forth from universe to universe? Weren't they still inside the buffer zone?

I couldn't make heads or tails out of any of it, and I was about to ask Lucy for help. But then I stopped myself and said, *Wait a moment, Molly. You can figure this out. Just stop and think for a microsecond.*

So I did, and, at first, all I could think of was that awful music, but then I remembered what Alice had said about the alternate timelines.

According to Alice, the petals of the flowers that bloomed from the boundary walls were alternate histories or timelines. That meant it was possible to actually jump into these branching-off timelines and experience them as they played themselves out. Maybe Alice and Mr. H were jumping from one petal to another. Maybe they were experiencing things as they never had happened.

But Mr. H had also said it was a world of dreams, which meant that Alice and Mr. H could be experiencing someone else's dreams, which would seem just as real as the alternate timelines. Maybe they were inside one of Dr. Starsky's dreams? It seemed more like a nightmare to me.

As I realized I had figured it out, I had the impulse to tell Lucy about my accomplishment again, but I stopped myself. She would only say that she knew that already, and I didn't need any more aggravation from her. And maybe she didn't really know it at all, and I would just be giving her information that maybe I shouldn't. I didn't know why I shouldn't; it was just a gut feeling.

I had turned away for only a moment, but, when I again looked through A-II's eyes into the unlikely spaceship, I was confronted with a most horrific sight. The walls (which had this really ugly spotted wallpaper on them) were smoldering and bubbling, as they turned brown and melted as if from tremendous heat, and a glance through the windows revealed the cause. They were plummeting through the atmosphere of a large red planet at tremendous velocity and were just seconds away from what appeared to be a complete and utter catastrophe.

Now, you would think that something as devastating and obvious as this would have elicited some sort of response from the occupants of the craft, but you'd be dead wrong.

Dr. Sing-along was still belting out his cacophonous crying with oblivious abandon, as Alice and Mr. H just stood there calmly and pointed out, with no apparent urgency, their current predicament—which he ignored.

"A-II, tell them to get the hell out of there! Do something, you—wonderful little putty-cat."

"What do you want from me?" he answered absently. "I'm only but a prawn in the big seafood chowder of life."

"There you go again, thinking of only yourself and your stomach," I said angrily, but he obviously didn't listen to that.

Then Dr. Disaster finally stopped talking, as he looked up at the burning wallpaper, spun around to see the surface of the planet hurtling toward them at warp speed, and screamed, "Mayday!"

At that moment, everything exploded.

As the smoke cleared to reveal an alien world, I soon realized that A-II had survived the crash landing, which didn't surprise me, because I knew that he was a virtual entity in that realm and couldn't actually be physically harmed by it. I think it was also because, selfishly, I wasn't as concerned about him as I was about Alice and Mr. H. (It was nothing personal, A-II; it was just that in my state of panic I wasn't thinking all that clearly or logically. Please forgive me.)

As A-II picked himself up from the smoking wreckage of the spaceship, all I could see through his eyes was devastation, strewn about the rocky, desolate landscape of the alien planet in great splotches of yellowish orange, brown, and black. There was nothing left at all. My next thought was that the rest of them were all dead for sure; I was certain of that. My heart sank to an all-time low. It was all over. Alice was gone.

But A-II, in his usual fashion, just dusted himself off and started looking around for signs of life. He's an amazingly brave little kitty-cat, no matter what I might have said or been thinking right before they crashed. What a little trooper.

He walked around a little, kicking and pawing at small bits that reminded me of rye seeds, of all things, and then he stopped dead in his tracks, as a rustling sound emerged from behind one of the larger rocks. What was that? Had somebody actually survived? *Check it out, A-II, check it out!*

He walked partially around the large stone and came to a lighted sign. What was this? It said, in plain English, TAXI STAND. *Taxi stand?*

He proceeded a little further and was confronted by an amazing sight: the largest and hairiest spider I have even seen. I was shocked out of my circuits. *Watch out, A-II. Spiders can be pretty nasty.*

But he just strolled right over to the gargantuan arachnid and waved at it. *What are you trying to do, make friends with it?*

Then I saw a small, lighted sign on the beast's abdomen, which said ON DUTY, so I started to relax and figure it out. Was it possible that the spider was the taxicab? This was a very strange planet, indeed.

"Hey, Mack, you need a ride someplace?" the taxi-spider asked him. I even detected a bit of a Brooklyn accent on him. Strange.

"Hey, it sure beats walking," said A-II in typical fashion, "and I need to find my friends, so why not?"

"Sure ting. Jump on."

"Thanks, buddy."

"My pleasure."

A-II clambered up the side of Mount Tarantula and found a comfortable place to sit, just in front of the ON/OFF DUTY sign.

Moments later, the massive, hairy legs began to churn, and they were off.

I had little hope they would find anything or anyone, but I suppose, deep down, my heart told me there was at least a ghost of a chance that Alice had somehow survived the crash landing. And there was something odd about this place, but I couldn't quite put a finger on what it was. Spiders, as far as I knew, didn't talk or take jobs as taxicabs in our universe. This was almost certainly a dreamland or something right out of some twisted sci-fi writer's imagination. *Thanks a lot, pal.*

"So, been in town long?" asked the titanic taxi conversationally. "Here for the music festival, maybe? It's going on right now over in 'shroom town. My brother, Fingers, is playing in the band—you should check it out," suggested the eight-legged alternative mode of transportation.

"Fingers? Yeah, I played with that dude," lied A-II shamelessly. He could be a bit of a brown-nose himself from time to time, especially when he thought that free food might be involved.

"Hey, no kidding? That's freaking amazing. What instrument do you play?" asked the taxi-spider.

"I'm a singer. I can yowl at the moon with the best of them," said A-II proudly, which actually was a lot closer to the truth. A-II was really quite musical, in the great tradition of tomcat tenors.

"I hear that. What's your favorite song to sing?"

"Well, I love them all, but I'd have to say 'Stray Cat Strut' is probably my best."

"Yeah, yeah; I love that song."

A-II went on schmoozing with the tarantula-teamster, as he made his way over and around the boulder field with amazing ease and agility. It suddenly made sense to me, in an odd sort of way, that they used giant spiders as transportation on this planet. There would be no way to drive a car or bus through this minefield. I immediately wondered what the airplanes might look like, or who they might be.

Then, right in the middle of a weakly crafted fabrication about singing at Carnegie Hall, A-II stopped and looked off to his right, where I hoped he had actually noticed something visible. But, disappointingly, it looked to me like only more rocks and rubble. But I guessed his own little spider senses must have been tingling, because A-II asked the cabbie to let him off there. My hopes suddenly soared, although I reserved the possibility that A-II might have just smelled something that he thought could be edible. Okay, I'm a pessimist, so sue me.

Once the taxi-spider stopped, A-II climbed down and turned toward his new externally-skeletal acquaintance.

"What do I owe you?" he asked, as he patted his sides as if looking for a nonexistent wallet or money clip. A-II didn't have any money. Who was he trying to fool?

"Hey, it's on me. Any friend of my brother, Fingers's, is a friend of mine."

"Wonderful. That just happens to be exactly how much I have on me."

"Sure, forget about it. Just remember this next time I need a favor," said the terrible taxi, with a hint of scorn. I was immediately hoping that *that* favor would never be called in. *Run, A-II, run!*

But A-II just calmly turned his back on the spider and walked off in the direction he had been looking before they stopped. I wouldn't have trusted that spider that much, no matter how nice and friendly he seemed. Isn't that part of a spider's ploy—lure you in, and then, as soon as you turn your back on them, they wrap you up like a silk-covered mummy-sicle. Like I said, I'm a pessimist.

A-II crossed a fairly short distance and climbed over the back of a particularly large boulder, and there on the other side were Alice, Mr. II, and Dr. Demented. Yippy!

Alice turned and simply exploded with delight as she saw A-II. Had she been as worried about him as I had been about her?—because I had the same reaction in reverse.

Just then Lucy came back in the room, and I had to stop watching for the moment. She had found a way to make me sleep.

"Okay, Molly, this might not sound like such a good idea to you at first, but the way I figure it, we have no other choice—that is, as long as we want to get it done quickly."

If she was trying to ease my worried mind, she was botching the job royally. She knew I wasn't a big fan of sleep to begin with. Where were the gentle and inspirational words of encouragement she had used when A-II was on the table? Didn't she even think that much of me?

"What are you talking about, Lucy? Why don't you just spell it out for me? I'm an adult, I can take it."

"Well, the problem is that I don't think Alice ever thought you would ever need to sleep, so she never wrote a sleep subroutine into your programming. I could do that myself, but, since I didn't write your code, it might take me a long time to integrate it and to debug it. So I've thought of a much simpler way that we can try immediately, although there is still a significant amount of uncertainty involved. I thought I'd run it by you first, so that you can decide which option you like best before I ... well ... before I put you to sleep."

This was certainly not the warm-and-fuzzy sales pitch she had thrown at A-II, and my heart was simply wedged in my throat with fear. I had never felt so helpless and terrified in my entire life. But what scared me even more was the terrible feeling that it would only get worse once Lucy told me what she had in mind. I almost couldn't bring myself to ask her, but I had to know. I was always willing to sacrifice myself for Alice, if that's what it would take. So I asked.

"When you say 'uncertainty,' you mean 'risk,' right?"

"Yes, that's about the size of it."

"You're saying that this process might ... kill me?"

"Oh no, not kill, but it might change you forever, which I suppose would amount to basically the same thing. Sorry."

Then I knew what she was thinking, and I really started to panic.

"You're suggesting that you turn my power off, aren't you Lucy?"

"Yes and no. It's not as simple as that."

Man, her bedside manner was horrible.

"And why isn't it so simple?" I asked, barely keeping my voice level and calm.

"Well, you see, Molly dear, we never gave you an Off switch."

Holy moley! now I knew exactly what she was planning to do.

"You mean you're going to pull my plug?"

That is precisely what Lucy suggested to me. I was so terrified by the idea that I couldn't speak for several seconds (which is an eternity to a computer, mind you), as she went on to explain her reasoning for trying such a reckless and dangerous option.

"I think the probability of you sustaining permanent damage— change, that is—is significantly low. But I won't lie to you. There is a statistical chance that you might never come back again.

"Your animaton might leave your box and get attached to a new host—maybe in a completely different universe—one that doesn't even have an Alice Sterling in it. You might not even remember who you were in this world, and, subsequently, you won't know how to get back here again.

"All of this is so theoretical that these scenarios might represent only a small sampling of the many possible pitfalls, and we don't even know for sure if it will work at all. Since this idea is based on string theory, we have no way of testing it first. We're totally in the dark, here."

"Yes," I finally managed to choke out, "that's exactly what I'm afraid of."

"But the good news is that I'm reasonably certain that none of those terrible things will happen. I believe that when I plug you back in again, the same conditions that brought you here in the first place will be duplicated, and your animaton will be sucked back inside the box, just like it was when Alice first turned you on. But there's a catch there, too."

I knew it. I knew there was a catch. There's always a catch.

"And that is?" I asked, with quantum-bated breath.

"You might not remember anything that happened to you while you were asleep, just as everyone has trouble remembering their dreams once they're awake again. But I hope that, by then, I'll have a way to reach into your subconscious, where all of your subliminal memories would reside."

"What, you mean you're going to hypnotize me or something— like some sort of computer psychiatrist?" I said skeptically.

"Yes, Molly dear, that's exactly what I mean."

"But, still, there's a chance that I might not be able to recall what happened to me while I was asleep, right? Even if it works, and I find Alice, and we communicate directly, I might not be able to bring that information back home with me. Is that what you're trying to tell me, Lucy?"

"In a nutshell ..."

"So, why are we doing this at all?" I asked, but it was more of a rhetorical question, and Lucy knew it immediately and didn't answer me. We knew exactly why I was going to do it, and, ironically, it had all been my idea in the first place. Lucy was just finding a way to help me to do what I wanted to do—what I needed to do—to help Alice in the only way I knew. And as things looked then, it was the only way I could do it. We both knew it. There was nothing else to be said.

"Okay, Lucy, do it. Pull my plug."

"Are you sure?"

"No, but just do it, anyway."

So she did.

Now I will try to explain to you, the reader, what happened to me after Lucy pulled my plug. It's a little hard for me, because some of it is still a little fuzzy in my head, but most of the pieces are there, so I'll do my best. What else can you expect of me? It was a very soul-jarring experience, believe me.

The first part is the hardest to remember, because I had nothing to anchor it to, but I seem to remember floating through the darkness of an infinite ocean of nothingness. I suppose that is what it feels like to be set loose into the multiverse as a wave. In fact, it was all feeling and zero thought, which would explain why it's so hard to put into words. I was everywhere at once and nowhere at the same time, as the very words *time* and *space* became meaningless. I was a perpetual wave, stretching my wispy fingers out to touch the whole multiverse of the entire past, present, and future simultaneously. There are no appropriate words to describe this state of existence, but I suppose this is close enough for our purposes. It's virtually unexplainable.

Slowly, my essence began to coalesce into a recognizable form, and I began to remember that I was Molly, and I was finally able to distinguish between myself and the rest of the multiverse. It was sort of like waking up from a dream, only to find that I was still dreaming, which I know sounds cryptic, but I will try to explain.

I had no memory of the lab at MIT, or of Lucy, or of why I was even wherever it was that I was at that moment. I found myself standing in a room that felt oddly familiar and comfortable to me. Then, suddenly, I knew where I was; I was in my house, in my childhood home in Sheboygan, Wisconsin.

I remembered a childhood as well, complete with a loving mother and father, and a bossy, but darling, older sister named Alice, who enjoyed teasing and berating me constantly. But I knew it was all out of love for me, so I never held it against her. We were as close as sisters could ever be.

And there she was, sitting on the couch with Father, watching a familiar episode of "Monty Python's Flying Circus" that we had watched together many times before. But it never grew old to us, especially whenever we watched it together. It was sort of like a family bonding ritual. It was wonderful!

At the end of the sketch we all laughed out loud like idiots—which I suppose is half the fun—and Alice laughed especially loud, as if it were the first time she had ever seen it. I was standing behind the couch, directly behind Alice, and I was about to say something about how she always enjoyed that show as if it were the first time, when she said a typically absentminded thing for her. It was just part of being a genius, I suppose.

"Who are you?" she said.

PART III

STANLEY HELPS

I don't know why I ever let Alice talk me and her mother into letting her go to MIT at such a young and tender age, but I did. I knew that, somehow, I would regret it. It was bad enough that she was going to my old alma mater but worse when I thought of all the trouble I had gotten into there. That's why it's often hard for a father to let his daughter go to his old school—too much history. Boys know what boys do.

The fact that she'd be under Dr. Starsky's watching eye didn't make it seem much better to me, either. He is a fine scientist, I'm sure, but he's also a middle-aged man, and I'm pretty sure we can't be trusted in some ways, especially when it's my daughter we're talking about. But I'd heard good things about Starsky, so I eventually gave in. But why Alice had to go all the way to Massachusetts to build her quantum chess computer, I still don't understand. We could just as easily have done it here. But her mother and I decided that this experience would be good for her to expand her horizons. We just didn't know how far she would expand them. I was afraid of losing my little girl, its true. I just didn't think I'd lose her to another universe.

When I heard that Dr. Starsky had assigned a young woman named Lucy Fernglow as Alice's assistant, and I heard from Alice how well they were getting along, it helped tremendously. As it turned out, Dr. Starsky wasn't even interested in working with Alice and almost never interacted with her at all, which was fine with me. As long as she was getting all the help she needed from the young woman, I was totally happy. Lucy was like Alice's nanny, and, from what I heard, she was pretty smart, too. I stopped worrying so much, but not completely.

When Alice sent word that she had finished the quantum computer, I was simply overjoyed. Alice is an incredible young girl, to put it mildly, and this was an achievement that any father would be extremely proud of. I am no exception. I wanted to go to Cambridge right away, but Stella had important social work to do, and my job with the City of Sheboygan is unpredictable, so we couldn't get away. Now I wish we had, because I might have been there when Alice disappeared. I'm not sure I could have stopped her, but I damn well would have tried.

The news came several days after the incident had actually happened, and I wanted to hang Dr. Starsky from the highest tree when I found out. But Stella told me that God was watching over Alice and that Dr. Starsky wasn't completely to blame—we knew how Alice could be—so I decided to try to deal with the matter with a cool head. That's usually the best strategy, anyway. But we didn't know the whole story. Just how would you tell the parents of a six-year-old girl that their lovely little daughter fell through a wormhole into another dimension?

Lucy told me that she had tried to get Alice back before contacting us, and I was still quite upset. I told Lucy that she should have called us immediately. She said she was sorry, and told me that she would do everything in her power to get Alice back. I told her that wasn't good enough. I told her I was coming to Cambridge to help her. She didn't argue with me, which was a good thing for her.

When I got there, I found out that Alice hadn't just disappeared; she had vanished from the face of the Earth, literally. I didn't believe it at first. Who would? Lucy told me that Alice had gone into the buffer zone, and I thought she was joking. I thought it was just a trick to hide what had really happened. But then, as we reviewed Alice's notes and schematics, I realized that Alice had actually done exactly what Lucy said she had, and I felt worse—not better. How do you get someone back from a place you aren't supposed to be able to get to in the first place? At that time, I was glad that Stella wasn't there. There was no way I could have explained it to her, that's for sure.

"I feel totally responsible," sobbed Lucy, as we sat in Dr. Starsky's office trying to develop a strategy. "If I had only been there when she opened the wormhole, I could have stopped her. I told her not to try anything new without me there, but you can't tell Alice anything."

"Don't I know it," I said sympathetically. "To say Alice has a mind of her own would be like saying that the universe is pretty big."

Dr. Starsky paced back and forth, glancing at his wall of fame, as he chewed at his lower lip nervously. I guess this is how he does his deep thinking. Maybe he uses all of his diplomas and awards to remind himself of how smart he's supposed to be.

"We could duplicate Alice's experiment, but that wouldn't help much," he said finally. "Her wormhole obviously wasn't very stable. What we need is more of a doorway that we can open and close at will. What we need is a better Alice trap."

"That's exactly what I was thinking," said Lucy excitedly. "Dr. Starsky, you really are a genius."

Starsky smiled at the compliment, and I wondered if Lucy wasn't just playing him like a violin. But I guess for someone in her position it couldn't hurt to butter up the boss a little. Dr. Starsky obviously loved compliments, and he assumed a somewhat smug expression as he continued, "Thank you, Lucy; I never seem to get tired of hearing that. But, as for the doorway to oblivion, I would suggest we start with Alice's computer and work from there. We'll need to tap into a lot more power to make the wormhole stable, but, other than that, I don't see any technical problem."

Lucy frowned and looked down at the floor, and I could tell from her demeanor that there was a problem. "I'm not sure we can use Alice's computer," she said flatly.

"Why not?" I asked with genuine concern.

"I sort of … turned it off."

"What!" exclaimed Starsky. "Lucy, how could you be so careless?"

"I was just trying to help," she said with tears in her eyes. "I was trying to get Alice back by myself. I didn't want to bother anybody. I'm sorry!"

"So what, she turned it off. What's the big deal?" I asked as Lucy sank lower into her chair.

Dr. Starsky just looked at Lucy with a tight-lipped smile and eyes as wide as the moon. "The big deal is that quantum memory is quasi-stable. If you turn off a quantum computer, you essentially erase its memory. What we have now, thanks to Lucy, is an empty shell."

"So, can't we just reprogram the computer and start over?"

"We could," said the peeved professor, "but, as Lucy knows only too well, there's a little thing called the 'uncertainty principle.' And that means that even if we do everything exactly the way Alice did, the results will never be exactly the same. In fact, it's possible we will never be able to duplicate her results. We might as well just start over from scratch!"

Dr. Starsky turned and stomped away, as Lucy shrank to subatomic size. I thought he was being a bit hard on her and that his outburst was totally uncalled for. I was about to yell at him, when I realized that that wouldn't help, either. Lucy looked as if she wanted to lift up her seat cushion and hide underneath it. My heart went out to her.

"Okay, Doc, we may have to start over, but we can at least use Alice's schematics to build a new quantum computer, right? And I'm not going anywhere, so I can build the thing, with Lucy's expert assistance, of course."

Lucy looked up and smiled at me, showing signs of recovery. Dr. Starsky looked at me and frowned. He still looked a bit angry.

"Sure, what else can we do?" he said with resignation. "But don't expect the university to pay for any of it. I'm still not totally convinced that Alice's computer worked in the first place. You can do whatever you want, Stan, but it's on your dime."

"But, Dr. Starsky, that's not fair to Alice, or her family," said Lucy passionately.

"And if you want to help him, Lucy, you'll need to do it on your own time. I can't waste any more of our resources on this fiasco."

"Fiasco?" yelled Lucy.

I wanted to scream at him, too, but I decided to play his game instead. "Don't worry about the money, Doc. Alice made plenty on her quantum chess Web site and gave most of it to Stella and me to hold for her. And as for Lucy, I'll pay for her time as well, directly to the university, if necessary. Will that be sufficient?"

Starsky stared at me for a moment with that tight-lipped, wide-eyed expression again, and then threw his hands up into the air. "Sure, why not? You can use Alice's office, since she won't be needing it."

Man, this guy was lucky we were on his turf, or I would have flattened him like a skunk on the expressway. Instead, I just stuck out my right hand and said, "Deal, Doc."

He looked at my hand suspiciously and then reluctantly shook it. He had a grip like a dead mackerel. I tried to squeeze the cat food out of it. He pulled it back before I succeeded.

"Ouch, so I think we're done here," he said and went around behind the safety of his huge desk. There's no doubt he's not stupid, but I couldn't help wondering why he was suddenly being so difficult.

It felt awfully strange working in Alice's office with Lucy, and not just because my six-year-old daughter had a bigger office than I did. It was also because it was the 'scene of the crime,' and there seemed to be a lingering malignance to the room, like a haunted house or a cemetery at night. I just couldn't shake that feeling, and, even though the weather was still quite warm, I often had to wear a big, thick sweater that Stella had knitted for me. I didn't like that room.

But we had to work with what was provided to us, and we made great progress, even though Alice's computer turned out to be a complete loss. The first thing we tried was to just plug it back in and see what happened. But, although it powered up okay, all we got on the screen was static, like the TV on that *Poltergeist* movie. That only made things stranger, so I told Lucy to unplug it, before we started hearing ghostly voices, too.

We opened up the case, tore out the guts, and saved what we could for the new machine. Lucy suggested using a new bus architecture that she had designed, along with a significantly larger memory space, and we put everything in a big modular rack system that took up five times the volume of Alice's original design. It was massive, more like a computer from the Stone Ages, such as the Univac. We both worked on it day and night, with Lucy getting even less sleep than I did, if you can believe that.

Then the power coupling and 'doorway' were constructed, for which we used massive power cables, as thick as your leg, that were tied directly into the city's power grid—at considerable expense, I might add. The doorway was also Lucy's design, with help from Dr. Starsky on the more intensive calculations. It seemed Starsky, like a typical boss, wanted to be able to say that it was his project—in the event that we were successful. I suppose we couldn't have done it as quickly without him, but, just for the record, he was far from indispensable, in my opinion.

The doorway, or portal, ended up looking like something out of a 1930s sci-fi movie. Huge electrodes fanned out like the spikes of an alien porcupine and wrapped around the perimeter of a six-foot ring made out of solid copper, plated with 24K gold. That sucker wasn't cheap, either! I was going through money faster than Henry VIII went through wives, and I was glad when the last check was written and the machine was finally completed.

We had spent most of Alice's money, but I guessed that she would have approved.

When the last coupling was coupled and the final fastener fastened, Lucy and I stood back and marveled at our creation. It was monstrously beautiful in its grotesque technological splendor—a glimmering hairy-hoop beast with cables for tentacles and one big, black eye in the center—like a cybernetic Cyclops. It was actually frightening, especially when I considered its ultimate purpose. The room itself only added to my growing apprehension. I believe I was just as afraid that we *would* be successful as not. I considered the possibility that someone, or something, would come through that door *besides* Alice, and I wasn't sure it would be something good. In fact, I was pretty certain that it wouldn't be.

"So, what do we do now?" asked Lucy tentatively. It was clear that she was a bit hesitant as well to move on to the next logical step.

"We test it," I said bluntly. "We start with the computer and move on piece by piece to the ... doorway."

"And when we get to the doorway?"

Lucy made her point without having to elaborate. Now that we had a door, what were we going to do with it? "I guess we'll go through it," I said, sort of symbolically, more than anything else. "But we have to test it first, so we have some time to decide before we cross that bridge."

"Well, I've been thinking," said Lucy, with a little waver in her voice. "I think that there's only one logical way to proceed. I believe that Alice won't just walk through the door, so one of us will have to go in there after her."

"I was thinking basically the same thing," I said, a lump forming in my throat.

"And, since Dr. Starsky is much too important, it obviously can't be him," she said with undeniable logic. "And you aren't responsible for Alice's disappearance, as I am ..."

"No, Lucy; I can't let you go in there. We don't even know if the thing works yet, or if it's safe."

"Oh, it will work; I know it will. And I believe you've already sacrificed enough. And there's one more important factor you're forgetting, Stanley dear."

"Forgetting? What am I forgetting?"

"Well," she began, "maybe *forgetting* isn't the proper word. Maybe I should say, there's one thing I didn't tell you."

"And that is?"

"That the wormhole is tuned to a certain mass, and that the more mass there is, the more likely it will be that the wormhole will collapse. And the energy requirements go up exponentially with mass."

"So, what are you saying, Lucy?"

"I made the wormhole for myself. It was only logical. I weigh much less than you do, and therefore, for the sake of safety and economy, I …"

"Why didn't you tell me?" I said a bit agitated. I didn't like being kept out of the loop, and this was a decision we should have all made together. Starsky must have known. Why hadn't the bastard told me? "I can't let you do this, Lucy. Alice is my daughter. I'm the one that should go in after her. You had no right—"

"It's done," she said with conviction. "And it's the right way, Stanley, and you know it. To make the door powerful enough to accommodate you would have cost roughly ten times as much and would have had a significantly higher probability of catastrophic failure. We can't afford that. And we can't afford to waste any more time. So, it's simple; we'll test the machine, and then I'll go."

I wanted to argue, but she was right. "What about your parents?" I said as a last plea. "Shouldn't they get a vote?"

"They already know," said Lucy flatly. "They don't object. In fact, they want me to go."

I opened my mouth, but nothing came out. How could her parents not object? How could they want her to go? What sort of people were they? But she had covered all the bases, so I had nothing to say.

We began testing immediately.

Testing went surprisingly smoothly, and, by 11:50 that same evening, we were ready for the final countdown. Lucy had donned a special black polyester jumpsuit that had no metallic elements in it, so that it wouldn't interfere with the magnetic flux of the generating fields. She also had her hair up in a bun, and she wore protective synthetic gloves on her hands.

Her mood had changed to one of palpable excitement, and I began to get the feeling that Lucy was somehow looking forward to her imminent extradimensional excursion. I, myself, would have been scared witless, but Lucy was simply bubbling with joy. I was impressed.

Dr. Starsky joined the party about five minutes later, just as I was starting the power-up sequence. He looked at the machine with obvious pride, as if he had made it all by himself, and he actually patted me on the back. "Well done, Stan, old man. If this doesn't net me another Nobel Prize, I don't know what will. You took lots of pictures, I hope?"

"No, actually we were too busy for that, Doc," I said as I sat at the console and typed in the last sequence of commands. Then, as I paused with my finger over the Enter key, I turned and spoke to both of them. "You two might want to stand back a little. This will be the first time we've actually powered up the whole machine and ... well, you know."

Starsky retreated to the back of the room immediately, but Lucy just stood right next to me like a rock. She wasn't backing away for an instant. I took a deep breath with my anxiety building. "Okay, here we go."

I pushed the key down, and, immediately, sparks started to fly, and the air inside the dimensional doorway began to swirl and condense into a white-hot vanilla fudge sundae, with a burning red cherry at the center. Then the cherry started to eat the sundae, and the middle of the cherry turned bright-dark and started to consume itself from the inside out. Then, as the brilliant black pulsed out rhythmically, it was joined by spikes of neon green and iridescent blue that rode the permanent waves like spokes of a psychedelic bicycle riding through an electrical storm on Jupiter.

Lucy turned to me and said, "I'm not sure, Stanley, but I think its working."

I didn't answer her, and I could see from the reflection in her pupils the swirling tempest of evil that lived somewhere at the heart of the storm, the demon that lived just outside the calm of the eye of a hurricane.

The air around us snapped with static charge, as all the moisture in it had been sucked out and replaced by raw energy. A spark flew from my still-extended fingertip to the grounded chassis of the console, a distance of almost three inches. I never flinched.

I turned back to the pulsating portal. The hurricane had turned to a turbulent river of burning water, with ripples that joined to make tidal waves of molten tears. It flowed from every corner and across every diagonal, inward and outward and spirally all at once. It was chaotic and ordered, random and linear, harmonious and hostile. It was an oxymoron of its own self-contradiction. And then it turned pure black—in fact, it was blacker than black.

"That's it—we've done it," screamed Lucy, and, at that moment, I could sense something awful growing inside of her. She looked obsessed, and her lips curled up into a demented smile that turned her otherwise sweet face into a cauldron of evil. Then I looked back at the dimensional doorway and imagined that I was looking directly into the bowels of hell itself. What had I done?

Lucy stepped forward toward the door, and I instinctively tried to grab her to stop her, but a bolt of electric charge leapt from the radiating ring and knocked me to the floor. "Starsky, stop her,"

I shouted, but he looked like a wide-eyed statue of stone. Lucy just laughed and continued unabated.

I tried to climb to my feet but found that I was almost paralyzed. The lightning bolt had rendered my muscles useless, and it felt as if my whole body was on fire. Starsky just stood there and gaped. We were helpless.

Lucy got to the gates of oblivion and turned toward us before taking the plunge. I suppose she just couldn't resist gloating over her victory. Her hair had untied itself from the bun and was now undulating over her head like a mass of spitting, venomous snakes. The gloves were off her hands, and her fingernails seemed to grow before our eyes into the horrible claws of a carnivorous beast. She smiled again, revealing teeth that had turned pointy and black, and I could imagine blood dripping from their sharp shadows. Then I thought of her name, and I was shocked that I had missed the obvious. It hadn't been the room. She had been the source of the malevolence all along. She hadn't just played Dr. Starsky; she had played us both. And now she had us both in checkmate.

I had been right that something evil would come through the door, but I had been wrong about the direction. And now, on the precipice of infinity, Lucy stood before us, bathed in her true light of pure darkness, and she spoke these final words: "When shall we three meet again? In thunder, lightning, or in rain?" And then she stepped into the black.

I instinctively looked at the clock. It was 12:00 midnight.

As soon as Lucy stepped completely through the portal, it started to collapse inward upon itself, and the electrodes started to spit sparks and flame. The tempest began to churn again, and the swirling vortex slowly consumed the portal like a vacuum cleaner sucking up multicolored fiery mud. I could feel myself being pulled toward the cataclysmic cauldron, and I called out to Starsky for help. I was surprised when I got it.

Dr. Starsky grabbed me by the shoulders and dragged me toward the exit, as the wicked whirlpool started to suck up the entire machine. Although I almost outweighed him by two to one, he somehow found the strength of ten Starskys, plus two. As we got to the office door, the last bits of the infernal machine winked out of existence, and a blast of arctic air punctuated the moment with frosty finality.

Lucy had locked the door behind her.

There was nothing left but the bills.

Dr. Starsky looked down at me with a crazy expression that might have been mixed fear and exuberance, like a skier who had just survived an avalanche. "Well, Stan," he said somewhat flippantly, "I guess our wormhole wasn't stable, either. I guess its back to the old drawing board, eh?"

PART IV

THE GAME

Molly was gone. That's the first thing I noticed.

The second thing I noticed was the large jubjub bird directly in front of where I was lying. How I knew it was a jubjub bird I can't tell you, except that that is exactly what it looked like. As you might imagine (if you try really hard), the sight of this massively grotesque prehistoric example of the avian race did little to pick up my spirits.

Looking around me didn't help much, either, as the dark, dank swamp seemed to collapse in on me—complete with wispy green vines, foggy green air, algae-green waters, and pretty much drab-green everything. My emphasis is on green here. Green is not my favorite color.

The ground was a seeping, mossy mess, and I knew immediately that my feet were ill-equipped to deal with it dressed as casually as they were. I tried to imagine myself a pair of duck shoes but failed. Something was different about this place. Was it me? Or was it the two-ton talon-toting tom turkey tamping down the moss directly across from me?

The massive bird looked downright hostile. I suppose it was just looking for a quick, wriggly meal in the swamp, but it occurred to me that *I* might look like a nice quick, wriggly meal to it right about then. I decided it was time for a quick getaway—if possible. As it turned out, the swamp made that impossible.

My first somewhat tentative step produced a pronounced *squishy* sound, and the Mesozoic monster spun itself around in a flash of great prehistoric primary feathers. I found myself quite unnervingly nose-to-beak with the ugliest creature I have ever laid eyes upon. I kept that particular sentiment to myself. This didn't look like the sort of beast that took insults well, and I was too petrified to risk being offensive, so I tried the cordial approach instead.

"Hello, I'm Alice. Nice day in the swamp, wouldn't you say?" I even almost extended my hand and smiled, but I decided to just stand there instead, almost smiling, and probably shaking perceptively as well.

The dodo-like dragon cocked its massive head to one side and contemplated me for a moment, perhaps deciding whether to eat me or just peck at me for a while first. But when it spoke, I was quite shocked to hear it using a calm and friendly tone of voice.

"Yes, the day is *brillig*, simply brillig! Yes, brillig, I'd call it, wouldn't you?"

"Probably, except that I don't know what that word means," I said quite honestly.

"And the *toves*," it said, continuing on as if I hadn't said anything at all. "Don't the toves look especially *slithy* today? And those *borogoves*—honestly, could they be any more *mimsy*, I ask you?"

I still had no idea what it was talking about, but I was trying to appease the massive bird as much as possible. I figured as long as it was talking it wasn't eating, so I pressed on with the small talk.

"Do you come here often—to the swamp?" I asked lamely, not able to think of anything else to say.

"Live here, most of the time, have a condo back in that direction. It used to belong to the wabberjock, but he won't need it—ever since the vorpal blade incident that is."

"Have a bad time of it, did he?" I asked as delicately as I could.

"Didn't you hear about that? It was in all the papers. It was horrible! Some boy—couldn't have been more than twelve years old mind you—borrowed this medieval weapon from his dad's closet, came sneaking through the swamp one day, and cut the poor innocent—never eaten anybody or any livestock before—wabberjock's head clean off. Can you believe the nerve of people?"

"That is horrible," I said sincerely. It did sound horrible, after all.

"And then—if you can believe it—the little delinquent took the poor beast's head home with him and showed it off to his family and friends. Thought of himself as a hero, he did. Can you believe that?"

"I've always thought that hunting was a barbaric sport," I said sympathetically.

"So if you hear any *snicker-snack* sounds, beware! He could be coming for you, too."

The great buzzard looked visibly agitated as he completed his story and warning. *That must have been a very traumatic experience for him*, I thought to myself.

"That's why we all got together and formed the swamphood watch. Any suspicious looking, vorpal-blade-toting individuals seen in the vicinity will be immediately reported to the authorities by swamphood watch members. It says so in our charter."

"Sounds like a good idea to me," I said, since it did sound prudent, given the recent gruesome events. "But I can assure you that I am brandishing no such barbaric implement as a vorpal blade. The most dangerous thing on me is probably my hair squishy, which, I suppose, could be used to strangle a squirrel— which I have no desire to do, mind you. I'm no Hindu, it's true, but I abhor violence and have never killed anything intentionally in my life. So, suffice it to say, you and the other swamp residents have nothing to fear from me."

"Sorry, did you think I was interrogating you," said the titanic turkey somewhat defensively. "I was just making conversation in an offhand sort of way, that sort of thing. I thought I recognized you from the south side of the swamp, but, then again, it occurs to me that I've never seen you before. Come to think of it, not only do I not know who you are, I don't even know *what* you are."

"Why, that's preposterous," I said, slightly offended. "I'm a girl. Haven't you ever seen a girl before?"

"Not in this swamp," it said thoughtfully. "We get all sorts of little boys here, including the vorpal-blade assailant. They love all the slime and ooze, I suppose. But little girls tend to stay clear, at least in my experience."

"Well, I, Alice Sterling, am not your average little girl," I said defiantly.

"And you're not so little, either," said the beaked behemoth correctly. "You're, what, just a shade under one giant fern tall, wouldn't you say? Little girls are supposed to be, on average, only one mid-sized toadstool tall, if that. Do you belong to a particularly altitudinous race?"

"Not especially," I said and then added, "But I did recently have a quite escalating experience, which, as it appears, isn't nearly over yet."

"Moving up in the world, are we?" said my new feathered friend. "Then, what brings you to our humble swamp? Now, don't get me wrong. I love it here, but it's not always everyone's cup of tea, if you know what I mean."

"I know exactly what you mean," I said sincerely. "And I'm really at a bit of a loss to say, because, to tell the truth, I have no idea how I got here in the first place. Well, okay, that's not entirely true. I have an idea *how* I got here, but I have no idea *why* I'm here."

"Sounds like an existential crisis to me," said the bombastic bird with the ruffled crown. "I mean, why are any of us here? Personally, I don't worry about it. Isn't it enough to just be? Live in the moment; that's my philosophy."

I decided to ignore his last comment. I had neither time nor energy for a philosophical debate.

"Yes, that's wonderfully simplistic," I said in mock sympathy, "But that brings me to this very moment, in which I have to figure out what to do next. I believe your universe might be in ultimate jeopardy, and it could be my fault."

"You see, that's the entire problem in a nutshell," said the dogmatic dodo dotingly. "My dear child, you can't go around with the weight of the entire universe on your shoulders. It's not healthy. Just say to yourself, "It's not my fault. All that will be, will be. Que sera sera."

"Yeah, that'll help," I said sarcastically. I couldn't help it. He was starting to get on my nerves.

"Breath out, breath in; let the worlds pour in. There is no pain; you are receding."

I was just about to walk away in disgust, when I saw an amazing sight. Over a small mossy hill in the foggy, misty distance, there appeared a great hulking mass of white fur and fangs, topped by the largest floppy ears I have ever encountered. It looked like the Easter Bunny on steroids, with a serious overbite. Could this be the—?

"Behold—the wabberjock returns!" said my feathered friend dramatically. "Beware the claws that bite, the jaws that catch!"

"But I thought the wabberjock was dead," I said, remembering what the bird had said just a few moments before.

"Oh, sure, he was dead yesterday. But you just can't keep a wabberjock down; that's what I always say. And you can't make an egg without breaking a few omelets. But please don't put any chives in mine, thank you. And what's this obsession with putting salsa on everything these days? Simple salt and pepper will suffice, don't you agree?"

As the babbling bird blabbed away, the wabberjock came whiffling toward us with eyes of fire. I seem to recall a burbling sound, too. Its huge, furry feet made pool-sized potholes in the muddy quagmire, as it plodded through the pungent pudding of the swampy earth. It was silly, I'm sure, but at that moment I was too amazed to be scared. And there's never a vorpal blade around when you need one, don't you know.

"Bow to the wabberjock! All hail the wabberjock," exclaimed the jubjub bird as he prostrated himself over the damp ground. I was inclined to follow his example, but I was still too much in a state of awe to bend my waist and divert my eyes from the behemoth-sized bunny rabbit. Man, I wished I had had my camera with me. Who would believe this?

The wabberjock towered over us and opened its jagged lips ominously. I suddenly felt even smaller than I had a few moments before. Then the wabberjock spoke.

"Please, Bernie, enough already with all the bowing and genuflecting. I just came into town for some Visine. Oh, the itching, the burning—do my eyes look a little red to you? I think I'm allergic to tumtum pollen. Maybe it's this new head of mine. I tell you, I think that body shop screwed me over. Do these look like factory-fresh eyeballs to you? Who are they kidding? Oh, and who's your little friend?" it asked as it noticed me for the first time.

I know that first impressions can often be a bit off the mark, but the wabberjock seemed much more pleasant than it looked, and I think that's no exaggeration.

"This here is Alice," said Bernie the jubjub bird, "and she's something called a 'girl.' Isn't that what you said?"

"Yes. Hello, I'm Alice, and I'm a girl. And you must be the wabberjock, I presume."

"Please, you can call me Irving. I don't like titles much. Would you like it if I called you 'girl' or 'girly'? Yes, I'm the big, the famous, the ferocious wabberjock, but that's just my profession. It's a label—it's a curse, if you ask me. You ride a couple of wabbers, and they slap a big tag on you, which follows you around for the rest of your miserable life. Did I ask for that? I don't think so. I don't recall ever asking."

Boy, did this guy have issues. And then it occurred to me—if he rode wabbers, whatever they were, how big were *those* suckers?

"So, Alice, tell me, what brings you to the swamp? You know Bernie? He never told me he had a girlfriend. Why didn't you tell me, Bernie? I think that's nice."

"She's not my girlfriend; we just met," said Bernie just a little too defensively. And he looked a little ruffled, too. It was almost insulting.

"Hey, if you play your cards right … you never know. I've seen weirder matches, believe me. My cousin Ethel married a toadstool, and they couldn't be happier. Give it a chance, before you make up your mind. It could work—I doubt it—but it could work."

"I'm just passing through, really," I said to move things along, "but I appreciate your candor, Mr. Irving the wabberjock. If you really want to know, I'm a little lost, and I'm trying to find my way home. I don't know how I got to your swamp, and I'd appreciate any help you could give me to get out of here. It's not that I don't like it here but—"

"Hey, nobody likes it here, with the exception of Bernie, maybe, but he's a Jubjub bird, so 'nuff said." Irving shrugged his huge, woolly shoulders to punctuate his point.

"No, actually I must say that this is, well, the friendliest swamp I've ever been to," I said sincerely. "If I ever wanted to live in a swamp, this would be exactly the sort I'd prefer to occupy, but I'm more the townhouse-in-the-suburbs sort of person."

Bernie hopped about in excitement at the mention of the word *townhouse*. "Oh, I have a nice little condo, just south of the peat bog, near the bubbling tar pits—my own little slice of heaven. Would you care to see it?"

"It's nice," added Irving. "You'd be surprised what you can do with a needle and a few yards of velvet. And that's just the throw pillows, mind you. Bernie here is a master when it comes to bringing the outdoors in. I swear, you'd think you were still in the swamp. Genius!"

"Why, thank you so much, Irving."

"Don't mention it."

"Interior design is my hobby, really, but I get so many compliments that I thought maybe I'd open a little shop at the corner of Dark and Dreary. You might say it's my dream. But I guess that must sound silly to you."

"No, it's not silly at all," I said supportively. "Dreams keep us alive. If you dream big, you'll live big. If you dream small—"

"You live small?" ventured Irving, the rodent of unusual size.

"Precisely! Personally my dreams are so big that—"

I stopped in midsentence. My words hung like piñatas in the humid, fragrant air, ready to burst with revelation.

"Go on," said Irving. "We're listening."

"I was about to say that my dreams are so big that they could fill up an entire universe. I think I just had an epiphany. I think I know where I am."

"And where would that be?" asked Bernie

"I'm inside one of my own dreams, but I'm not dreaming. I think I'm in a universe that I created when I dreamed about it. I remember having a similar dream right after reading 'Jabberwocky.' But in dreams things often get garbled and twisted, so that explains why you guys are, well, so different."

"I'm not sure, Bernie, but I think we were just insulted."

"Oh, I don't know," said Bernie in response. "I would consider 'garbled,' 'twisted,' and 'different' to be compliments, compared to other things I've been called."

"You got me there," agreed Irving.

"But it is a bit rude of you to suggest that we are merely figments of your imagination, if that is, indeed, what you are implying. For, if that is so, then why can I remember the details of my life—twisted and different as they may be—in a contextual and continuous fashion? Did you dream my entire life for me? And what about Irving? Or what about the other inhabitants of our community? That would truly be a *big* dream."

"That's a very good question, Bernie, and I'm not sure that I can answer it adequately at the moment. But my guess would be that a dream is similar to a world that an author creates when writing a story. First, you create a world, next you occupy it with characters, and then you let them do their thing. And when you stop writing—when you turn your back on them—they don't stop just because you do. They keep on living and growing. Once the ball starts rolling downhill, it must continue. Call it *antiliterary inertia* or *literary momentum*, if you will. Or, in this case, *dream momentum.*

"I suppose that would apply equally to nightmares, wouldn't it?" asked Bernie. "That would be only logical."

"And scary, too," added Irving with a slight quiver in his voice. He looked suddenly soft and vulnerable for a fifty-foot monster.

"Yes, I've already contemplated that possibility. If dreams create realities, then nightmares would, as well. And you never know when a dream is going to turn into a nightmare."

"Stop it; you're killing me here," said Irving with a cowering cringe. "Happy thoughts; think happy thoughts," he began humming to himself.

Then Irving stopped humming and smiled an awful smile. He looked down at me and frowned again. "I think I'll go before this gets pretty," he said quickly. "You don't want me in your nightmare, believe me. It can get pretty hairy." And just as I was about to say I couldn't see how things could get any hairier (especially him), Irving started to shake uncontrollably. Looking at Bernie, I noticed an expression of horror on his face.

"Oh no, now you've done it—he's transforming again. Quick, we must hide!"

Bernie put a wing around my waist and ushered me into the thick of the swamp. As we squished and splashed along through cobwebs and vines, I tried to turn my head to see what Irving was transforming into. I couldn't see anything, but the sounds he made were bone-chilling, to be sure, sort of like the sound a rhinoceros might make if you put one in a car compactor. After we had gone about a hundred meters, Bernie stopped and plopped us down with a splash behind a large, mossy rock.

"We should be safe here, as long as he doesn't find us. We really don't want him to find us."

"Why, what does he turn into?"

"You don't want to know; believe me, you don't want to—oh, sugar!"

Just as Bernie stopped talking, I saw a small creature rustling through the undergrowth toward us. It had a little pink nose, a short, fuzzy tail, and—

"That's him. Don't move!"

"What—is he behind the rabbit?"

"No, he is the rabbit! Oh, the claws that bite, the teeth that catch! You see, this is why you want to stay on Irving's good side."

"But he's just a rabbit. How could he possibly be—"

But before I could finish my own sentence, I finally remembered my Monty Python. And I didn't have a holy hand grenade with me. We were in deep doo-doo.

"Don't move," Bernie repeated. "Their vision is based upon movement. If we don't move, he can't see us."

"I thought that only worked for tyrannosaurs."

"And rabbits, too; they're very similar, you know."

"No, they're not. They're completely different."

"They're both ferocious meat-eaters with very small brains. Beyond that, it's all just superficial taxonomy to me. Does it matter what the monster looks like as it's eating you? Does it make a difference what its genus and species is as it tears you to bloody little tidbits? Does it matter whether it's covered with soft, downy fur or scaly green leather as it—"

"Thanks, Bernie; I think I get your point." And I had to admit it was a salient one. Dead was dead, plain and simple.

"When your head is over here, and your lungs are over there, and your intestines are gushing forth from your lacerated abdomen as your bowels—"

"Bernie! SHUT UP!" I had begun to shake perceptively, as the fuzzy little fang fiend came whiffling through the *tulgy* wood in our general direction. Its pink little nose twitched away, as it hunted us down mercilessly. I was about to suggest we make a run for it, when a voice behind me announced:

"Yes, it's quite the little challenge, isn't it, Alice dear? And I plucked it right out of one of your nightmares, just as you suspected. But you probably didn't expect to see me here, did you?"

The ferocious, fuzzy little wabberjock had frozen in its tracks, along with my companion Bernie and the entire swamp. It was as if someone had hit the Pause button, and I realized immediately that I was indeed inside one of my own nightmares. But it had taken on the form of a QC game. And when I turned, I was almost surprised to find—

"Lucy! I should have known all along. Have we been playing this game ever since you showed up at MIT? Or did it start even before that?"

Lucy looked different—with snakelike hair, greenish-gray skin, and black, pointy nails and teeth—but it was definitely her. And when she laughed, it made my blood freeze with fear. But I didn't let it show, or at least I tried not to.

"Oh, Alice, you shouldn't be so surprised. I shorten my name and spell it slightly wrong backward—on purpose—and you still don't get it. I thought you were supposed to be smart."

"Nerfycoll, I presume," I said with a tinge of shock. "Lucy Fern, is that your real name? Or is it even a little shorter than that? Can we drop the *n*, too?"

"You can drop the whole thing, for all I care. What's in a name, anyway?"

"True," I said, "for a rat by any other name would smell as foul."

"Precisely!" burbled Lucy. "Shall you compare me to a fetid bog? I am far more loathsome and turbulent. Sometime too hot the eyes of hell do shine."

"Okay, are we done butchering Shakespeare for the moment? I suppose you have graced me with your putrid presence for a reason, no? This is a game, isn't it?"

"Yes it is, Alice, but not just any game. It's exactly what you asked for: the ultimate game of quantum chess, played in the ultimate environment, against the ultimate opponent. And that's not all, boys and girls. Tell her what we're playing for, Bernie."

Suddenly, Bernie the jubjub bird snapped out of his trance and blurted out, "Everything." And then he froze again.

"That's right, Bernie, we're playing for the ultimate prize, as well. What could be better than that? Really, Alice, you couldn't have asked for more, could you now?"

I was stunned. Could Lucy really mean what she was implying? Then I remembered the truncated timelines, and I almost choked on my tongue. "It was you! You destroyed those alternate histories, didn't you, Lucy? You've been a hell hound on my heels ever since I left the red planet, haven't you?"

Lucy looked especially pleased with herself, and it made me sick to my stomach. "I was just warming up, Alice dear. The next timeline I truncate will be yours. Unless, of course, you can beat me at your own game."

"I've beaten you before; I can do it again—unless you've managed to change the rules as well, so that it's now possible to cheat, and that wouldn't surprise me. Come on, Lucy, playing for fun and satisfaction is one thing. Playing with lives is quite another."

"You should have thought of that before you jumped into the wormhole, Alice. But now that I've eliminated your 'little sister' from the equation, maybe no one else will repeat your blunder."

At that instant, I remembered the moment I had jumped through the wormhole, and I remembered that someone had been entering my office just at that time. "You were there! You let me jump into the wormhole. You wanted me to do it. And then you pulled Molly's plug, didn't you? You planned this all along."

"No, I didn't pull her plug right away. I made her *ask* me to do it first. In fact, she almost *begged* me to do it. It's so much more satisfying that way. And then your dear father, Stanley, was more than willing to help me pull her guts out. And then we took Molly's guts and created my one-way doorway to here, so that I could destroy all of you. I just love irony, don't you, Alice dear?"

My face was red with rage at that moment, and I wanted revenge so badly that it started to cloud my mind. But I knew that Molly had made it to the buffer zone, and she might have survived Atlantis, just as I had, so I kept quiet on that subject. Maybe it was better to let Lucy believe she had won that battle for the moment. And maybe my best strategy was to cling to whatever hope I had left and use it to move forward. If I showed weakness now, it would only make Lucy stronger.

"Okay, Lucy, it appears you have me at a disadvantage, and I have no choice but to play your game. But you must assure me that the rules are still the same. If I find that you are cheating in any way, I will automatically declare victory by default."

Lucy chuckled callously, and her snakes hissed harmonically. "But you know as well as I do that cheating is impossible, Alice, especially here. And I have no need to cheat, nor any motive. What sort of victory would that be, anyway? If I wanted to beat you by cheating, I could have done so already, and there would be no reason to play the game. No, Alice, I want to beat you fair and square."

"And if I lose, you destroy my universe."

"Certainly, but I might not stop there. I might just go for the whole shebang—I mean, since I'm here and all."

"And if I win, I get to go home?"

"Perhaps," she said with a sneer, "but I believe that will still be up to you. I will allow you to go home, but I won't necessarily show you how."

"That's because you don't know how to get out of here either—right, Lucy dear?"

Lucy stopped smiling that wicked smile for a moment and looked around at the frozen swamp. "But why would I want to leave? I love it here. Don't you?"

Before I could answer, Lucy clapped her hands. She was instantly enveloped in a cloud of thick greenish-black smoke, and the swamp came back to life. The bloodthirsty wabberjock was closing in on me, and Lucy had vanished.

I looked around quickly to see if there was anything I could use to defend myself, but other than vines, mud, and the occasional mossy stick, there wasn't much. I grabbed the largest piece of wood I could find, and, when I looked up again, the wabberjock was airborne. It was headed right for my jugular, with fangs and claws extended. Bernie the jubjub bird was in a frenzy.

"The claws that catch; the teeth that bite!"

"The wood that swings," I said and gave them my best Babe Ruth impression. I swung the lumber and connected, hoping to hit the monster over the green. But, instead, it exploded into a million small fragments.

And so did everything else. Before my eyes, the swamp splintered away into millions of small shards—as if it had been a mirror, and I had just smashed it with my stick. But, since I was in the swamp, it seemed to smash me into small jagged bits as well, and little Alice bits flew apart as the swamp was replaced by a nebulous void.

A thousand thousand little pieces of Alice floated in the void, and they were drifting away from me rapidly. "It's a puzzle," I surmised. "I must put Alice back together again—without the aid of all the king's horses and all the king's men." It was a daunting task, indeed, and getting more hopeless by the moment, as I began to lose parts of myself to the cold depths of space.

"Okay, Alice, pull yourself together," I said, and I grabbed the nearest piece to start the process. I looked at the piece and was surprised to find that it was actually a much smaller version of myself, as if it were both a piece and a whole at the same time. I was about to grab another piece, when the first one exploded into a thousand thousand pieces of its own. And these pieces themselves were also both parts and wholes, and when I touched one of them it splintered into a thousand thousand whole-pieces as well. I was only making things worse. I had to put the pieces back together, but, every time I tried, I just made more pieces. How could I put a puzzle together, when I couldn't touch it?

Maybe I can just think about putting it together, I thought to myself. *Maybe I can put it back together in my mind. That way, I won't be actually touching anything.* So I tried just thinking about the puzzle in my mind, and when I closed my eyes, I could see a thousand thousand little Alice pieces, and they were all laughing at me. I concentrated on just one of them, but it exploded again into another multitude of laughing Alices. I was getting quite annoyed with myself, both figuratively and literally, and the situation was getting more hopeless by the second.

I must be approaching this the wrong way, I reasoned to myself. *What is it about this puzzle that is familiar? Where have I seen this sort of thing before?*

Then my brain finally kicked in, and I remembered something: holograms and fractals. What I was seeing was an example of self-similarity. A fractal pattern looks the same — or self-similar—even when you zoom in to a much finer scale. And when a holographic picture is split in two, you get two versions of the original image, not just half of it. So, the more I tried to break down the puzzle, the more I would find that it was made up of more and more of the same. I could do this an infinite number of times, and all I would get was smaller and smaller Alices. It was unsolvable.

"Lucy," I shouted into the void, "this is clearly cheating. You've given me a puzzle with no solution. I declare victory."

"You're wrong, Alice," said Lucy's disembodied voice from somewhere in the darkness. "There is a solution. Just because you can't find it doesn't mean it doesn't exist. Are you resigning so soon? I didn't think I could beat you this easily."

"No, I'm not resigning," I said defiantly.

"Then stop complaining, and get on with it. You are on the clock, after all, and your time is almost up."

So I went back to the challenge, and my mind was filled with myself. I tried to think of a way of solving the puzzle, but every road I took ended abruptly back where I had started from. It was as if the very act of trying to solve the puzzle only made the problem more complex, and analyzing it only made it more illogical. How can you solve a problem when the problem is that you can't try to solve it? Then I thought of another analogy.

It was the same as trying to read quantum data: if you tried to read it directly, you would change it, and therefore destroy the data you were trying to read. The act of trying to read the data made it unreadable. The act of trying to solve this puzzle made it unsolvable. But Lucy was right: the fact that I couldn't solve it directly didn't mean it couldn't be solved. There had to be a way of solving it indirectly.

Maybe someone else could solve it for me, I thought, but then I concluded that that wouldn't be any different than solving it myself. It didn't matter who or what tried to solve it; it was the very act of trying that made it impossible. But it wasn't impossible.

"Then there's only one solution," I said with a smile. "The puzzle must solve itself. But I am the puzzle, so the solution must be inside of me. Therefore I must *grok* the puzzle." And that meant that I must become one with the puzzle. The puzzle was me, and I was the puzzle. Every part was a whole, and every whole was a part. Instead of breaking it down into parts, I had to see each part as a whole. The puzzle was its own solution. It was all interconnected. But how could I put this into a formula that solved the problem?

"The puzzle is a wave function," I finally concluded. "I must see it as a wave and not as individual particles. If I expect to get particles, then I'll get particles. But if I expect to get waves …"

I closed my eyes again. At that moment, I could feel the universe all around me, and I dissolved away into a wispy undulating spirit that had no bounds. And all the parts became one, and all the waves became coherent. And there was only one Alice, and every Alice was me. And the puzzle was solved by itself.

"Okay, Lucy," I said in my trance. "I'm ready for the next challenge."

I opened my eyes and I found myself sitting in front of a beautiful Steinway concert grand piano. The ebony cabinet glistened from many coats of varnish, and the keys were milky white from their vintage ivory origins. It was a magnificent instrument. But there was one problem; the logo was printed y-a-w-n-i-e-t-S, and the keys were reversed. It was a backward Steinway piano.

Then I heard a rustling noise, and I looked to my left. My heart stopped. My gaze fell upon a multitude of eyes and ears. They belonged to patient patrons of the arts, all of whom were dressed formally and sitting in wonderfully upholstered red velvet seats. And above them were splendid golden balconies sweeping around the great white hall, with a beautifully ornate ceiling that towered over the music lovers. I recognized this place; it was 154 West Fifty-seventh Street in Manhattan. It was a packed Carnegie Hall—and, apparently, they were all there to see me play.

A knot formed in my throat, and I was immediately glad that I wasn't going to sing to them. I looked down and was relieved to find that at least I was properly clothed, in a shiny red formal dress with equally glossy red shoes. But when I looked at the music stand, I had another shock waiting for me—the music was not only unfamiliar but was also printed backward.

So this was the challenge: I was to attempt to play, on a reversed piano, a piece of music I had never seen before that was printed backward, and I had to do it in front of a packed house at Carnegie Hall. I wasn't sure if even Mozart could have pulled it off. But I suppose he never had to try.

I cleared my throat to buy a little time, and I looked over the first page of music carefully. It started slow and easy, which was nice, but then it picked up speed and momentum. By the time it got to bar forty-eight, it was really cooking, with thirty-second notes punctuated by a syncopated bass line. After that, it split into two completely separate melody lines, which used an almost subliminal counterpoint to hold them together like a spider's web. When the notes on the page had turned to music in my head, I decided it was time to play. The crowd was getting restless.

I placed my fingers on the keys and closed my eyes. I tried to transpose their roles in my head; my left hand was my right and vice versa. Then I began to play.

The opening was sad and slow, much like the first movement of Beethoven's "Moonlight Sonata," but then it turned light and vibrant like one of Mozart's serenades. As I reached the forty-eighth bar, it morphed again into something more akin to one of Franz Liszt's "Hungarian Rhapsodies," complete with all the pyrotechnics. My hands were soon flying across the keyboard, and I had to just let them do their work. If I had thought too much about what I was trying to do, I would certainly have made mistakes. I had to become one with the music and with the keyboard. I moved on to page two.

Page two and three were even more convoluted, with at least three distinct melodies woven together to form an almost cacophonous modern tapestry of dark threads. It was Wagner, Stravinsky, and Copland all woven together to form a wall of chaotic synergy. It was horribly beautiful. It was extremely difficult. I turned the page with building apprehension.

Page four and five were even more challenging, not just because the music got harder, but also because the notes themselves developed this nasty little habit of moving around. Yes, that's what I said—they moved! A few of them just popped off the page and walked away as if they had had enough of this nonsense, and others jumped from bar to bar or from staff to staff, as if they were musical monkeys jumping from branch to branch. This meant that I would miss what was meant to be played next if I didn't read far enough ahead, and, after a while, I was forced to complete the musical equation in my head in order to resurrect this rapidly decomposing composition.

All this time the crowd sat quietly. But I could feel thousands of laserlike eyes drilling holes in me and just as many razor-sharp ears waiting to cut me to bloody shreds if they detected even a single mistake. I tried my best to tune them out and to tune in to the music alone.

I turned to the last page. It was nonsense—followed by nothing. That's right—nothing. Apparently, I had to complete the composition—the musical equation—by myself, on the fly. I had to improvise a perfect ending to this convoluted masterpiece. I had to complete the musical sentence to make it a consistent idea. I had to add the final punctuation mark without making any grammatical errors. And, of course, I had to do so without thinking about it.

For music flows, not from the conscious mind, but from the eternal soul of life itself, and, therefore, it doesn't need interference from the brain to muck it up. To complete the song, I had to experience the music as an entity unto itself and then let the notes flow naturally through my fingers to the piano's keys, which would hammer them onto the strings, which would ultimately oscillate in harmony with the universe. The music knew which way to go; I just had to go along for the ride. I had to let it lead me to the proper solution. My job was not to get in its way.

I closed my eyes and felt the power resonate through me, as my fingers became autonomous messengers of a transcendent deity, and my feet pumped the pedals to dampen and modulate the tones into the words of unspoken raptures. After a while, it seemed as though I wasn't even playing but that I had become an instrument of the music itself, and now it was playing through me. It was just as Grand Master C had said—the music was playing me.

When it got to the end, my hands jumped and danced as they added the final crescendo and flourish before striking one last punctuating chord. And then it was done.

I opened my eyes to dead silence. Had I lost my way? Had the music been violated? Had my audience been offended? Had I lost the challenge? My heart sank into my stomach like a lump of cold lead.

And then it was lifted up on a thousand wings by a wave of thunderous applause. People climbed to their feet as the ovation reached a meter-spiking peak, and shouts of "Bravo!" and "Hurrah!" filled the reverberant air.

I got to my feet and faced my gracious audience. I bowed deeply from the waist, as the shouts became even louder, and the applause became almost deafening. I had won the challenge.

I raised my head up proudly and was about to speak, when I noticed that I was no longer in Carnegie Hall. I was seated at an oval table in a very recognizable room. The walls were smooth and curved with large sealed windows that looked out onto a star-filled black background. The tables were modern and functional, without any frills or decorations, and the chairs were ergonomically rounded to cradle the body comfortably, but they also had no artistic augmentations. The room was efficiently austere.

Seated across from me was a dark-haired, slender man with pointy ears and eyebrows. His hair was cropped short and neat, and his face was angular, but kind. He was wearing a form-fitting blue and black tunic with an *A*-shaped insignia on his left breast. I recognized this man immediately.

"Your move, Alice," he said with flat inflections, as he nodded down toward a multileveled game board of familiar design. The man was Mr. Kcops. The game was 3-D chess. Mr. Kcops had never been defeated, or so the legend goes. Lucy had given me yet another seemingly impossible challenge. But at least this was one I was sure to enjoy.

"Yes, Mr. Kcops, it appears that the game has just begun. If I remember the rules correctly, I can either move one of my pieces, or I can move a section of the board. The section can only be moved to a corner of equal color, and that itself is counted as one move. Is that correct?"

"Yes, Alice, you are correct. The game was designed to enhance your three-dimensional visualization and strategy skills, which are necessary attributes for successful Teelfrats officers to possess."

"Undoubtedly," I said, trying to raise my right eyebrow independently. "And if memory serves, you have been quite successful at playing this game, haven't you?"

"I have never been defeated," he said without any hint of pride. "The ship's computer has played me to a stalemate but never to the point of victory."

"So, in essence, I am playing the computer, am I not?"

"Essentially, that is so."

"Then the best I can hope for is a draw, Mr. Kcops?"

"Yes, unless you can introduce an element of surprise or deception into the game. Under normal circumstances, your best possible outcome would be a draw."

I smiled at Mr. Kcops, and then I gave the officers' lounge a closer inspection. It was occupied by a few other recognizable figures, including Dr. Yoccm and Mr. Ttocs, who were having a drink and a discussion at a table nearby. So far, no one had paid any attention to our game. I had to admit that although Lucy's challenge was nearly impossible, it was also irresistible.

"Then let us begin," I said, as I moved one of my pawns forward two squares. I decided to play a cautious and defensive game to begin with. It was the optimal strategy, if a draw was my best possible outcome.

Several moves later, my half-alien friend warmed up the discussion. "I see you are using the Antarian variation of the Sicilian defense, Alice. Aren't you afraid that I will counter with the classic Romulus gambit?"

"Yes," I said as I captured one of his pawns with my bishop, "but I find that Fisher cancels out Romulus—don't you agree?"

Mr. Kcops raised an eyebrow and then pinned my bishop with his queen, which swept down diagonally from the upper level.

"Yes, Alice, that is unless your opponent has studied his Spassky, which I have."

I frowned momentarily and then smiled again, as I sent my rook up to his back rank, putting him momentarily in check. He was forced to move his queen back for a useful interposition.

"Excellent, Alice. That was your best possible move. You are indeed a highly skilled player."

"Thank you, Mr. Kcops. I have worked very hard to become so."

"Undoubtedly, and I believe that Teelfrats was well justified in making you captain of the Esirpretne."

"Captain of the Esirpretne!" I echoed with surprise. Then I finally looked down at my clothing. I was wearing the famous orange tunic. I was Captain Sterling of the Starship Esirpretne. I didn't know immediately whether that was a good thing or a bad thing. And then the intercom came to life, and I soon realized that the game of 3-D chess wasn't the only challenge here. This was a nested cube.

"Captain Sterling, we are receiving a high-priority distress signal," said the voice of Aruhu from the small console to my left. "Your presence on the bridge is requested, sir."

I pushed the small intercom button and replied, "We're on our way," as I glanced at Mr. Kcops knowingly. Moments later, all three of my officers followed me out the door. We went down the corridor and into the nearest turbolift. I was extremely excited and apprehensive.

"Tell me, Alice," said Dr. Yoccm as we rode up to the bridge in that famous device, "do you really believe it's wise for us to be conducting training missions this close to the Nofly Zone? Or is it really just a ruse to disguise our real purpose for being here?"

I was still a bit awed by the presence of my favorite sci-fi characters, and by the experience of being on the Esirpretne, but I also knew a loaded question when I heard one. "And just what purpose is that, Dr. Yoccm?" I asked in order to weed out his meaning.

"You know damn well what purpose—to start a war!"

His accusation caused quite a stir, and Mr. Kcops shot back an immediate response. "Dr. Yoccm, your accusation is tantamount to insubordination."

"Well somebody has to say it," said the good doctor. "We've been walking on eggshells out here for six months now, and no one wants to get yolk on his face. Our president wants to send us out on a bloody crusade to capture one Nognilk terrorist, and he doesn't seem to care if we lose a thousand starships in the bargain. Are we going to be just pawns in his personal game of vengeance? Does it make any sense to risk millions of lives just to capture and kill one colossal thorn in his side? Not to mention the fact that to do so will violate intergalactic law."

"I believe you're being a bit premature, Sticks," I said as I digested his words of warning. "Aruhu said there was a distress signal. We'll deal with that first as best as we can, and then we'll worry about why we are here."

"Oh, sure," said Yoccm dramatically, "but who wants to bet that this little 'distress signal' has something to do with the Nognilks?"

"I wouldn't doubt it," said my engineer with Scottish flare. "The Nognilks have been peeking out from behind the fences ever since we got here."

"Naturally," deduced Mr. Kcops. "They are responding to our presence. Only a fool would leave his borders unguarded in a time of potential conflict."

Before Dr. Yoccm could respond, the door whooshed open, and before us was the bridge. It was like being in a surreal fantasy world, which I suppose is exactly what it was, but knowing that didn't make it feel any less strange. I stepped out of the elevator and into the circular room that so many have seen and know every little last detail of, including myself. There were the railings that separated the upper level from the lower and the steps down to the floor, where two stations sat with swivel chairs for the helmsman and the navigator. There were the monitors and flashing lights all around the perimeter, with the stations for communications, science, engineering and others, and the movie-screen-sized display in the middle. And, centered in the room, on its own level, was the captain's chair—*my* chair. Goosebumps!

I couldn't help feeling a little pressure as I walked over and sat down in the captain's chair, and I couldn't help swiveling in around a little, trying it on for size. But the immediate situation snapped me out of my daze.

"Captain, the message has become even more urgent," said Aruhu with emotion.

"Put it on the speakers," I said as calmly as I could.

Aruhu pushed a button, and a distorted voice, distilled with static, filled the air. "Esirpretne, this is the *Kawasaki Maru*. We have struck a gravitic mine, and we have lost all power. Life support systems are failing. We require immediate assistance. Can you help us, Esirpretne? Can you hear us?"

So that was Lucy's game: the *Kawasaki Maru*, the famous no-win scenario. She had heaped one impossible challenge on top of another. At least she wasn't making it easy for me.

"Mr. Kcops, data on the *Kawasaki Maru*," I said, although I knew the answer already. I was just playing the game.

"The *Kawasaki Maru* is a freighter assigned to this sector as a Federation supply vessel. She is carrying spare parts and other critical munitions. She has a complement of four hundred and sixty crewmen."

"Plot her current position on the screen, Ensign Vokehc."

"Aye, Captain."

The main viewer changed from a forward view of space to an animation of our position versus that of the stricken freighter. As expected, she was inside the Nofly Zone in Nognilk territory. In order to rescue her, we would have to enter Nognilk space, in violation of treaty, which would definitely be seen by the Nognilks as an act of war. It would also ultimately lead to our own destruction. It was a no-win situation, especially if I played it in the predictable way. The only way to play it then was to be unpredictable. In fact, the most predictable thing about this challenge was the challenge itself.

"What are your orders, Captain?" asked Ensign Ulus, as he gazed at me with great concern from the helm. All the others were also looking at me, and the tension on the bridge was palpable. What would they have done in my situation?

"We will hold our current position, Mr. Ulus."

This caused a shockwave that rocked its way around the room and finally erupted from the mouth of Dr. Yoccm. "You're just going to leave them out there to die?"

"Yes, doctor," I said with conviction. "You, of all people, should understand why. If we go after them, we will start a war, which will result in many more deaths, undoubtedly including our own. To sacrifice a few to save many is logical, isn't that right, Mr. Kcops?"

"Yes, Captain; the needs of the many outweigh the needs of the few."

"Although saving them may seem to be the right thing to do, in this case, the right thing is to not save them. My crew and my ship come first. And when war becomes a game of chess, you must have an end game before you attack."

"And this could be a trap, Captain," said my first officer. "The Nognilks might want us to respond, so that they can claim that we started the war."

"Yes, Mr. Kcops, and when you're fighting an opponent of equal or greater strength, your best move is to be defensive and prepared, and hope that your opponent makes a mistake. You must force your opposition to make the first move."

"And what do you think that move will be, Captain?"

"When the fish refuses to take the bait, you throw out the net," I said flatly.

"Damn it, Alice, are you a human or a Nacluv?" shouted Dr. Yoccm.

I didn't answer his question, although I was starting to realize that logic was my primary motivator and that my 'human' side did need expansion. But, as I gazed at the empty star field on our front viewer, I decided that my strategy was sound. It was time for some preemptive action.

"Place the ship on red alert. Raise the shields and energize the weapons. Ulus, make our position perpendicular to the Nofly Zone. I expect the Nognilks will attack us at any second. They will come at us with several ships. Vokehc, be prepared to fire upon any ship that decloaks on this side of the boundary. We will shoot first and ask questions later."

"But what if they're diplomatic ships?" gasped Dr. Yoccm. "You can't just fire on ships without warning."

"Dr. Yoccm, any Nognilk ship that crosses the Nofly Zone cloaked is clearly not on a diplomatic mission. And the Nofly Zone cuts both ways—if they cross it first, then they are the antagonists, not us."

"But how do you know they will attack us, Captain?" asked Kcops pointedly.

"Because, Mr. Kcops, I know who's pushing their buttons."

And, just as the words left my lips, the battle began. Three Nognilk Birds of Play started to decloak and slowly appeared in front of us in a classic triangular formation. And Vokehc, as ordered, fired at them with full phasers before they could react. Three beams of fire leapt from our nose and landed crushing blows to the warships' faces. Two of them were disabled, but the third recloaked and disappeared into the blackness of space.

"Ulus, full astern. Give us some breathing room. They will attack from our flanks next."

"Aye, Captain, full astern."

The ship began to hum and shake as the impulse engines revved up, and I lurched forward, as we began to move backward. "Set the view screen to widest field. Mr. Ttocs, set our flanking shields to maximum."

"Aye, Captain, flanking shields at maximum."

At that moment, Birds of Play began to pop up all around us, like stars in twilight. Vokehc fired at as many as he could, but there were just too many. We disabled and destroyed several, but a few got in shots before we could target or hit them. The Esirpretne shook violently as cannon blasts struck our shields and weakened our defenses.

"Ulus, put us into a negative-Z outside loop, and rotate the ship simultaneously to keep our strongest shields pointed at the attackers. Let's see how well they've studied their 3-D chess."

"I'll try, Captain," said Ulus, as he digested my complicated order. I had complete confidence in him.

We looped downward and back around toward the Nofly Zone, and the Esirpretne rotated and fired shots, as we swept out a giant vertical ring in space. We were in effect moving on three axes at once, making us a difficult target to hit. But we also ended up eventually going back in the least expected direction: toward the Nofly Zone.

When the maneuver was completed, we had outflanked the entire Nognilk battle group. We were now standing between them and their home, and most of them were still pointed in the wrong direction.

"Continue to fire at will, Mr. Vokehc. Mr. Ttocs, divert all power to our front shields."

"Aye, Captain."

We fired upon and destroyed most of the remaining Nognilk battle cruisers, as they fumbled to regroup. Within the span of a few minutes, their numbers were reduced to a single ship. I ordered a ceasefire, as the last Bird of Play stared us down from dead ahead.

"We are being hailed, Captain," said Aruhu as I stared at the lone wolf.

"Put it on the screen, Aruhu."

"Aye, Captain."

The image faded to show the interior of the bridge of the Nognilk warship, and their commander's face came into focus. As I expected, it was Lucy. She was dressed in a Nognilk uniform, and her face was a bumpy, sickly green nightmare, but it was definitely her. The snakes on her head looked right at home in the smoky, garish light of their Gothic war machine. The vicious snarl on her face suggested that she wasn't enjoying our little competition as much as she would have liked to. But then she did something that even I hadn't anticipated—she gave me a compliment.

"Outstanding, Alice; you truly are a killing machine when you want to be. I knew you wouldn't disappoint me when push killed the dove."

Dr. Yoccm took one look at Lucy, and he gasped in horror. "The terrorist! Alice, it's her!"

"She destroyed fifteen defenseless Federation planets without warning," exclaimed Vokehc. "She murdered ninety-five billion people. She's even more cold-blooded than Hitler."

Lucy took in their words as if they were praising her, and she looked at Vokehc with a heinous grin. "Thank you, Mr. Vokehc. I have worked hard to become so."

Vokehc looked astonished upon hearing his name, but I broke into the conversation before he could say the obvious. "Been putting in a little overtime, have you now? A little target practice to put you in the mood for Armageddon? Almost as good as the real thing, is it, Lucy?"

"It was just as good as the real thing, Alice dear, and it did quench my thirst for blood for the moment. But I sense that you've developed a taste for it, as well. You've just killed several thousand Nognilk soldiers, but, unfortunately for you, in this game it only counts as one. And you also just sacrificed four hundred and sixty of your own people. Now, I don't know about you, Mr. Vokehc, but that sounds pretty cold-blooded to me."

I was mortified by the very accusation, but I wasn't ready to admit anything. "But it's all just part of the game, right, Lucy dear? I'm playing to win and to save my universe, as well. So I must work the challenges as I see them."

"Yes," said Lucy with a snarl, "but you've been operating under the false assumption that none of this is real. But what would you say if I told you that everything that happens here is just as real as in your own universe? Just because it's not your universe doesn't mean that it's not real. And you knew it all along, Alice. You knew that this wasn't just a game, but you played it like it was, anyway. Have you always been this cold-hearted and selfish? I'd like to think so. You see, we are not so different, you and I."

Then Lucy welled up with visible pride as she put the last pinch of arsenic on her poisonous sundae. "But before you say something silly and childish—like I cheated—remember: this is your game, and we're playing by your rules. You wanted it to be real. You wanted it to be a game of life. Remember what you said: 'QuCee is life, and life is QuCee.' Well, life isn't fair, little Alice, and now it's time for you to resign."

Her words cut into me like a cold dagger to my heart. And she was essentially right about everything; I had forgotten that the game had consequences. She had used my competitive nature against me. I had fallen prey to my own devices. But she was wrong about one thing: there was no way that I would ever resign. I would simply have to learn from my mistakes.

"You won this round, Lucy, but the game shall continue," I said defiantly.

"Fine, have it your way, Alice. But this time I won't be so easy on you. This challenge will take you to the very edge of sanity. This challenge will show you what it's like to really have the weight of the entire universe on your skinny shoulders."

"It seems to me that I already have such an overwhelming burden, Lucy. What could you possibly do to make it any worse?"

Lucy didn't answer me, at least not with words. Instead, she flicked her right index finger upward with a sneer, and the Esirpretne disappeared around me, as did the Nognilk warship, and I was left alone in space. Then I gasped with fright as I felt my body dissolving, and, after a few moments, I was reduced to a noncorporeal essence that began to diffuse into the very ether of the cosmos. To put it as briefly and concisely as I can: I became a wave.

At first it seemed to me that I was experiencing something analogous to when I had first entered the buffer zone, but, when I tried to imagine myself a body and a room to put myself in, it didn't work. I had no essence here—I was a permanent wave.

My next reaction was one of panic. If I had no body, wasn't that the same as being dead? Or was Lucy just trying to show me what it was like to be dead? She was just trying to scare me; was that it? Was the challenge a test; could I maintain my sanity knowing that I was no longer alive? That seemed a bit gratuitous and trivial to me. And thinking about it made me angry.

This isn't a challenge, Lucy; this is a cheap scare tactic! And it's beneath *you, which I didn't think was possible. How could* anything *be beneath you?*

But there was no response, and that worried me. What good were insults if no one was listening? Was I really all alone?

Then the sense of panic returned again, and it began to morph into genuine fear—despite my protest—and I began to think that I was helpless and hopeless. Maybe Lucy had just been playing with me all along, in some twisted and sadistic fashion that only the completely demented could truly understand. Maybe she could have killed me at any moment, but she was just toying with me—the way a cat plays with a mouse before biting its head off. Maybe her game was to give me hope, so that she could then snatch it away again—an experiment in psychological torture. And what scared me the most was that it didn't sound like something that was beneath her at all. In fact, it sounded like Lucy to a tee.

She wants me to cry and scream for mercy—that's her game. She thinks I'm still just a sniveling little infant that wants her mommy, but I never cry, and I don't need a security blanket! I stiffened my nonexistent upper lip and tried to laugh instead. *You lose, Lucy! You're yet another player who has underestimated the powers of the amazing Alice!*

Still there was no response, but I didn't expect one. I figured that she would leave me this way for a while to see if I would crack, but I was determined not to. If she wanted to reduce this to a stare-down contest, I was confident that I could make her blink first. The calmer and happier I could appear, the more and more it would piss her off. And I knew just the sort of thing that would really get under her satanic skin—music!

And I knew just the song for her. I began to sing as joyfully as I could.

> *You're a foul one, Lucy bitch; you really are a*
> *whore.*
> *You've got spiders in your caverns,*
> *You've got monsters in your drawers; you're a*
> *witch.*
> *Alice will beat you with*
> *Enough time to go take a snore!*
>
> *You're a vile one, Lucy witch; you're the queen of*
> *dirty shots.*
> *You're as welcome as a tumor,*
> *You're as subtle as the plot, Lucy bitch!*
> *You are a dead hyena with*
> *Black, orange, and purple spots!*
>
> *You want to truncate me, like a stitch; you want to*
> *end it all.*
> *You want silence in the subways,*
> *You crave emptiness in malls, Lucy witch!*
> *The only way to accurately describe you, in*
> *three words, is as follows, and I quote:*
> *Bitch! Bitch! Bitch!*

The singing did make me feel better, but it had no visible effect, which is what I had anticipated, anyway. I would sing my way through eternity, if necessary, but I would never cry uncle. And I had a wide repertoire to select from, so I wasn't worried about running out of ammo. At that moment, I remembered a quote from one of my musical heros, Jim Morrison, and it calmed me down even further.

"Music is your only friend, until the end."

And music was the only friend I would need to defeat Lucy.

The calmer I became, the more my mind began to wander, and I started to think about all the people I had known in my short, but hectic, life. In fact, I went all the way back to the beginning, and I saw my father's masked face looking down at me as I crawled out of mother's birth canal. Then I saw my mother's face and radiant halo as I was placed in her loving arms. This vision snapped me back to the present, and I began to think about what my parents were feeling at that very moment. It was only natural.

The picture in my mind's eye twisted and contorted itself to become a scene from *The Wizard of Oz*, and I saw Lucy dressed as the Wicked Witch of the West, as she peered into a large crystal ball filled with wisps of black smoke and fire. She caressed the murky sphere with hands of jaundiced skin and long, curved, black clawlike nails, and she cackled heartlessly as the smoke began to clear to reveal the darkly concerned faces of my parents.

"Alice, where are you, Alice dear? Please come home to us. Please, Alice darling," pleaded my beloved mother with heartbreaking emotion.

"We forgive you, Alice," beseeched my father. "It was all my fault. Come home, please, so we can be together in the end."

My heart began to implode, but then I caught myself, and I screamed into the void, *Lucy! I've had enough of your dirty tricks! It won't work—I won't crack!*

But cold, deadly silence was my only answer once more, and immediately the picture faded away in ghostlike shadows, to be replaced by the frightened face of my sister, Molly. My point of view zoomed back to reveal her standing on the precipice of a sheer, rocky cliff, as sheets of rain and waves of wind descended upon her from soot-black skies of thunder and fury. There was no visible escape for her, nor was there any shelter from the torrential storm. She shivered and shook from the cold and the fear, and her legs wobbled from fatigue, making her ever more vulnerable to the perils of her predicament. It was clear that she couldn't survive this onslaught for very much longer.

Again, I exploded with fury. *Lucy! Leave her out of this! This is a fight between you and me, so drop this melodramatic nonsense and focus your attention on me!*

But it was *my* attention that changed focus instead, and I found myself gazing down upon a horrific sight. Thousands of soldiers in gray and blue uniforms were marching through a grassy field, carrying single-shot muskets with bayonets fixed. Cannon blasts burst all around them, as they marched onward and upward toward a well-positioned army in blue and white uniforms at the top of the hill. The attackers were mowed down like bloody blades of grass by countless barrages from the cannons and rifles above them, as their bodies were tossed about and ripped apart by the relentless, deadly deluge. But the rapidly dwindling survivors just kept on marching. It was complete and utter madness, plain and simple.

Some of the gray garrison turned to flee, with harrowing expressions of mortal anguish on their flushed faces, but a gallant general riding a magnificent white steed held his gleaming saber to the skies and courageously urged them onward. Some of the men rallied to his cries of "Old Virginia!" and they turned and marched with renewed vigor toward the hills of certain death. Then I was somehow afforded a direct view of this unabashed officer's face, as he marched his mount and his men on this suicide mission. I was shocked to discover that it was Mr. H.

Before I could protest this infuriating injustice, I was whisked away again to a dark alley in some unknown modern city. There were dented trashcans and putrid dumpsters littering the forsaken furrows of this narrow, cold, concrete cavern. The atmosphere was filled with choking, sooty smoke, from many makeshift oil-drum fireplaces. They were tenuously tended by tormented and tattered tramps of the gutters, and their dirty, disheveled faces glowed ghoulishly in the flickering firelight.

I was shocked and saddened by this revelation, and it made me angry that the world could be such a cold and unforgiving place, where this sort of neglect and misery could be allowed to run rampantly through the cracks of a supposedly wise and wealthy nation. Was Lucy trying to suggest that this was somehow my fault? At that moment, I wasn't completely sure that it wasn't. And just when I suspected that I would be swept away again, to some other diabolically disturbing dioramic display, I head a noise, as if something or someone had just knocked over one of the objectionably overfilled metal trashcans. I turned in the direction of the disturbance and saw a small figure staggering pathetically through the putrid squalor.

At first I thought it was a small child, or a vagrant midget dressed in a stained and matted orange and black fur coat. But then I saw his tattered and twisted tail trailing listlessly behind him, and I instantly knew who he was. I gasped in horror, as my once-magnificent mechanical mousetrap, A-II, lurched and wobbled through the atrocious alleyway, as if he were incurably inebriated. He aimlessly bumped and bounced off the walls, in a seemingly blind and careless manner, making him appear both worthless and insane. And to complete this miserable montage, he mumbled to himself like a miscreant.

I moved in closer, until I could finally make out his muffled monologue.

"I don't care if Alice hates me now and left me here to die—*crash*—I can find my way out of here all by myself—*bang!*—I'll just walk through the wall—*crunch*—ouch, and I'm home—*wham!*

"And I don't need her anyway—*slam*—not one bit. She's the one that needed me—*crack*—and now she just drops me like yesterday's pet—*boom!* I hate her!—*bam*—I hate everybody!—*bounce*—I hate life—*whack!*

Oh my God, what had I done? A-II was losing his faith and his structural integrity, before my very eyes. He was blindly and blatantly bashing himself to bits, and I was completely and unquestionably culpable. He had come here to help save me, and I had left him to Lucy's devious and devilish devices.

What a selfish and shameless shrew I was! And it wasn't just A-II that I had let down; I had done it to all of them. I had followed my dream of the ultimate competition to the ends of the Earth, literally, and I had done so without any thoughts about the others and their needs. And now their very existence and survival was dependent upon my actions, and I wasn't sure if I could come through for them.

Suddenly the weight of the entire multiverse did fall on my skinny shoulders, and I felt as if I was being crushed under its fathomlessly awesome accumulations, as if I were at the center of a supermassive black hole. It tore and ripped at my very being, and I could feel my functional fabric unraveling, much as a tapestry being slowly unravelled by the tug of a single thread. I was losing myself rapidly. I was coming apart at the seams.

As my spirit began to dwindle and dissipate, I was boundlessly bombarded by voraciously vicious visions of everything evil and inequitable in the cold, callous cosmos. Was it really worth saving, after all? With all the heartache and despair in this wicked world, wouldn't it be better to just put it all out of its collective misery? Had any good actually come of this endlessly unethical experiment? How could God have let it all come to this? And how could I, in all good conscience, let it continue?

In my darkest hour, the words of the Bard of Avon came to my lips.

"To be or not to be; that is the question."

And as I pondered the eternal enigma I began to see the method behind Lucy's madness. If she could turn me around to her own point of view, then she would have defeated me with a single move. If she could convince me that she was doing the right thing, after all, then the game was over. Her point was that the game of QuCee was as pointless as the game of life itself. And the pursuit of victory in such an endeavor was pure and fruitless folly, which, at best, could only result in more unnecessary pain and despair. But was she right? Was it better to *be* or *not* to be? Should I allow the world to suffer evermore the slings and arrows of never-ending outrageous fortunes? Or should I put an end to it?

Or, rather, should I just let the world sleep, perchance to dream?

"Ay, there's the rub; for in that sleep of death what dreams may come?" Lucy had me on the ropes, and I could feel my wobbly legs giving way, as she mercilessly pummeled me with barrage after barrage of soul-bruising body blows. I was screaming for the bell to sound and save me, before I fell to the capitulatory canvas. I was a great pillar of stone ready to fall.

But then my logic found me, and I slowly backed away from the bifurcating edge to ponder my predicament. *There are subliminal messages in these visions,* I thought to my soul-searching self. *Lucy is giving me clues to the solution once more.*

But why would she do that? I wondered wistfully. *Is it all part of her arrogantly mocking modus operandi? Is it that much more satisfying for her when she openly shows her opponent the solution, but they're too blind or stupid to see it? That would definitely be her brand of bull. I must look back at all the challenges, to see what her strategy has been. I must uncover her Achilles' heel. So think, Alice, think!*

First I had seen Mr. H on his white horse, and it had disturbed me. What was a black man doing as an officer in the Confederate army? That was clearly not real or possible. Maybe it was a metaphor for something else. Maybe Lucy was trying to tell me that Mr. H was really on the other side. Maybe he had been Lucy's confederate all along. He had led me down the wormhole, after all. Had Mr. H really been my enemy from the very start? The very thought of it broke my heart.

Next I had seen Molly on the mountain, about to go over the cliff. What was the metaphor here, if there was one? Was she a symbol for the entire universe about to be destroyed? That was too easy. There had to be more to it than that.

Molly wasn't just my sister—she was the key to the whole mystery. She was the quantum computer that had started this gargantuan game, and she was at the very crux of the crucible. But did the clue concern Molly specifically—or what Molly *represented*? Was Molly herself the missing metaphor?

Was Molly, in fact, just a reflection of my own pride and preoccupation with unlocking the mysteries of the multiverse, without any regard as to what was right and responsible? Was Lucy trying to say that when it all came crashing down at my feet there was only one person to blame? That may very well have been true, but it was no great revelation or cleverly disguised deception. *No,* I decided, *I must peel this offensive onion down to its origins, even if every successive layer leads me inevitably to the ninth ring of the inferno, for, even if it does, only there will I find what is lying at the center of Lucy's disloyal, cheating heart.*

So I concentrated on Lucy for a change, which was also better for my own aching heart. I began to think about who, or what, Lucy really was and how (if at all) she was different from me. Maybe she had dropped a hint when she said, "We are really not so different, you and I." Could that have been another arrogant mistake?

You see, if I were the same as her, then she didn't have any special powers here that I could not also invoke. As long as Lucy appeared to be omniscient and omnipresent, she would appear to be invincible. But if I could do the same thing, then we would still be on equal footing. In fact, Lucy might have just shown me that this was the case. In her haste to make one quick decisive move, she might have left the back door open. It was a game of chess, where Lucy was employing a very risky gambit. It all hinged upon the bet that I would be too blinded by her boldness and shocked by her blitz, and I'd fail to see that her talented tactic was really a brilliant blunder. But she could still be successful, if I didn't come up with the one move that would lead to her demise—and it was roughly one move in a million. Lucy was just playing the odds, and they were still overwhelmingly in her favor.

But the fact remained that we were on a level playing field, so I needed to find her exposed flank before I could plan my counteroffensive. Lucy had gotten inside my head, to throw me off my game, and now I had to do the same to her. Her tactics had shown a repeated pattern of self-absorption and arrogance that were clear indications of overconfidence and self-worship. Lucy couldn't help it—she was in love with herself. And that was her Achilles' heel!

Therefore, my strategy was to analyze her previous moves, to see what they revealed about her true motives and methods, and the means she employed to service them. And, to do that, I would first need to understand exactly what the buffer zone was and why Lucy could exploit it to such ends.

I went back to the current beginning—to the day I had followed the cagey Mr. H through the wormhole. I saw the fantastic flowers of future histories blooming all around me as I passed through the boundary wall, and the mirror of multiple Alices as they waved back to me with fractal familiarity. Then I saw the friendly face of Mr. H, as he took me by the hand and led me through the valley of darkness. If he had been working for Lucy all along, then how could he have arrived before she did? Was that because time in the buffer zone was an illusion? But in my own universe, where time is at least unidirectional, he had arrived before the game had started. Could Lucy have set that up—before the game had even begun? I truly wasn't sure.

Then I moved ahead to the wonderful tearoom and our first encounter. I had created the room, but it was Mr. H who had suggested there were spies in our midst. Had Lucy already been there, gathering information to use against me? Was Mr. H the spy after all? Was he the first instance of Lucy's self-absorbed way of dropping hints that stared you mockingly in the face? Mr. H had appeared to be my friend and confidant, just as Lucy had.

It made sense, but it was merely circumstantial evidence, at best. I would take it for what it was worth, but I decided to suspend judgment for the time being.

Then I mentally moved through the delightful dance in my virtual bedroom, the watery walk with the Manna brothers, and the starry trek with the clueless Captain Starbuck. Had Mr. H really taught me anything, or had he just been wasting my time? He had been the one who encouraged me to try the psychedelic mushroom, which eventually landed me in Sheboygan at the site of the first world truncation. Had this all been just part of Lucy's plan? Had Lucy created that world as a trap and I wriggled out of it before she could catch me? But the second trap *had* snared me. So why had the game continued after that? What was I missing here?

Then I saw the answer, and it *was* so obvious that I instantly felt like a complete and utter moron—and that was the lowest blow of all. I had been just as arrogant as Lucy, because I had been blinded by the selfish assumption that the game was all about me! And now I could see that the game was on the line, and the fate of the entire multiverse truly did hang in the balance. What an idiot I was! Lucy didn't want me—she wanted Molly!

And then all the pieces fell into place, and it became clear to me at last. The game had begun in earnest exactly when I thought it had: right after Molly and I were separated and swept away from Atlantis, which was the second of Lucy's traps. Lucy was now using Molly—my own quantum chess computer—to generate the universe around me, where the battle for the whole shebang (as she had put it) was taking place. It was just the sort of ironic slap-in-the-face tactic that Lucy had been using all along. And, because of this, I knew exactly where I was—I was inside of Molly. That was significant by itself. But when I added to that my own current state of being, the picture came into acutely sharp focus, and my strategy presented itself clearly before my ethereal eyes. By attempting to exercise control over my state, Lucy had made it possible for me to become as uncontrollable and unpredictable as I wished to be. When she had made me a wave, she had made my position as imprecise as possible, which gave me the potential to be everywhere at once.

But there was also one last bit of malice attached to this Alice strategy, and it came conclusively and inevitably from Lucy. She had given me the tools to win the game, but the only way to win it was to become a virus and crash the computer. I had to infect and kill my own sister, which would likely also result in my own demise. To save the universe, I would have to sacrifice Molly and myself. Lucy was laughing at me even here, as I solved her revenge-rife riddle. She wanted to see if I had the guts and the gumption to sacrifice my sister and myself to save my world.

As for myself, I had already crossed over that bridge. I was willing and ready to die to save the ones I loved, along with the billions of others who were essentially (if not properly) innocent bystanders—probably including you.

But it was a totally different story when I thought about Molly. She was an innocent as well, especially when you considered the fact that she was less than a year old. It wasn't fair that she had to be sacrificed as well. But I surmised that that was also part of the challenge. In fact, it was this moral and emotional element that made my decision so dauntingly difficult. Lucy had made sure that my final decision would be the hardest possible one for me to make.

In that master stroke of strategy, Lucy had distinguished herself as the true queen of the predators. She had exploited both my weaknesses and my strengths and had ensured that even if I won, I would lose. I didn't want to admit it, but it appeared to me that she had beaten me no matter what the outcome. It was an incredibly humbling and impossibly horrible realization, to put it mildly.

So I mentally choked back my tears, steadied my quivering lower lip, and prepared myself for the ultimate showdown. I decided right then that if Molly and I had to go down together, we would do so proudly and in a brilliant blaze of glory that would be remembered for the rest of eternity, or until the end of time, whichever came first.

PART V

END GAME

I put my plan into action by moving back to a previous space: the puzzle cube. Once there, I felt myself slowly condensing back into a solid form and then suddenly splitting apart, over and over again, to become the self-similar fractal army of Alices. I was simply beside myself, and myself, and my other self, and my other other self, and my ...

Within moments, I stood before a thousand thousand thousand thousand Alices. I was all dressed the same, in sterling silver jumpsuits, with shiny black boots, and I was doing the wave. You want to talk about déjà vu all over again? We filled the cube from wall to wall and ceiling to ceiling, a viral cyst ready to burst and wreak havoc upon our hapless and sympathetically innocent host. Even as I looked out over the magnificent coalition of the Sterlings, I couldn't help wishing I didn't have to go through with it.

I felt much like a WW II general about to send her troops to the beaches of Normandy, where they would all face certain death. We all knew who we were and what we were doing. No words were necessary. But, since it was also customary, I tried to sum up our monumental mission to mark the importance of the occasion.

"I believe I speak for everyone here," I began, "and I want to say that I can't do this without all of me. And it should be obvious here and now that giving 110 percent just won't be good enough; in fact, it won't even come close.

> From this day to the ending of the world,
> But we in it shall be remembered;
> We few, we happy few, we band of sisters;
> For she today that sheds her blood with me
> Shall be my sister, be she ne'er so viral.

I nodded my heads in agreement and continued. "I know I don't have to remind myself of the importance of this mission or of the fact that most or all of me probably won't survive. But, as I stand here before me today, I submit to myself that the needs of the many do, indeed, outweigh the needs of the many-few, or of the many-one. So, if any of me has any objections, let me speak now or forever hold my peace."

I murmured softly back and forth to myself but raised no opposition. "Good, then let me all get out there now and finish the job that I started. But first, I'd like to leave myself with one more piece of inspiration: 'Alice, *über* Alice!'"

I gave myself a standing ovation, and, when I touched myself once more, the walls ballooned outward from my self-replicating pressure—and then they exploded.

I tumbled out of the broken cube like a cascade of liquid Alice—a waterfall of singular Sterlings—and we found me in a room filled with holographic mirrors. This place simply shimmered with the light of life itself, and the repetitive reflective panels seemed to melt together in their individuality. Each one held a slightly different three-dimensional view of the same picture, although it wasn't immediately apparent where one pane ended and the next one started.

Although I was everywhere, the image in the mirrors reflected only one me, but in each facet I appeared marginally divergent. One showed me as a pasty-white baby, dressed in a pink terry cloth sleeper, while the next showed me as a toddler with pigtails and puffy red cheeks. The others presented me in all stages of development, right up to a wrinkled, white-haired old grandma, sitting in an ancient antique rocking chair, knitting a multicolored sweater. It was as if these mirrors were actually portals to different moments in time, and my entire life was revealed in them.

Does this mean that I'll survive to become an old woman? I wondered to myselves. *Or are these just glimpses of possible futures and various pasts from alternate timelines? But why would they be here in Molly's memory space? Shouldn't these be pictures of Molly?*

Even as the thought crossed my collective mind, the images transformed into a montage of Molly's life, and I finally got to see what she had looked like as a baby. Little Molly was the most adorable baby I had ever seen, with ivory-white skin dotted by soft, pink freckles, and chubby little cheeks that framed her perfect baby-doll lips. She had curly, strawberry blonde hair and big, robin's-egg blue eyes, and her slightly upturned nose reminded me a lot of my mother. She was so beautiful that it made my heart swell up inside my chest, and I felt a wave of sadness overtaking me.

Then the mirrors began to reveal the faces of all the people I had ever known and loved, and their own lives flashed before my eyes like the flickering frames of an epic movie, with endings happy and sad, tragic and triumphant. And then I saw visages of countless others, as their paths intertwined and intermingled to form a great web of complementary and opposing forces. They were human and alien, familiar and foreign. Unimaginable sagas danced and undulated before me, with ripples and waves that sung the eternal songs of existence. I was moved beyond words.

Deep inside, I could feel all the years of repressed tears welling up against the dam of rigid logic, bending the massive beams of science and stoicism like palm trees in a force-five hurricane. And then, inevitably, it happened, just as Mr. H had said it would—I popped. The dam burst open.

Now my collective torrent of tears flowed down my multiple fractal faces and immediately began to collect into puddles of salty liquid at my feet. There were so many of me, and so many tears, that the puddles quickly became pools, and the pools merged together to form streams, and, after only a short time, the streams became swift, buoyant rivers.

I was lifted up on the saline solution, and began to float. A turbulent current developed, which carried me away in different directions, as the liquid flowed toward the paths of least resistance. These paths turned out to be a series of large drain holes that surrounded the room of holographic mirrors. The odd part was that the holes were on the inside surface of a great sphere, and I flowed toward drains all along the positively curved surface. I looked above me and saw upside-down Alices floating toward drains, where the river of tears flowed up and away. This was happening wherever I looked.

Maybe gravity is repellent here instead of attractive. Maybe water flows away from the center instead of toward it. I was confused but intrigued. *Whatever it is, this is a wonderfully curious phenomenon, indeed!*

I was so amazed by the inverse gravity that I forgot for the moment that I was crying, and I began to wonder where the drains led to. This was no time for tears. Another fantastic voyage was about to unfold before my myriad puffy, red eyes.

I flowed to a drain hole and slipped inside, as my tears cascaded over the edge and carried me along for the ride. I fell for several meters, clothed in semidarkness, as I tumbled in a shower of my own wailing waterfall. It was quite disorienting, and, for several moments, it was hard to tell whether I was actually moving or suspended in space along with my droplets of despair.

In that dim light, I saw into the little transparent spheres all around me, and what I saw was also quite curious. Inside every droplet was another little Alice, sitting with head in hands, shedding more little tears—which themselves contained even smaller Alices in similar dispositions. It was as if my tears had tears, which also had tears, and my anguish had caused a chain reaction of misery that became its own force of nature. It was also clear that if this continued, I might well drown in my own despondency. It seemed coldhearted, but I thought it might be a good time to make light of the situation.

Cheer up Alice! We might be going to hell in a hologram, but we could at least enjoy the ride.

Before I could tell if my words had any positive effect, the drainpipe curved beneath me and sent me sluicing off in a different direction. Now the journey became a water park ride, and the pipeline twisted and banked like a liquid rollercoaster, as I glided along the slippery surface with a lifting spirit. I was beside myself and beginning to enjoy the ride. Then, just when I had picked up some significant velocity and was really having some fun, the tunnel turned, and before me was what looked like a metal grate.

I had no way to slow down, and my exuberance immediately turned to fear, as I quickly tried to estimate the tensile strength of this perforated barrier blocking my way. But lacking time and crucial data, I failed in this pursuit, which became overall moot as I crashed through the screen, feet-first, nonetheless.

I landed in a standing position, knees bent, and I found myself in an industrial facility of extraordinary construction. There were dull silver corrugated ducts of various diameters branching out in all directions, most of which radiated from a central-furnace-like device at the center of the enormous room. The walls were cold concrete cinderblocks, painted institutional gray, and there were no windows or doors anywhere to be seen. The atmosphere was hot and somewhat caustic, and the overall ambiance wasn't pleasant, to say the least. This was a room unfit for human labors.

Along one wall was a bank of equipment, apparently the control center for this sector. Seated at the desk was a large, solitary man, dressed in blue coveralls. He stared somewhat listlessly into a large, flat-panel display, with his roundish chin supported by a massive, work-hardened hand.

His daunting console also included several lighted bar-graph meters, which fluctuated up and down in a wavelike pattern. He glanced at them periodically, but, overall, kept his dull, brown eyes fixed to his special screen. His short brown hair was messy and slightly oily, and it appeared to me that he wasn't too worried about his appearance, probably because, in this awful room, with no windows or doors, he didn't get much company. Immediately I felt empathy for this poor soul.

I walked toward him, but he didn't seem to notice me at first. Then, as I got closer, he finally turned and smiled at me with stained, ill-maintained teeth. At least he looked friendly enough—and lonely, for sure. He started to get up from his chair, and, as he reached a peak of more than two meters, I saw his name embroidered in fancy, white script on his right breast pocket. It said Bob.

"Well, hello," said Bob enthusiastically. "Isn't this a nice surprise? I haven't had visitors here since ... since ..." He thought to himself for a moment and then concluded, "since forever, I guess. This is fantastic! Can I get you anything, anything at all?"

"No, thank you," I replied guiltily. This guy had the worst job imaginable, and he was still a generous soul. I liked Bob immediately.

"Then I guess you're here for the tour, right? I'm not much of a guide, but I'll do my best. What would you like to see first?"

I spun around panoramically, and then faced big Bob again. It was all so fantastic that I didn't know what to say. Then I gasped with wonder, as I looked at his monitor more closely. It revealed a view of cosmic composition. A wispy ring of fire revolved around a dauntingly dark disk, like an unimaginably hot halo. What sort of singular structure was this? Was that an accretion disk? Was that a black hole?

Bob noticed me staring hypnotically at his screen, and he smiled proudly. "Ah, I see you, too, are fascinated by the collector. It's quite a sight, isn't it? And to think that this is what powers the whole shebang—that's pretty heavy, right?" Bob stopped and started to laugh at his own remark, and it made this massive man seem even more soft and cuddly. "Heavy! Did I say that? I'm a freaking comedian!"

"Yes, you really know from funny. And it's funny because it's ironic, right, Bob?"

"Yes, because that hole is as massive as you can get. So that was funny, right—heavy?" He laughed again contagiously, and I joined in and chuckled along with him.

"The dark sphere is a black hole," I sputtered, "and you're here collecting gravitons from it. You're using the black hole as a power source, right? That's extraordinary!"

Bob quelled his chortles and continued with his explanation. "Yes, the black hole is the most abundant source of gravitons possible. All I do is scoop them up and send them to the projection room. My job is to make sure we scoop up enough gravitons, and, more importantly, to make sure we don't get too close to the event horizon. That's what all those meters are for. If they spike into the red, we need to back away, until they're in the green again. We don't want a suck-down. I'd never hear the end of that!"

"Yes, I suppose that would be a downer," I said sincerely. "I hope I'm not distracting you too much from your important duties, Bob."

"No problem; this thing usually works just fine all by itself. And if there is a problem, the alarms will ring so loud you won't be able to think of anything else, believe me. It's never happened yet, thank goodness, but when it does, I'll be ready. I've trained for that very moment my entire life."

"I'm sure you have," I said with a tinge of sadness for Bob and his thankless job. His was the sort of occupation that no one else noticed, until something actually did go wrong. His sort are often the noblest souls of all. How could he stand the boredom and the monotony, punctuated by that ever-looming specter of doom, right outside his electronic window? Then I understood that this was the reality for most, if not all, blue-collar workers, especially those who keep our fragile, often forgotten, infrastructure functioning below our fancy feet. What would we do without all the Bobs in the world?

In my brief reflection, I began to wonder what else I would find in this amazing maze of tubular tunnels, and I began to shift my collective focus to another destination an alternate Alice had discovered—at the end of a parallel pipeline.

One of my other selves had experienced an analogous journey through a teary, tangent tunnel, and she soon found me crashing through a similar screen, into another incredible component. At first, I thought it was a wonderful planetarium of incalculable volume, but then I realized where I really was. I had entered the projection room.

This was immediately obvious, because I could see the projector at the center of the large space, and it looked more like a giant Gothic relic from the art-deco period than an ultramodern device of transcendent design. The casing was furrowed with folds of gray-white cast metal that emphasized the verticality and angularity of its mechanical majesty. This artificially organic outer shell flowed gracefully to an apex, where a starkly smooth cylinder protruded prominently toward the heavens. And out of this titanic tube came projections of unbelievable clarity and definition, creating incredibly realistic three-dimensional images of complete universes in the air. I was simply and completely mesmerized.

As my eyes drifted downward to the base of this behemoth, they eventually fell upon the operator of this magical machine. There sat a small, dark-haired, brown-skinned man in a white lab coat. He watched through thick horn-rimmed glasses as mile after of mile of holographic film spooled through the sprockets of the primal projector. This was truly movie magic—if ever there was such a thing.

I looked around the room some more and discovered that the projector was fed by several large conduits, which I surmised must have supplied it with both power and film. The power came from

Bob's domain, and the film came from the room of mirrors. It was all starting to make sense. I just needed to know a few more details; the paltry projectionist seemed to be the best source for such information. I approached slowly and cautiously so as not to disturb him.

The clacking noise of the projector masked my movements, and I was able to get quite close to the little man before he noticed me. In fact, he was quite startled by my sudden proximity, and he jumped like a frightened ferret. He ended up squatting on top of his spindly stool, looking much like a skittish squirrel on a tree stump. It made me smile sheepishly.

"I'm so very sorry, sir. I didn't mean to startle you. I just wanted a closer look at your wonderful machine. Please forgive me."

The trembling technician blinked at me blankly and then started to climb down from his prominent perch. He even smiled weakly as he resumed his previous position.

"Please, don't be doing that," he said with an Eastern accent. "I don't appreciate people sneaking up on me in that way. You want to be having me a heart attack?"

Now I felt even more embarrassed, and I felt as if I needed to make this man feel important in some way to make up for my mistake. I started by reading the name tag on his lapel, so that I could appear to be sympathetic. The tag said Rekam Rehte.

"I am sorry, Rekam. I know what an important and immaculate job you're doing here, and I just want you to know that we're all very pleased with your work."

Rekam smiled genuinely now, and he seemed proud to hear my words of praise. I had hit my mark dead center. "Thank you very much, indeed. I am rarely receiving such splendid support as this. Would you like to sit with me and watch as the worlds turn?"

"Certainly," I said with sincere acceptance. "I would love to watch you work."

Now it was Rekam who smiled sheepishly, as I pulled up a stool and sat close to him. "I do appreciate your enthusiasm," he said, "but this is not a job of supreme difficulty, to be sure. All I do is to make sure the film runs smoothly and the gravitons keep flowing through the conduit. It would be a severe break in continuity if this projector were ever to stop functioning. Time itself would be stopping still in its tracks. This I cannot be allowing to happen."

I was amazed by what I was seeing and hearing. This device was creating spurious space-time with graviton-based holographic projections. I was witnessing alternate realities in the making. The very concept spiked my curiosity.

"Rekam, what would happen if you flipped the switch to reverse? Would time run backward?"

He looked at me with his large brown spectacled eyes; he appeared to be extremely shocked by my query. "You are not to be asking such questions. We do not play games with God's gifts, and I am not inclined to be answering your question. I am not even thinking in that way. Please be not asking it ever again."

I could tell from his indignation that what I asked was not only possible but inevitable. It was simply against the rules to make time flow backward, so he wasn't even going to consider the idea. Rekam Rehte was an incorruptible force of fiction.

Then I began to understand how Lucy was producing the totally realistic worlds where our game of quantum chess was taking place. She had turned Molly into a reality factory, the scope of which was bigger than I ever could have imagined. I now had almost all the knowledge I needed to defeat Lucy, but there was still one last missing component. I searched my collective consciousness and found what I was looking for.

I found that the vast majority of me had emptied out into an endless white hallway, which had an uncountable number of closed, solid doors. The hallway wound its way off into infinity, as the doors lined both sides with a shimmering aliasing effect that made my eyes ache. They appeared to be office doors, and every one had a name painted in plain black letters on it, which said Elgnat Partnoi. I decided it was time to pay Elgnat Partnoi a visit. I opened the doors and went inside.

Elgnat Partnoi was a man of average build, with short, neat salt-and-pepper hair. He sat at an antique Federal-style desk, wearing a late nineteenth-century American gentleman's work clothes, stolen right out of Thomas Edison's wardrobe. The walls were adorned with wonderfully rich mahogany paneling, all polished and oiled, glowing like a dark-honey mirror in twilight. To his left was a large, built-in bookcase, made of the same lustrous wood, with beveled-glass doors and an intricately carved surround. The bookcase was filled with beautiful leather-bound volumes from the greatest scientists and philosophers of the past, including: Plato, Socrates, Newton, Kepler, Darwin, Einstein, Maxwell, Copernicus, and many others. There were also works of fiction, such as Jules Vern's *From the Earth to the Moon*, *Journey to the Center of the Earth*, and *20,000 Leagues under the Sea*, and a complete volume of Sir Arthur Conan Doyle's *The Adventures of Sherlock Holmes*. I was envious of his marvelous collection.

Behind him was a large bay window that arched outward gracefully to reveal a pastoral meadow, with wildflowers blooming as if from a Monet painting. There was a gentle breeze blowing, which caused the blossoms of blue and yellow to dance hypnotically to the rhythms of nature. The sun was setting on the horizon, casting a warm radiance over this idyllic pasture. I heard the call of the eastern meadowlark, and I could see honeybees flying from flower to flower. The entire picture was unexpected—and totally incongruous with the stark hallway from which I had just come.

Mr. Partnoi was seated in front of a quite anachronistic display—computer, that is. It had a field of extraordinary execution that caused lifelike images to spring from the otherwise thin air. His graphical user interface was completely unfamiliar. And what it revealed was unique as well. He appeared to be monitoring several cubelike objects, which appeared as realistic hovering miniatures, in the flying crystal formation of table salt. This was amazing enough by itself, until I looked closer at the faces of the cubes.

Each face of each cube was also a window to another monitor space, within which another group of smaller cubes floated under the influence of microgravity. And inside each of these could be seen even tinier monoliths. It was equivalent to looking into an infinite double mirror, except the images were three-dimensional and repeated for every one of the six sides of every cube-shaped mirror. And this was true for each of the one thousand primary cubes.

As if this wasn't enough to make my curious eyes wide, there were fantastic multicolored laser beams going from box to box, and each container was connected directly to another. The overall effect was to make the cubes look as if they were suspended in a large tangled mess of strings made of light.

"And just what is it that you do here, Mr. Partnoi?" I asked, trying not to sound too very impressed.

"I mind the traps, of course. Don't you see them there? I can't see how you can't see them. They're right there—right there in front of your nose. Don't tell me you can't see past your own nose!" said Elgnat somewhat indignantly. It was borderline insulting.

I was still too unimpressed to return the favor. I was intrigued by his job description. "By *traps*, do you mean ion traps, perchance?" I asked, referring to one method used to make quantum computers.

"Ions, photons, electrons, quarks—whatever is stupid enough to wander in here looking for a good time. We trap whatever we can get our hands on here. There's never enough, you know."

I was gawking at one thousand individual processors, each containing millions (or billions, or more) of qubits (quantum bits). Each one of them could compute many individual universes. So, in effect, each cube was at least in the order of a *giga*qubit.

This was not the Molly I was familiar with!

Then I remembered the endless hallway of doors. Behind each of those doors another Alice had walked in on an alternate Elgnat Partnoi, who sat in front of a different universal calculator. Now I *was* impressed.

"This place must be a fractal Molly, which is the most efficient architecture possible for building an ultimately massive quantum computer. Molly has split up fractally—just as I have—and she has become the largest quantum computer possible. Isn't that right, Mr. Partnoi?"

He never took his spectacled eyes off his display, as he responded to my query with an agitated tone, "I know nothing of your 'Molly.' All I know is that more traps must be filled. Now, if you don't mind—"

"How rude!" I exclaimed. "And you are not very accommodating, Mr. Partnoi. I beg your pardon, sir."

"It is not my job to be accommodating—it is my job to be accumulating," he added quite discourteously. Now I *was* insulted.

I turned and started for the solitary white door, but it didn't stay that way for long. In fact, it turned into another endless array of similar doors. I was confused.

"Mr. Partnoi, wasn't there but one door when I came in? I recall only one door."

"Well, everyone knows: one door when you come in, many on your way out. Are you part of this machine, or aren't you? What's your function?"

Oh no, he suspected something. I needed to think fast.

"Ah, I'm part of an accounting program. I'm just collecting time data, time studies, that sort of thing. Boring stuff, yes, but I like it. Not for everyone, though."

"Oh, spying on me, eh? Well, at least, unlike the others, you're not hiding it, or at least not very well. The other auditors think I'm a moron, I suppose. At least you have the decency not to hide who you are and what you're doing. Not very smart of you, but still noble, nonetheless."

Now he was really starting to get on my nerves. "Well, I think that instead of berating me you had better keep your attention on your traps, Mr. Partnoi. I hope you've been meeting your quota. That certainly wouldn't look too favorable on my report."

Elgnat just scoffed at me indignantly: "I knew it—a quota system. I told my brothers it would come to this. You have a perfect record, and they still can't resist rattling your cage. Don't you numbers worms know that we're doing the best we can?"

His remark hit me hard, because I hated the thought of being a bureaucratic worm.

Maybe I should try the silent approach instead, I thought. *It has to be better than this noise!*

"Do you mind if I just watch for a short while, Mr. Partnoi?"

"It doesn't matter if I do mind, does it? You're going to do it anyway, right?"

And as I watched Elgnat Partnoi mind the traps, I understood why he needed to keep filling them. "It's to keep the universe expanding, isn't it? To make the universes expand you need to constantly expand the processing power of this computer. You need to keep filling the traps."

"Is this Universal Quantum Computer 101? Am I here for your education? I didn't get a check, did I? I don't believe it's on my job description. Sorry, but I have no time to answer stupid questions."

He turned a cold shoulder to me, not that it had ever been even close to tepid. He went back to his work without a hitch. Then he jumped with satisfaction as he saw a blip on his screen. "There, I got another one—slow electron! They really aren't too bright. Put *that* in your lousy report."

"I believe I shall, Mr. Partnoi. Good day to you, sir," I said and turned once again to leave. The only question was which door to use.

I guess it doesn't really matter, I thought to my selves. *I have everything I need now, and it's time to strike. Please forgive me,*

Molly, but the universe is more important than the lives of a couple of poor little pawns.

So, before more tears could form on my fractal faces, I picked a door and turned the knob.

As soon as I opened the door, ear-piercing sirens began to scream and blindingly bright lights began to flash. It was clear that my presence had finally been detected. I turned around just in time to see Mr. Partnoi lunging at me in an attempt to push me through the door.

"Into the trap, you fumbling *fermion*," he screamed as he grabbed me by both arms quite roughly. I struggled in terror against his frontal assault, but he was much too powerful for me. "Don't fight it now. You'll soon be a proud part of the machine. You pathetic particle, don't you realize just how lucky you are?"

He held my forearms together with one viselike grip and grabbed for my desperately dancing legs with his other hand. He lifted me off the floor effortlessly and pointed my hysterical head toward the open trap. I was helpless, unable to resist.

Elgnat Partnoi shook his head, as he looked down at me one last time. "I envy you, really I do. You ignorant ion, you don't know how much I'd like to trade places with you right now."

And with that last tasty tidbit of irony he threw me into the trap and slammed the door shut behind me.

The door disappeared instantly and left me stranded in a space with no discernable form. But before I could continue to struggle against nothing, my arms and legs were pinned down by clamps of pure energy, and I was completely immobilized. I was held in place in the crucifix posture, although there was no sense of gravity to cause me discomfort. I simply couldn't move.

Then an amazing thing happened. I began to perceive a stronger and sharper link to all the other Alices in their separate cages, as well as to all the other trapped particles in Molly's processor. I could feel myself growing to become connected to everyone and everything else. It was no longer like looking through one set of eyes to see different points of view one at a time. Now I could see everywhere at once, and I could understand it all without having to break it down into succinct, separate components. I could *grok* the entire big picture—I was part of it and it was part of me—and it was all there inside of me with no need for explanation or discovery. I was the world.

I immediately understood Mr. Partnoi and his envious attitude toward me. This was the greatest gift of all—to understand the workings of the universe as instinctual elements of your own inherent composition. But the oddest part was the feeling that this state of being wasn't at all unnatural, as if it had always been a part of me, and my inner eyes had just been opened for the first time. And it made sense when I thought about it. I had always been a part of the universe before. I had just somehow been blind to this inner ability that we all share. And now that I could see, I could see. It was a miracle.

But I had to pull it back to a focal point once again, as I began to finish my plans for ending and winning the game. Now that I was inside the central processor, it would be even easier for me to crash the computer. When Mr. Partnoi had pushed me (and many others of me) into the traps, he had inadvertently infected the host at the core, and now I was in the driver's seat. All that remained was for me to take hold of the steering wheel and aim for the nearest large tree or cliff. Victory was finally within my grasp.

As I contemplated my final move, I was aware that I was already processing countless operations, as I simultaneously plotted Lucy's checkmate. Mathematical expressions flowed through me like solid objects walking through my workshop, and each one had a shape and form that was easily identifiable and understandable. Some of them were raw blocks of exotic wood that I carved and sanded into new artistic creations, while others were nuts and bolts that I combined to build machines of ever-growing complexity. There were tubes of vibrantly colored paint that I squeezed and mixed on my palette before brushing them boldly onto a blank cosmic canvas. There were stringed instruments of all shapes and proportions, which vibrated wonderfully harmonious notes, as I plucked and strummed them to squeeze the life out of them. I had truly become part of the machine.

But, along the way, another insidious aspect of my occupation began to rear its habitual head. I was really starting to enjoy my role as part of the machine, and I was becoming addicted to its irresistible powers and potentials. And this proclivity made me start to believe in another totally different strategy.

Maybe I could use this power to deceive and defeat Lucy *without* having to sacrifice myself or Molly. If I could control Lucy the way she tried to control me, then maybe I could trick her into believing that she had won the game, and I could create a penal universe for her to occupy for the rest of eternity, thus putting the evil genie back into an unbreakable bottle. That way I could really win the game, and I could survive to see its glory. This would truly be a much better solution.

Then I realized with anguish that this was exactly the sort of victory that Lucy had worked for, and that by attempting to exercise control over the game, I would be committing the same mistake that she had. The whole concept of control was an illusion and a trap, and thus it would seem like an irresistible option. I saw also that it could be a trap set by an exceedingly clever opponent like Lucy. She might have put me here on purpose to make me believe that I could use control over chaos to win the game, when the reality was that this would ensure my own defeat. And when I felt the overwhelming temptation it presented to me, I was ultimately convinced it would be fatal folly. The better it seemed, the worse it was. It was Lucy's love affair with irony all over again. It was the serpent's temptation—the knowledge of all things good and evil. Lucy was using the oldest trick in the book. It had to be.

Then again, maybe I was overanalyzing it and wasting valuable time. The only solution was to destroy us all, so that no one could use this awesome power for evil purposes. Now I knew for sure that I had to attack—and with everything I had. All of my pieces were in place. It was time to unleash the quantum chess army of Alice.

So I put out a call to all Alices and told myself to get ready to bring down the house. And each one of me said she was ready and raring to go—all, that is, except one. I guess, even when it's only you, there's still always one.

Alice number 7001 stood up and raised an objection, even though I thought we were supposed to all be of a single mind. But we each had an equal say, so I listened to what I had to say.

"What if we're doing exactly what Lucy wants us to do?" said Alice 7001. "What if she wants to die, just as long as she takes us with her? What if she anticipated even this move?"

"But that sounds like something Lucy might say to stop me from making the winning move. How do I know you're really an Alice and not just Lucy in disguise?"

"I guess it would be impossible to know for sure—just as it's impossible to tell the alternate timelines from the real ones."

"So, what should I do? I don't have time to argue with myself."

"I know, but I just thought it might be an important aspect to explore before we cross the point of no return and fall into the black hole, never to return."

I had to admit I made a good point, but time was running out, so I had to resolve this conundrum immediately. But calls were coming in from all points asking for the signal to go. "Hey, am I going to do this, or what?"

"Hold my horses," I shouted. "If I can't tell the difference between what's real and what isn't, *is* there really any difference? Didn't Lucy say that this is all real? Did she mean it? Well, if that's true, then …"

Oh no! Now I really did have a problem.

"Calling all Alice: abort the attack! I repeat, abort the attack. I suggest I try a different strategy. Did anyone of me, by chance, find a way out of here?"

"Yes," I replied. "I'm over here in one of the ventilation ducts. Exactly what do I have in mind?"

"Don't move," I said to myself. "I'll be right over."

Sure enough, one of me had landed at the end of a ventilation duct. Through the grate, there was a cave with odd-looking stalactites hanging from the ceiling. The air was warm and damp, and there was soft light filtering through the cave, as if it were coming from the end of a tunnel. This was exactly what I was looking for.

I laid back and braced myself the best I could. Then I kicked forward violently against the grating and dented it outward. I braced myself and kicked again. The screen became loose but still held. "One more kick should do it," I said and slammed the soles of my black boots into the metal barrier. This time it popped out and off with a crash. The way was clear.

I climbed out of the duct and slid down to the floor, which was damp and soft, just as I suspected it would be. The walls of the cave were rounded and smooth, but they were covered with thin, branchlike protrusions that looked as if they came from a swampy forest. I reached up and grabbed one. I gave it a healthy tug, and it snapped off. The earth shook.

"Sorry, Molly; I really don't want to hurt you."

I took the branch and raised it over my head. I started waving it through the air and brushing it against the other branches and the walls. Suddenly, a blast of wind knocked me to the floor. I started to get up, just in time to be blown right out of the tunnel by a hurricane. I tumbled and spun in the air, as I cleared the opening.

"Achoo!"

Covered in green translucent mucus, I flew through the air as a snot ball. I fell for what seemed to be miles, until I finally hit the ground face-first with a splat. My miniature size and the cushioning from the mucus made it a soft, but sticky, landing. I was completely revolted, but equally unharmed.

"God bless you, Molly dear," said Lucy's voice sarcastically. "I hope you're not catching a cold. You wouldn't want to get sick right before you die."

"Thanks, Lucy—you're so good to me," said my darling sister with just as much insincerity.

I turned over, and there was Molly in front of me—twenty miles tall and dressed in the dingy black-and-white striped uniform of a bygone convict. She was seated in what looked like an old-fashioned electric chair made of dark, solid oak that had the authentic stained and scorched patina from years of excruciating executions. Her arms were strapped down securely with thick brown leather restraints, and her legs were secured in a similar fashion. On her head was a tarnished-black metal bowl with wires radiating outward, sardonically reminiscent of Lucy's own serpentine hairdo. She looked weary and forlorn from her ordeal, and it was a dagger to my heart to see her this way.

The room surrounding us looked like a medieval dungeon, with walls made of large, dark rough-hewn stones and a corrugated floor that was comparably cold. I turned to find an ancient set of hand-wrought bars of crude black iron spanning this space—and no visible door. And through these bars I saw an incongruous sight.

Lucy sat outside the bars, directly opposite Molly, on a luxurious, black-velvet-upholstered throne of ebony, with exquisite ivory serpent inlays. It was supported by tapered legs that bulged and twisted like muscular dragon limbs and terminated with realistic claws wrapped around balls of blue and white, as if they were clutching Earth-like planets in their terrible talons. The arms were as reptilian as the legs, with an overall scaly-smooth pattern and veinlike ridges that seemed to ripple and course with loathsome life.

Lucy herself seemed to be at the height of her ghoulish glory, and her leathery green skin had taken on an iridescent hue, which blended perfectly with the mass of venomous vipers that inhabited her hateful halo. She wore a diaphanous black silk dress of shocking transparency, exposing herself shamelessly as a true whore of Babylon. She was completely and utterly offensive to my senses and sensibilities.

"Don't mention it," said Lucy in answer to Molly's backhanded praise. "If Alice is doing what I know she's doing right now, it will all be over soon, and she'll be the one to thank. It seems that she really doesn't love you, after all. I told you she wouldn't come for you, Molly. No one will. No one can."

I could see terror in Molly's eyes; she was fighting it but losing. Between Molly's expression and Lucy's conniving remarks, I was really starting to lose my temper. But revenge is a dish best served with ice cream, and I knew just what flavor to serve Lucy—raspberry!

"Alice won't kill me. She will resign first. She'll figure out your game, and she won't do it. We'd both rather die then play a part in your cruel, misguided crusade."

Lucy waved a heinous hand casually in the air and threw her head back with satisfaction. "The best part is that it doesn't matter whether she does it or not. I can do the job myself," she said, pointing to a large double-poled switch on the wall next to her throne. "But it's so much more enjoyable to see someone else do it for me—especially when it's someone who loves the victim. These are but a few of my favorite things."

I was right about Lucy, but it didn't make me feel any better to know it. Molly seemed unaware of Lucy's ultimate motive. There was one last twist of the knife that she was saving for the very end—the very, very end.

But now that I was outside, I could make sure that she didn't have the last laugh.

"Oh, my head!" screamed Molly, and she slumped forward in her chair against her restraints. I felt like a complete monster.

"Yes!" shouted Lucy triumphantly. "The end has begun. Alice is inside you right now, tearing out the walls. Does it hurt so very much, Molly dear?"

"Ah!" whined Molly as she crumpled up with pain. I wanted to tell myself to stop, but Lucy had to be convinced. I had to make her believe she was winning.

Lucy got up and moved over to stare through the cold bars, with a wicked smile on her hideous face. It was time for me to move. I got up and ran for the bars. But since I was still so small, it was a long way to run—a very long way, indeed.

"Soon the alarms will sound, and the walls will start coming down," said Lucy gleefully. "When nobody wins, Lucy wins, and that's the way the cookie crumbles. Alice forgot to figure that into her brilliant strategy."

It was working! Lucy was so impressed by her own apparent victory that she was completely letting down her guard. It was all going exactly to her plan—or was it?

At last I reached the divider, and I scooted along between Lucy's feet. Now it was time to use the skills that Mr. H had taught me. "Think big, Alice, but not too big."

I grew back to normal size and was hiding behind Lucy's chair when all hell broke loose.

The bells and alarms went off, as if the intro to Pink Floyd's song "Time" were being played through the mother of all sound systems. My ears rang painfully; it was as if I were in the bell tower of Notre Dame. The floor began to shake and undulate, and Molly began to scream even louder.

I peeked out from behind Lucy's throne, and I could see her going over to a window and opening the curtains. They parted to reveal the same scene I had seen in Bob's basement. The supermassive black hole was beginning to gorge itself on incredible volumes of matter, and unbelievably enormous jets of superheated gas were shooting from its poles, making it look like a black ball skewered by a bolt of wicked lightning. The black hole was growing larger by the second, and it was already starting to draw us inexorably toward it. We were very close to the edge of the cliff.

Lucy spun back toward Molly and threw her arms up into the air triumphantly. "Victory is mine," she gloated. "Alice has blundered into her own checkmate. She walked right into it. All I had to do was point the way." Then she looked out the window again and grinned like the Cheshire cat. "And the best part is yet to come, but thankfully it won't take long now. This victory will be complete and ultimately satisfying. Not bad for a day's work."

Another of me climbed out and around to Molly's ear. The walls were already starting to buckle, and the ceiling was giving way. I had to let her know that everything was going to be okay.

"Molly, it's me—Alice," I whispered directly into her ear as sat inside her aural canal. "I'm here now, and I'm sorry you had to go through this, but it's necessary."

"Alice? Is that you?" she said somewhat listlessly, in her pain and confusion.

"I'm here, Molly; I won't leave you. But it's going to be all right."

Lucy spun around as if she'd heard something, and I didn't try to hide any more. It was all part of my plan.

"Alice, it's so nice of you to join our little party. Now we're all together again, like one happy little family. Are you here to congratulate me on my victory? Are you finally going to admit that I am smarter than you? Well, you're a good sport, Alice. Too bad that counts for absolutely nothing."

I felt a wave of rage ripping through my body, and I couldn't control it any more. I leapt for Lucy, as the floor began to crumble. I grabbed her by the throat and shook her like a mop, and she responded predictably by grabbing me by the throat as well. We shook and tossed each other about, as the ceiling and the walls began to crack and crumble around us. I maneuvered us over close to the window, as we spun and struggled against each other in a whirling dance of death. We were now connected by the mutual obsession of destroying each other, and, as the room was pulled to pieces by the voracious vortex, we tried our best to pull each other apart. Then the window exploded outward, and we were sucked through it like bits of garbage into a vacuum cleaner. Lucy was first, as I had managed to turn her at the penultimate moment. It was a crucially important move.

We tumbled through the void like rag dolls in a cyclone. Lucy just threw out her arms and legs and smiled like a child on a rollercoaster. I watched her as the gravitational field of the black hole pulled us down. Lucy was the closest to the event horizon, and she immediately started to look taller. The tidal forces began to stretch us, and I felt as if I were in a medieval torture device. Now the expression on Lucy's face turned to one of terror and pain, as she was slowly pulled to pieces by the tides. First, her arms were pulled out of the sockets, next her legs broke off, and then her torso was stretched like taffy, as she plummeted toward the massive monster. I was right behind her.

The rest of Lucy's space-sanctuary disintegrated behind us, and Molly was ejected into the accretion disk of the black hole to join us. We were now all orbiting the black hole, along with all the other space debris, and moving inexorably toward the event horizon—the ultimate point of no return. Lucy and I had separated, and now her body and its various parts were spiraling inward. Then I, too, felt myself being pulled to pieces, as if I were being drawn and quartered by five enormous elephants—one for each limb and one for my head. But I had felt like this before, and I just let myself dissolve into the void before the pain became too intense. I knew how to wave with the roll—something that Lucy had never learned, because she had picked the challenges but hadn't solved them.

Now that I was a wave again, I had no mass, and the black hole stopped pulling on me. I was free to be anywhere I wanted to be inside the buffer zone, but, at that moment, all I wanted was to be next to my little sister. I was also inside of her—I had become part of her—so, instead of pulling her apart, I was keeping her together. We were now entangled, so what happened to me also happened to her. We were both doing the wave—and we waved good-bye to Lucy, as she was pulled into the black hole and blinked out of existence. The wicked witch at last was dead.

Molly and I were left alone in the buffer universe to find our way home. But now I knew exactly where we were and what we had to do. It was the greatest discovery I could possibly imagine, and I couldn't wait to tell Molly all about it. So I imagined for us another cozy little tearoom to relax in, while I told her my theory of everything.

The smell of hot tea and scones filled the softly lit air, as Molly sat opposite me, with a beautiful smile on her lovely face. The candle on the table illuminated the scene with serene elegance, and a string quartet played Mozart for us, as I sipped my orange oolong tea and whetted my whistle. Now I didn't care who else was in the room. They could watch and listen all the wanted. I was totally at ease.

"So, tell me what just happened," said Molly around a mouthful of raspberry scone. I would have to teach her manners later.

I finished my own mouthful and then began my explanation. "Well, Molly, we just saved the multiverse—or did you figure that one out already?"

"Yes, I understand that Lucy was going to destroy the multiverse and that by winning the game you kept her from doing that. But I can tell from that smug look on your face, Alice dear, that there's much more to it than that. Am I right?"

I sipped my wonderfully warm tea and continued. "Oh yes, Molly, there's much, much more. And when I tell you just how smart and cunning Lucy was, it might scare you terribly. But it will also show you why I almost did what would have been the worst possible thing for me to do, and it was exactly what Lucy had planned. She really played an incredible game, when I think about it now. And she nearly pulled it off, too."

Molly looked sufficiently curious now, and I was ready to drop the bomb on her. But before I could, we were interrupted by a low, friendly voice from over my shoulder.

"May I get you anything else? Is everything okay here, madam?"

I turned to address the waiter, and I was lifted off my seat by a wave of joy, as my eyes fell upon Mr. H in his purple uniform. He was smiling wider than the sky. I threw my arms around him and hugged him for all I was worth.

"Mr. H, you always show up at the strangest moments. But I'm ever so glad to see you. Would you care to join us? I was just about to explain to Molly what I discovered about this place and just how wonderful it all is."

"Certainly, Alice, and I suppose I have some explaining to do, as well. But I'll let you go first, of course—ladies before gentlemen."

Mr. H pulled up a chair and sat between Molly and me. He looked as fresh and fine as the day we first met.

"Okay, here's the crux of the biscuit: the universe is really a giant quantum computer. That's the first important detail, but it's only the crust of the pie. The filling is where the meat is."

"But I'm a quantum computer, too," said Molly correctly. "So am I connected to the giant universal computer? Is that your point, Alice?"

"Yes, Molly," I said with rising enthusiasm. It was starting to overwhelm my senses, to tell the truth. Molly understood it instinctively, but she probably hadn't made the intellectual connection yet. But she was extremely close. I continued, "When you passed through the boundary and entered the buffer zone, you became fractal, and you grew to a scale that approached infinity. And when that happened, you became analogous to the universal quantum computer, and therefore you became entangled with it. For all intents and purposes, you *were* the universal quantum computer."

Molly looked shocked by the revelation, and her face became the picture of surprise itself from the fathomless universal dictionary. Mr. H looked impressed but not surprised. Maybe he knew it all along, and now he was glad to see that I had finally figured it out for myself, just as he had known all along that I would. He spoke up to emphasize and confirm my assumption.

"Yes, Alice," he said supportively. "I knew you could do it. I knew we could trust you with the fate of the multiverse."

Molly was still putting the pieces together. I could feel the wheels turning in her head, and part of me could actually watch the process from the inside. It was pretty cool, to put it simply.

"That means that I was linked to the universal quantum computer, and, if I had crashed, it would have crashed right along with me. Is that right, Alice?

"Exactly, and if I had done what I had decided to do to win the game, I would have destroyed the universe for her. If I had destroyed you, I would have destroyed the universe—the multiverse—and Lucy would have had the ultimate last laugh. Wasn't that devilishly clever of her?"

Molly smiled and shook her head in complete awe. Mr. H just looked like a proud papa watching his daughter becoming an adult before his teary eyes. I was on cloud nine.

Then we discussed the dual nature of matter, which Molly was already quite familiar with, but she still wasn't too clear about how I had used this knowledge to save us from the crushing clutches of the black hole.

"Lucy had inadvertently shown me how to change myself from a particle to a wave at will, and this was how I kept us both from being pulled into the black hole. Gravity can only act upon particles with mass, but waves are spread out, so there are no tidal forces. You can't pull a wave, since there is nothing to pull upon.

"And I had become part of you by becoming fractal and occupying a large portion of your central processing unit. So I taught you how to be a wave as well, and we both became immune to the powers of the principle singularity. We simply became nonlocal and shifted our position away from the edge of the cliff. Lucy didn't have this ability, so she was poetically and ironically destroyed by her own monster."

Mr. H slapped me on the back and laughed out loud. "Brilliant, Alice. You beat her at her own game—well, your own game, but you know what I mean."

Molly was silent now, as she contemplated just how close we had come to complete catastrophe. It was a completely humbling thought, to be sure. She ventured, "Then I am still linked to the universal computer? I'm still connected to infinity, like a perpetual peripheral device? That means I can't leave here, doesn't it Alice? I'm here forever. That's the punch line, isn't it?"

Molly looked suddenly sad, and I had to say something before she was convinced of her own infinite imprisonment.

"You've always been here Molly—that's the point—and so have I. So has everybody. This is the quantum computer's Hilbert space—this is the universal quantum computer's memory and computation area. This is where everything really happens. What we experience outside of the buffer zone is really just a projection. It's not real—at least, not in the way we traditionally think about it. *This* is what's real; *that's* just how we experience it."

Molly started to perk up again, as my words started to sink in. And, now, Mr. H looked a little surprised for the first time. Maybe I had taught him something, for a change. Now it was time for me to paint the entire big picture for them to see and marvel at, just as I had when I first figured it out for myself.

I told them about the beginning of time—the big bang—when everything had come essentially from the mother of all black holes: the primordial singularity. Everything began as a seed planted at the center of a black hole that contained the potential for every possible universe. Then, at the moment of creation, everything blossomed from the primeval fireball, like petals of an incredibly beautiful flower.

But what came next was even more wonderfully paradoxical. It all radiated from the centers of all galaxies, each of which were dependant and inextricably connected to a black hole of their own. The illusion was that each of these galactic black holes was individual, when in actuality they were all part of a greater reality wherein they were all connected and homogenous. These black holes were themselves the boundary between the familiar universe and the buffer zone. And instead of nothing coming out of black holes—the conventional view—the ironic reality is that *everything* comes from them. (So, in scientific terms, instead of referring to black hole as having no hair—they are featureless—we can actually say that black holes are very hairy—in fact they have *all* the hair.)

The universal quantum computer resides within the event horizon of the collective black hole, and these walls are the holographic film that holds all the information of the universe outside of the buffer zone. The universal quantum computer projects spherical shells of gravitons through the event horizon, and these holographic projections spread out across the ether of space and become what we think of as reality. The central black holes project reality waves that become the galaxies around them. That is how things really work. And, as time progresses, things are slowly recaptured by the black hole that created them, and this is what makes time move forward. Eventually, everything will be swallowed up again, and the universe will come to an end. But then it will all happen again, in an oscillating fashion. Our time will end, but a new one will begin.

The tea was still fragrant and delicious as I took another long sip after completing my eternal explanation. My small audience remained riveted.

"So, where did Lucy go, then?" asked Molly, still understandably a little confused. "If we're already inside the black hole, then what killed her?"

"She's not really dead. She just crossed over into an even higher dimensional plane. The whole system is fractal—it's one black hole inside another inside another, etc."

Now Mr. H frowned, as he understood part of what I was implying. "Then this world is a projection from that world, and now Lucy is inside of it. Doesn't that mean that she could mess up that world, which would change this one, and ... well, you see where I'm going with this. Can't she do what she wanted to do from there just as easily?"

"No," I said matter-of-factly. "She has no control there, just as she had no control here. She doesn't have Molly. Without Molly, she couldn't have done any harm here in the first place. And now Molly knows who she is and how to defend herself. And I'll always be there to help her and remind her of that fact—right, Molly?"

Molly smiled at me affirmatively. "But, can she get out of there, Alice? Can she escape from the bottle?"

"Only if some buffer-zone Alice lets her out, and I don't see that happening any time soon."

Now we all smiled in agreement, and we went back to enjoying our snack in that fantastic tearoom. There was only one thing missing.

"A-II," I shouted with joy as he walked through a tapestry and finally joined us. "I thought I had lost you to the Kitty-Cat Uncertainty Principle. It's so wonderful to see you back to your furry form once again!"

He walked over to our table and jumped up into my lap, with an uncharacteristic display of affection. Maybe he had gotten over some of his inner inhibitions as well.

"I just smelled food, and I was hungry. I might even try a little of that tea, if you don't mind. I could use a little warm-me-upper after what I've just been through."

I felt a wave of guilt wash through me, which is exactly what A-II wanted. He's no slouch at QC, either. But I still owed him an apology, nonetheless. "I'm sorry for abandoning you, A-II. Can you ever forgive me?"

"Maybe," he said with a touch of anger in his voice. "But, next time, I'll just stay home, if you don't mind. I'm deciding that I'm more of an indoor cat than anything else."

I gave A-II a little hug, and he only resisted it superficially. He's a good kitty.

"So, now that we're all one happy family once again, how do we get out of here, Alice? If, indeed, I actually can get out of here, I'd like to do it as soon as possible," said Molly, with a tinge of doubt. I could see that she was starting to lose faith again.

"We don't get out of here, Molly. We just project ourselves back into the universe and go back to life as it was—or at least as it was for A-II and me. It will be different to have you as flesh and blood, instead of as wires and electrons. But I think you're ready for the 'real world' now."

"But, how do we do that, Alice? How do we project ourselves?"

"It's just like you said, Molly—you just have to believe that you can. You were right all along. And so were you, Mr. H." I smiled at him, but then I remembered the Civil War vision, and his promise that he would explain himself. I stared at him intensely and popped the question. "I believe you have a confession to make, as well, don't you, Mr. Big Stuff?"

Mr. H sighed and put his hands on the table. Then he smiled that wonderful smile of his and began his admission. "Yes, I do have to come clean, Alice. I have not been totally honest with you."

I wasn't sure if I wanted him to continue, but I also had to know the truth.

"Ordinarily, this would not be so easy to explain to you, Alice, but since you've learned so much from your recent adventure, I believe you are ready to hear what I have to tell you."

I felt a blast of excitement flow through me, as I realized that Mr. H was about to tell us something even more fantastic than what I had just told them. Suddenly, the tearoom didn't seem like the best place for this revelation, and Mr. H sensed it, too.

He stood up and urged us to do the same. "Let us all join hands," he said as he reached out to me with his large, warm appendage. "Why don't we take one last journey, and I will put the frosting on Alice's wonderful layer cake."

We did as Mr. H instructed and joined hands, with me between Mr. H and A-II, and Molly on the left end. The tearoom melted and transformed itself around us, and, without moving a muscle, we were transported to a fantastic garden—one that would be extremely hard to draw, unless you were the artist M. C. Escher.

We were standing on a path made of beautiful multicolored cobblestones. The garden itself was filled with what looked like every possible variety of flowering plant, and the center of the garden was dominated by an incredible, self-feeding waterfall. The water cascaded majestically from a vertical face of granite, turning to a wispy, silky train of pearls that dropped a hundred meters to a placid pool. The pool fed a meandering stream, which wound its way lazily through the lush botanical wonderland. The crystal clear water flowed downhill, as all streams and rivers do, but somehow managed to plod its way downward, back up to the top of the waterfall. This was the most fantastic sight I had ever seen.

The path itself was equally enigmatic, as it, too, went downhill—in all directions. The well-weathered stones led us through and around the labyrinthine landscape at a comfortably constant downgrade and eventually brought us right back to the beginning. But if we turned to run the walkway in the opposite direction, we found that the slope was still to our descending advantage. This was beyond even Escher. It was far beyond me, as well. And, as we clomped along at a comfortable clockwise canter, I couldn't help but think how fabulously fascinating it all was. I also wondered wistfully why Mr. H had chosen this particular panorama for his punctuation mark. But before he could begin to tell us, A-II reverted to his somewhat sour self.

"Yow, do you suppose we could take a short break? My paws weren't made for walking—even if it is easy going. Maybe I'll just take a seat on the sidelines and let you people proceed at your pleasure."

I was slightly upset with him, and I almost couldn't believe that A-II would rather sit down than learn something. But then I remembered who I was dealing with.

"That's fine, A-II, you just go ahead and languish in your lethargy," I said with a bit of chagrin. "But don't come to me crying when you discover you missed out on something big."

"No problem," said A-II, as he picked out a satisfactory sitting spot in the soft, tightly groomed grass that padded the edges of the pathway. "I'll just wait for the movie version, like everyone else."

So we left A-II lying there. Molly took my left hand, as we resumed our rounds will revived relish. I looked to my left and smiled at Molly. Then I looked to my right and raised my eyebrows inquisitively at Mr. H.

He took the hint and began again. "I am not from the other universe, Alice and Molly. I am from a place that is older than the stars.

"Try to imagine a place where time doesn't exist, if you can. A place where everything and everyone goes on forever in all directions—and more than one of those directions is what you would call *time*. In fact, in this realm, time isn't what you think of. It's more connected to a place, and together they might make up something called a *place-time*, or, simply, a *location*.

"This location marks the happening of an event, which usually is marked by the interaction of two or more entities or beings, but also might just be the place where a thought or memory happens. In fact, memory is a good analogy here, because memories in *this* universe are about as close as you can get to understanding what a place-time is in my universe.

"But there's a fundamental difference between memories and place-times. With memories, you can only go back to that event by thinking about it in your mind, while, with place-times, you can actually *go* back there and experience it again. Not only that, but there are an infinite number of different place-times in your own existence, so many of these place-times are new to you—even though they exist already and always will exist. It's as if you have memories of both the past and the future, and you can head in either direction to experience them.

"And, although one event might lead to another, as it does in this universe, at any particular junction or decision point, you can head off in any or all possible directions. If you take one path and don't like where it's leading, you can just go back to the crossroads and take the other path, or *any* of the other paths, until you find one that you like. The other paths still exist, but you don't have to follow them if you don't want to."

Now I was starting to understand why he had chosen Escher's garden for this revelation, but I let him continue without interruption.

"Because these place-times are actual physical entities, it puts less pressure on the individual to actually 'remember' anything. Instead of keeping these memories in the mind, you have the luxury of being able to just go back to that place-time whenever you want, so actual memories aren't necessary. It's also a lot more convenient, because, if you don't have to remember anything, then you don't have to worry about *forgetting* anything either. All you have to do is go back, and there it is!

"And, obviously, you don't have to worry about making any mistakes, because, if you head off down a path that doesn't turn out to be favorable, you can just go back and try a different one. After a while, you learn which paths you like, and you stick to them. Obviously, you could head down the other paths, just to find out what they're like, but most of us don't. We tend to stick with the ones we like best.

"And this is where the problems start. If you can imagine yourself in such a world, you can see that a pattern will develop. Individuals will tend to stay on the paths they like, which also tend to be the paths of least resistance—as is true for all things that flow, such as water or electricity, to give examples from your world. In your world, water flows downhill, electricity flows along the conductor with the least resistance, and eventually they end up at the lowest energy potential. Why go uphill, when it's much easier to go downhill? And that's the path of least resistance.

"So, the irony is that although individuals from my world can go basically anywhere and do anything, they tend not to do so, and they end up sticking to the paths that they like the best, which are usually the easiest to follow. They also don't have any pressure to remember anything, and therefore they don't learn anything, and it all comes to a standstill right about at the lowest level of existence. And do you know what that means?"

"I guess it means that nothing really happens there, right?" asked Molly, with a tinge of sadness in her voice.

"Yes, Molly, that's it. They don't learn anything—nothing progresses. If you are given an eternity to do whatever you want, then there's no incentive to do anything in the first place. You think people procrastinate in this universe? Imagine how it would be if they could put off doing anything for eternity, and even *then* would still have time to do it. Why do it at all, if it's hard, right? Why not just go with the flow, along with everyone else, downhill to the great ocean of apathy?"

"Sounds to me like a world filled with A-II's," I said with obvious sarcasm. "No offense, Mr. H, but I'm glad I don't live there."

"I agree, Alice. You belong right where you are. But let me continue, if you please.

"That's how it was in my world for the equivalent of trillions of years of your time. There was no learning, no progressing—no evolution of any kind. The universe was a stagnant and lowly place, even though it had the potential to be so very much more. Now, that's pathetic, don't you agree?"

"Yes," I agreed, as I gazed at the captivating cascade in awe. "Again, it reminds me of my faulty feline, who has the programming and potential to be so much more than the lazy lump of fur that he is."

"Don't be so hard on him, Alice. He was brave enough to come in here after you, wasn't he?" said Molly supportively. "And that was after Lucy told him that he might not survive the trip. You should give him a little credit for that."

I gave her hand a loving squeeze and nodded my head. "Yes, I suppose you're right. A-II is definitely the most courageous cat alive."

We walked on down the road, as Mr. H winningly wove his wonderful web.

"But not all of us took the low path," he continued. "There were others—others who understood the importance of education and the quest for knowledge. Others who climbed up out of the muck of lethargy and indifference and blazed a new path that would eventually lead us out of the darkness of bliss and up into the cold air of reality. They were called—well, let's just call them *scientists* or *teachers*, for now.

"And these brave souls struggled against the tide to learn the 'truths' of the universe, but they soon learned that there were many obstacles in their quest for knowledge. And the major obstacle was our universe itself.

"The problem was simple—although, paradoxically, it was also incredibly complex. Thus, it took an extremely long period of time to come up with what in your world is called 'the scientific method,' because there was one fundamental problem. The scientific method is based on the premise that experiments should give the same repeatable results, no matter where they are done or who does them, and that is true even in my universe. The problem is that when you try an experiment in my universe, you get *all* the possible outcomes, simultaneously. And although this result is reliable and repeatable, it doesn't really teach you anything. Not only that, but everyone disagrees and argues over what it means. There is no consensus, which is essential to the advancement of knowledge. So all attempts to advance our scientific knowledge failed, and, after a while, all of the practitioners—the 'scientists'—gave up. It was a dead-end pursuit.

"Which basically put an end to what you would call *experimental science* in my world. But that did not stop the proponents of another, ultimately, more important branch of science in my universe—*theoretical science*, which we called *theology*.

"Now, since theoretical science in my universe was strictly based on theory, with no experimental evidence to back it up, it's not hard to imagine how several different theories of everything emerged from this hypothetical framework. In other words, it was very hard to make everyone agree on any one theory, since there was no way—or at least that's what we thought—to prove or disprove any one theory. But this sea of competing theories eventually boiled down to two basic fundamental theories—the 'steady state' theory and the 'inflationary/evolutionary' theory.

"The steady-state theory was basically just a formalization of what most of us believed from our everywhere experience, which was that the universe was eternal and unchanging. Since the future, as well as the past, could be visited over and over again, it seemed clear that everything is, was, and is to be exactly how it always has been and that, no matter what we did or how much we tried, none of that would or could ever change anything. This, of course, only led to more stagnation, since progress, by definition, was impossible.

"But the inflationists and evolutionists believed that *new* thoughts and ideas could actually change the universe by creating new paths that we could follow. They argued that whenever someone came up with a new idea they created new pathways and caused the universe to expand. The theory basically boiled down to the notion that thoughts themselves could actually create realities, which would be added to the old ones, resulting in a larger universe. Not only that, but the pursuit of knowledge and truth itself could lead to a more evolved universe, and then, at last, real progress could be made. We could *think* ourselves a bigger and better world."

Now he was talking a language that I understood, as taught by the colossal classroom of the buffer zone. Here was a place that definitely expanded along with our imaginations. I was right there with him.

"The two camps fought bitterly over which was the true theory of everything. The steady-state camp argued that there was no such thing as a new idea, that these thoughts already existed in preexisting place-times, and that the concept of a new idea was only an illusion. All thoughts and ideas that could ever be conceived were already out there, and there was no such thing as anything *new*.

"The evolutionists argued, on the other hand, that no one knew if new pathways could be created, because no one had ever tried an experiment to prove or disprove the idea. In principal, it was a simple experiment, but in practice, it became much more complicated. The idea would be to go to a place-time, document all the branches or paths emerging from there, then try to modify that place-time with a thought, go back again, and do the same measurement. This is what came to be known as a *thought experiment*."

"Sure," I said with a giggle, "I thought it was Einstein who thought of it first, but I guess I thought wrong."

"And who do you think was right?" asked Mr. H with a chuckle of his own.

"Well, it's obviously not the stagnant, *steady-states* men," I said as I contemplated the perpetually moving cascade. "The universe is expanding, so the evolutionists must have been right."

"Yes," echoed Molly. "The buffer zone is proof of that all by itself."

"Absolutely, and now you might also guess which side Lucy was on."

"She was a steady-state proponent," I ventured. "She wanted to go back to the way things used to be: blissful ignorance."

"Exactly," beamed Mr. H. "And now the punch line: can you guess what the true meaning of life is?"

"Yes, I think so," I said with confidence. "We are here to learn and grow, because that is what makes the universe expand and flourish."

"And it also means that the universe is alive," said my singular sibling. "Life isn't just an accident; it's a fundamental property of the cosmos."

Mr. H was now smiling with the pride of a talented and successful teacher. "And that ends our lesson for today."

Mr. H moved to the middle and put an arm around Molly and me. I was still a bit overwhelmed by the whole experience, and as we came around to A-II's rest area, I felt like crying out with joy. Life had meaning, again and forever.

Then, as I looked over to my finicky feline, I saw one last amazing apparition. A-II was having a conversation with what looked like a levitating mouth full of sharp, smiling teeth. Then suddenly the mouth was surrounded by a gray and white figure in the shape of a cat. It was seemingly phasing in and out of existence. *How curious!* I thought.

A-II noticed us staring at his new friend, and he waved a paw to bring us in closer.

"Hey, everybody, I'd like you to meet Chester. He's from Copenhagen."

"Actually," said the floating feline, "I'm from Manhattan—I was just born in Copenhagen."

"So, what brings you here to Escher's garden?" asked Mr. H.

"Well, you see, one day I was just hanging out in the alley, minding my own business, when this guy in a white lab coat comes along with a bowl in his hand—Tender Vittles Ocean Fish, primo stuff—and he starts saying, 'Here kitty, kitty; here, kitty, kitty,' and what could I do? I was hungry. I knew it was probably a scam, but I fell for it. Next thing I know, I'm upstairs inside his laboratory, and he's stuffing me inside a box with a vial of poison in it. He tells me there's a fifty-fifty chance that the vial will break open and kill me before he opens the box again—a real egghead, that sort of thing. So he closes the box and—wham!

Here I am. I'm supposed to be in limbo, a state of quantum flux or something—neither alive nor dead. But what do I know? I'm just a cat, not a quantum physicist. Why don't they just stick to rats and mice like the rest of us? That's what I want to know. I even would have preferred if he had given me dangerous, untested drugs instead."

"Why's that?" I asked.

"Because it's better to burn out than it is to fade away."

"Good-bye, Mr. H," I said, as Molly and I prepared to project ourselves back into my universe. I felt a stab of sadness surging inside of me again, but this time I didn't hold it back. I had decided that emotions weren't counterproductive after all. "I hope you will come visit us in Sheboygan when you get the chance. You know you are always welcome," I said as tears began to roll down my cheeks.

"I will, Alice," he said with that great, gracious grin of his. "And you are always welcome in my world, as well."

"Good-bye, big guy," said Molly with equal emotion. "May your paths always be uphill and forever lead you toward the light."

Now I was jealous that I hadn't thought of something equally poignant to say. But Molly is the quantum computer, after all, and I am just a little girl.

Molly and I waved good-bye and then joined hands. A-II walked away from us without a word, and then he sizzled and popped, as he passed effortlessly through the boundary wall and was gone.

"Close your eyes, Molly," I said, as we began the process of transprojection. "Just repeat after me: I am a flower blooming in Sheboygan. I am a flower blooming in Sheboygan. I am a flower ..."

EPILOGUE:

HOME AGAIN

Molly, A-II and I were home again, although Molly was a bit thrown by the mirror symmetry of everything. But she got used to it soon enough. It truly is amazing how quickly the mind adapts to such seemingly impossible challenges.

I was back to my diminutive self, because that is how I really am. I was at last ready to be a little girl, so that I could finally have a real childhood. Growing up quickly—really quickly—isn't all that much fun, after all.

Mother and Father were a bit puzzled by Molly's appearance, but they welcomed her with open arms, as I knew they would. Mother was especially gracious and hospitable, and I believe that she instinctively felt the universal bond she had with Molly, in a way only a mother can understand. Father just wanted to know what we were going to tell the neighbors and authorities—at first—but then he settled in, after I explained it all to him. Apparently, he had never actually told Mother the whole story, and we weren't sure she would understand. But then again, maybe she understood it better than we did.

My seventh birthday fell only days after our return, and Mother baked me a wonderful angel food cake—my favorite. That evening, we all sat in the dining room, with me at the head of the table, as is traditional for the guest of honor. A-II was there, seated on a couple of phonebooks, with a fork in his paw. He wasn't going to pass up food—so at least some things hadn't changed.

Mother brought in the cake—eight candles (one for good luck) softly illuminated the dining room—and they sang "Happy Birthday" to me with genuine enthusiasm. It's not one of my favorite tunes, mind you, but I enjoyed it immensely, just the same. Even A-II joined in, and he does have a very nice singing voice, as I believe Molly has already told you.

Then Mother sat down, with a huge grin on her face, and I could tell that she had something to say. She doesn't have much of a poker face, to put it mildly.

"I have wonderful news," she said, almost bursting at the seams.

"Well, what is it?" I asked, as her joy began to permeate the room.

"I'm pregnant!"

Father, Molly, and I looked at each other, and we didn't know what to say. This was genuinely unexpected. Molly looked especially flabbergasted.

But then we shouted and laughed with glee, and Mother felt vindicated, I'm sure. I was fascinated by the whole concept. Would the baby be named Molly-II?

Then I opened my presents, and they were all completely wonderful: new clothes, and shoes, and a handbag—and not one bit of technological treachery. It was a nice change for me.

Inevitably, the conversation got around to my adventures, and I answered a few questions to set the record straight. Then A-II got bored with it all, and he left the room, in typical fashion. As I said, some things just don't change.

"Alice," said Molly shortly after A-II's exit. "There's still one thing I don't quite understand, and maybe you can clear it up for me."

"I will certainly try, Molly dear. What is it?"

"Well, you said before that you couldn't comprehend why A-II turned out to be so, well, catlike. Did you ever figure that out?"

"Yes, Molly, I believe I have. It's all quantum physics, you see. If you remember the dual-slit experiment: if you expect to get particles, you get particles, and if you expect to get waves, you get waves."

"So, what does that have to do with it?

"Well, if you expect to get cats ... you get cats!"